# The North Wind Doth Blow

Rosemarie Leetham

*Dignity is a noble thing*

*But it is nothing*

*Without compassion and forgiveness.*

authorHOUSE®

*AuthorHouse™ UK Ltd.*
*500 Avebury Boulevard*
*Central Milton Keynes, MK9 2BE*
*www.authorhouse.co.uk*
*Phone: 08001974150*



*First published by AuthorHouse 12/18/2007*

*ISBN: 978-1-4343-4583-7 (sc)*

*Printed in the United States of America*
*Bloomington, Indiana*

*This book is printed on acid-free paper.*

Fly little bird into the night
The stars will guide you home
Though darkness has descended now
Another day will come.
So do not fret, nor shed a tear
Tomorrow you will see
The world anew and without fear
Tomorrow you'll be free.

# Skerra Kua

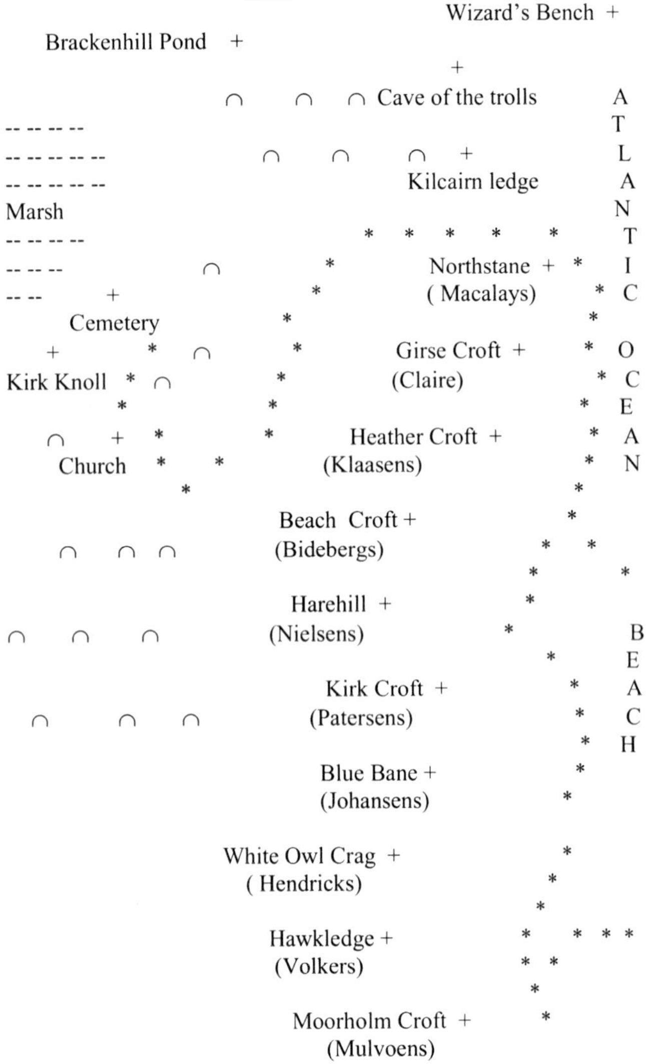


∩∩∩ Hills
***** Common Path

# Chapter 1

They were an odd pair to look at - sad, comical - yet no one seemed to notice it. It was never quite clear whether Siegund invited Maunsie or whether he invited himself, but he was always there, hobbling alongside her, trying his best to keep pace. Gentle Maunsie Nielsen was different from other folks. Between his shoulder-blades sat a skew-whiff hump like an obstinate witch's familiar, a deformity that stirred Siegund into regular bouts of pity.

'Blow me down, Maunsie, it's going to be a good day, indeed it is,' Siegund announced, making it a promise rather than a hopeful weather forecast. She drew deep, purposeful breaths of the chilly air and stretched herself noisily while her rosebud lips emitted chirpy sounds of infinite contentment. Her cornflower-blue eyes delighted in the mass of clouds chasing and being chased across the sky, her mind followed them with curiosity into the unknown distance where ocean and sky seemed to unite as one. There seemed nothing beyond it, nothing real anyway.

Maunsie ignored his sister's talk of the weather that was as changeable as her moods. He pointed down the common path with dismay where Roland the fiddler was coming towards them, walking tall and erect, neither leisurely nor in haste, yet with an air of great importance. That is to say – he walked reasonably tall and erect. He was on his annual mission, bringing his Yule Tide cheer and, hopefully, good fortune to the ten crofts of Skerra Kua, and receive a well deserved dram or two of brandy for his efforts at every door. With every call he made, his spirits rose - in more than one respect - and the quality of his musical performance fell by the same degree. His tune fled ahead like the wailing wind, lagged behind him like mourning shadows, filled the air like echoes of a thousand whimpering souls. No one minded his artistic shortcomings, for no one could do better, or even as well.

Roland Mulvoen's moth-eaten coat - once grand, no doubt - might have belonged to one of the Pilgrim Fathers or some other ardent observer of Puritan religion. Since it had become the fiddler's possession it saw daylight only on festive occasions. Its once great length, severely and haphazardly curtailed to combat the fraying edges, had dwindled inch by inch with the passing of the years, and yet, it still transferred a trace of its former sombre dignity to the present wearer.

The icy wind gnawed at the man's fingertips. For all his hardiness his temporarily immobilized hands now dug deep into shabby pockets for warmth; and while the fiddle halted its pitiful wails a worshipful serenity lay over this tiny speck of land in the Atlantic, this home of sheep and wild ponies, of puffin and auk, of guillemot and cormorant, a place overlooked by the world and forgotten by time.

'Good morning, Fiddler,' Siegund giggled. Her tall, wiry body twisted with amusement. Her giggles stopped abruptly. Roland's gaze was upon her as it so often did of late. Quick wit or not, she knew nothing of the fiddler's dreams and fancies, nothing of his fervent woos nor of his kind of love. His odd manners and his dark immobilizing eyes spoke of things she did not understand, eyes that did not exactly control her, but neither was she in control when they looked at her despite their temporary bleariness.

'Blow me,' she stammered more than a little embarrassed. She shook her long blond hair in defiance.

Roland pulled his black wide-rimmed hat snugly over his head, wedged his wooden companion under his stubbly chin and applied his bow to the strings with much vigour - and the fiddle cried out under its torture. Gallantly he attempted his most dignified stride, but he managed no more than a pitiful extended stagger as his legs buckled under the weight of the brandy.

'Ah, Siegund! She is not much more than a child, aye, that she is,' the fiddler admitted to himself, but still, his no longer youthful heart beat faster and his mind filled with fitful romantic imaginings. The lively breeze caught his steaming breath, instantly dispersing into nothingness this flimsy dew of his labours and aspirations. He gave a knowing smile and one corner of his mouth drooped a little as if to kiss the crying fiddle better. 'Aye, and I am not much more than an old fool,' he muttered, then fell back into a more manageable pace as he approached the Nielsen's cottage.

The Harehill cottage, neither greater nor lesser than the other homesteads, leaned its whitewashed flank defiantly towards the rebellious sea. Through the shimmering mist of blissful intoxication the cottage bobbed up and down one moment and swayed from side to side the next before the musician's temporarily ill-focusing eyes. He fixed his gaze on the twists of wispy smoke that rolled across the peaty roof until a playful wind took the tumbling vapours and shredded them into aromatic fragments. His only love in the past had been like smoke - flimsy, volatile and in the end only memories. Ah, but he had been a mere boy then.

He took a long, deliberate drink of brandy from his own provision, so long and deliberate in fact, it instantly obliterated the old memories and provided a good deal of encouragement. And once more he was ready to forgive the Kuans; they were his people - he was part of them in all their strangeness - proud, hardy people, ruled by the moods of wind and ocean, by brooding moors and wild superstitions. Isolation from the outside world and dependence on each other had shaped their characters the way only island life could. They knew how to share their losses and how to weep alone; how to share the fruits of land and sea and how to see to one's own. His thoughts swayed from a gloomy past to a dubious future. What good was it to know one's own mind in a community where other folks had the last word? The fiddler's Irish blood, or what was left of it after mixing for generations with the Nordic equivalent, deemed it unfortunate that in their grim sense of pride and dignity, upheld to the point of obsession, they mistook the precious gift of compassion for a detestable weakness. If at first glance there was a baffling sameness about the islanders, out-of-the-ordinary situations soon sifted the weak from the strong, the bright from the dull, the submissive from the impetuous whose hearts were larger than pride and dignity.

Roland played his Christmas greeting with all the sincerity and goodwill he could muster, disregarding the risk of chilblains; besides, reflection was difficult with a fuzzy head. Another two brandies later he was on his way again, fiddling as well as he could. At the best of times his music lacked refinement and harmonious quality - not for want of trying on the fiddler's account, it must me said - and indeed, the wailing notes in all their imperfection blended perfectly with the whining wind and the tuneless shrieks of birds. Ditty or dirge - whichever way one cared to interpret each tune - the sound befitted amicably the rugged landscape; it reflected with tragic-comical accuracy the islanders' constant struggle for coexistence with the elements, it lamented with fierce resilience the perpetual fight for survival.

But now his fiddling had gone totally out of control and his legs in tightly knitted hoses matched the fiddling. He was running along sideward, remarkably resembling a footsore fiddler crab, swaying this way and that. With squeaks and grunts, but without resistance, he kissed the much loved ground of Skerra Kua.  His fiddle gave a desperate screech.

'Nay, it's sad! It's wicked.' Maunsie's head gyrated on his scrawny neck as if it were made of soft India rubber. His sympathy lay entirely with the fiddle. He felt its pain and humiliation and grimaced in mental agony. 'Yay, I'd make the fiddle sing, not whine and shriek.'

'Blow me, not with a belly full of brandy, indeed not. A tipple or two at every cottage - I do declare, you'd have the substance of a jelly fish.' Siegund giggled anew at the sight of the music man who was still squeaking and grunting as he clumsily struggled back to his feet. He tried another tune, or something like a tune; it was barely recognisable.

'Nay, brandy is not for me.'

'Blow me down, by the time he reaches the Northstane he'd do better to let Malkie's piglets do the squealing for him. As for the fiddler - he ought to sleep it off in a sty; indeed, that would be better.'

'I want to be a fiddler,' Maunsie insisted. There was an air of absolute finality about his words as if convinced by the fiddler's artless endeavour of such necessity, or at least desirability. He would not go as far as to compare the fiddler with a pig, but he did feel more than a hint of resentment.

'Perhaps, when the fiddler dies…'

'Nay, nay, Siegund, how can you say such a thing,' Maunsie cut her short. 'Nay, it's not right, it's sad,' he complained. 'I've prayed....oh how I wish I had a fiddle.' The immense longing made the boy's bilious, square face twitch a little; the sadness that followed smoothed it back into a tense mask. He glanced across the foamy sea where treacherous rocks rose out of the waves. It was like standing at the edge of the world and at the end of hope for him. With one hand he pretended to hold the precious fiddle and with the other he worked the imaginary bow in wild erratic movements.

'Maun-sie the fidd-ler, Maun-sie the fidd-ler,' Siegund chanted and playfully began to dance to the soundless melody. Her face became strangely serious, her eyes dreamy and far away. She was no longer mocking him. Roland's tune faded into the distance. A different kind of music filled her ears; it filled her head - powerful, enchanting music that saturated the air. She could not identify the melody, nor its origin or purpose; she only knew that she had to dance, dance, dance. The wind whistled and whined, the turbulent sea roared as it crashed against the cliffs below. A whole orchestra came to life and invited brother and sister to be part of it.

On and on he played his invisible instrument, on and on she danced to the illusory rhapsody - a fiddler without a fiddle, a dancer without music, a performance without audience. For one magical moment they penetrated deep into the island's soul and its soul penetrated their minds. Skerra Kua claimed them, exposed their vulnerability, revealed to them with painful honesty the one's fickleness and the other's misery. It demanded their loyalty, their hearts; it warned, it hinted in monochrome hazy pictures which they could not interpret. They fell into each other's arms and wept because they were frightened of so much emotion. The music ebbed away, leaving their hearts in uproar and their minds in paralytic inaction. The bugle-like cry of a herring gull called them back to reality, and for a while brother and sister eyed each other in curious wonder.

'Blow me down, the air is laden with tantalizing spirits,' Siegund whispered. 'I can feel their hot breath tingling on my skin. Don't you feel it too, Maunsie? You must do - I know you do!' Her trembling hand ran hastily over her flushed face. She puffed her cheeks out and let the air escape noisily like pressure released from an inflated balloon. Maunsie was still in a daze. He blinked several times and tried to persuade his fluttering heart to be calm.

'Nay, you're dreaming again, Siegund,' he said evasively and shuddered. He would rather forget this unholy moment of pain and elation, of bitter truth and vague premonitions; they had glimpsed into the future, yet, had not learned their fate. His mind returned to the fiddle, or rather to the unlikelihood of ever owning such precious thing. Being of practical nature he envisaged profitable possibilities should one ever come his way and in his longing he felt a precarious sense of normality, of safety even.

'We'd give a good show, you and I, Siegund. We could go to the mainland and earn stacks of money, and Midder wouldn't have to work so hard any more.'

'Would, could!' Siegund taunted. 'Wood on the beach and cud in the cow's stomach! You call me a dreamer? Then I call you a fool.'

From his deformed chest came three short, shallow gasps that resembled the air hunger of a dying man; in Maunsie's case it was merely a sigh - Maunsie always sighed when he did not know what else to do. In his unshakable loyalty he forgave her the rebukes, admired her uncanny logic, thought her foolish and brave. Sometimes he felt enslaved by her, for she was tall and strong and he was small and weak, yet he followed her willingly even though trouble had a wicked habit of seeking her out.

Josefa Nielsen, hands on hips, stood by the byre door and called them in for breakfast. They needed no urging; the fresh air had made them hungry. In the *ben* a lively peat fire, encouraged by a few slivers of driftwood, dominated the centre of the room like a grand sun on which all else depended. Suspended over the heat hung a steaming cast iron vessel. A mouth-watering promise of palatable enjoyment rose from its contents. Josefa was presently engaged in lighting candles, clusters of them here, rows of them there, adhering the waxy tapers with painstaking correctness and with solemn expression to where ever candles might be adhered, each one receiving its life from the blessed candle, the princess of light, which burned graciously in the eye socket of a cow's skull perched high on a shelf. The bleached bones glared, the impressive horns curved outwards and upwards, majestically conveying unspoken words of power and protection. On the same shelf, which stretched from wall to wall, the neatly stacked food, pans and tools formed a peculiar contrast to the pagan idol; reality and myth, resolution and compromise clasped hands in sobering harmony.

Whirling peat smoke mingled with the profuse light of the flickering candles and shrouded the whole scene in a bluish-grey veil. Its biting aroma blended with the smell of sizzling bacon to which the close proximity of cows and hens in the byre added a flavour of comfort and reasonable prosperity. Windowless walls barred entry to daylight and fresh air - lack of chimney hampered the smoke from a swift escape, though gradually it would find its way through a small gap in the roof. Escape for the occupants could have been no swifter were the need ever to arise; their only way out was through the byre, past cows and hens. But it was a good home, a safe home and there was as much to be said for the cave-like dwelling as against; it helped to keep them warm during the harsh winters when the gales drove in from the ocean without mercy and swept across the treeless landscape - endlessly, untiring in its various moods, howling, screeching, whistling, moaning, and sometimes just gently sighing.

Josefa nodded her dark head as signal that her waxy task was completed and that breakfast could begin. They crowded around the driftwood table and sat down on driftwood chairs; all seven of them, which was by no means easy, and as always, young Maunsie was left with just one corner of the table, straddling his weedy legs either side. Josefa glanced at her brood, yet did not seem to see them. Her thoughts were with Erik, her firstborn, who was on some foreign ship or in some foreign land - that is, if he was still alive. Her tired face showed hazily the early signs of premature old age hastened along by a life of toil, of childbearing and of silently borne grief over too many losses. She was with child again. Jan stood by his chair, his back straight despite toils and troublesome joints. Straight and stiff too came his speech. His ice-blue eyes wandered steadily - with a certain degree of gratitude - from Josefa to his sons and daughters. Stony-faced he urged them to listen - and listen well.

'Today is the sixth day of January in the year of the Lord....' He was not sure what year it was. 'Sixteen hundred and forty, I believe. But the year is of no importance; what matters much is this day of the dawning when the sun begins to wake and return to us from the land of everlasting ice.' He prayed to the Holy Midder Mary, prayed to the Nordic gods and all the powerful forces on land and sea, calling by name and with immense respect all the unearthly Beings he could think of - all but the devil - and uttered his special regard for the trolls in the cave, those elusive little people who shunned all human contact. His white, strawy eyelashes fluttered briefly with uneasiness. He reached for a small earthen jug of brandy and began to pour a drink for each member of the family, and with every drink he poured he chanted a Nordic rhyme which combined prayers, blessings and a sacred formula against all evil. He sat down, gave a little smile, took Josefa's hand and squeezed it gently. Her startled face told him that moral decency demanded proper distance, and he let go of her quickly. In mild embarrassment at such lapse he brushed his hand over his straw-white hair, bleached by sun and weather rather than by his years. His face became sombre again - Josefa preferred him that way.

In the flickering candlelight the hollow eyes of the cow skull seemed to blink. Consequently, sixteen year old Krista, mousy-haired, mousy-eyed and of mousy character, shrank into a kind of defiant, sullen apathy. Sameness could hardly be applied to this family. Her over-lively, over-enthusiastic twin sister Siegund was instantly stirred into a restlessness that fuelled her longing to know the unknown. Helped along by the unaccustomed tot of brandy she plunged herself headlong into dare-devil fantasies and was instantly carried in speedy flight through a maze of imaginary adventures, out into the great world beyond the horizon, an amazing world of which Erik had spoken. In her naive way all lands looked like Skerra Kua with an abundance of peculiarities added. She saw mighty trees reach into the sky, saw dancing girls in quivering grass skirts, saw huge animals with ridiculously long noses, which reminded her of Konrad Mulvoen's wife Arlene. She saw turbaned people, brown people, black people, yellow people, red people; the colours were dazzling. A fleeting care for Erik's safety brought her back with suicidal rapidity into her tedious, small world. The drastic descent into reality gave her the painful sensation of a physical crash landing and stunned her into a brief moment of stupor.

'Blow me down, I wish I could sail the seas with Erik,' Siegund spluttered, filling her mouth at the same time. She loved Skerra Kua, knew no other place and was proud of her Norse heritage - except when the strange lands called to her. And they did call - often. They were calling now. They beckoned, tempted, teased and made an earnest bid for her affection by promising sweet reward. But instantly the power of the ancient Nordic sentiment folded over her like a heavy blanket - protective, soothing, yet rapaciously suffocating. She trembled in awe. 'I am of this island, yet I am not,' she proclaimed with uneasy conviction.

'This is were you belong, Tirrik, were you were meant to be. Ours is a good place if you heed the signs and warnings around you,' her father reproached her sternly with yet a hint of affection, bestowing on her the name of the buoyant-flighted tern.

'Girls never sail the seas,' Krista lisped in her short-tongued, short-phrased manner. 'No, never though,' she added under considerable effort, followed by a succession of diabolical facial expressions. Words never came easy to her, neither the kind ones nor the brutish types; pulling faces seemed the next best thing to compensate for her verbal inadequacy. No amount of coaxing would stir her into any kind of action. In Siegund's estimation, insults were almost as ineffective, but at least they instigated one of Krista's legs to kick out.

Maunsie's head gyrated with disapproval at the twins tedious quarrels. Although being the twins senior by one year, he lacked Krista's plumpness and Siegund's wiry robustness, so it was quite prudent of him to keep out of any disputes.

Twenty year old Rory, less tolerant than Maunsie, wrested a despairing frown from his expressionless face, but being a man of few words, respectfully, if somewhat impatiently, left the command to his father. And today Jan was in a generous mood, willing to ignore whispers, giggles, sighs, and scuffling feet until Josefa's silent glance demanded him to take control. She thought him far too lenient, though she would not say so.

And then there was nineteen year old Hegan with her father's ice-blue eyes and bleached- straw hair and with her mother's commendable and much appraised aptitude for a great number of useful occupations. She was fidgeting nervously like an ill-sitting hen on addled eggs; Hegan, who always seemed to be in control, had something to say and did not know how to say it. She coughed, cleared her throat, then coughed again.

'Fadder..., she stammered at last, and the naturally generous colour in her face deepened by several degrees. 'Duncan Macalay wishes to pay you a visit.' She swallowed hard and quickly continued lest the courage should leave her: 'Will he be welcome in your home?'

Duncan from the Northstane was a regular caller and a willing helper when help was needed. He had never required permission before, but this would be no ordinary visit. The flicker of joy that had appeared on Josefa's face vanished quickly under nervous restraint. Jan knitted his bushy eyebrows, closed his eyes as if in great pain and braced himself under the heavy load his daughter had placed upon his shoulders. There was much to think about - and Jan thought. He had feared this day, had seen the signs and had hoped that Hegan's good sense might prevail. She had no sense after all. Not that the Macalays, whose ancestors had ventured from their native Scotland generations ago, were not honest, hardworking people; no one could fault them in that. The problem lay in old Jock's legacy - the flame-red hair, which he had passed on to all his offspring and theirs after. Stubborn superstitions, interwoven with tales from the past, had cruelly obliterated all Macalay hopes of wedlock amongst the Kuans. It still burdened that good family today, though the redness at last showed signs of weakening.

Throughout the generations the blemished Macalay fledglings had left the island in shame and bitter disappointment never to return, all except one of each brood who brought back from the rugged Highlands the darkest flower to be found - not always a willing one, it was said. For some of the young Macalays, separation had been too hard to bear, but finding loneliness no easier option  had died of mysterious maladies or unexplained accidents, so rumours had it. But rumours are like sailors' yarns - a little added, a little lost as time goes by. Their graves were long overgrown now, but their grief was never forgotten; Donald, Matt, Kathleen, Marie, Bridie - all now ghosts from a troubled past. Then there was Marnie...., ah, but no one spoke of her. They would not speak of bad things until a safe time had elapsed, until pain, shame or uneasiness was no longer acute, but they did not forget. Each shadow, each cloud, each blade of grass held secrets from a past that lived constantly alongside them.

This is how it was, how it had always been; farewells, tears, losses, grief; each generation cursed and torn apart. The Macalays' childhood belonged to Skerra Kua, their womanhood to the Highlands, their manhood to the sea. And now Jan was faced with the incredible decision whether or not to allow the redness to taint the Nordic blood. With sombre deliberation he weighed up the matter with all its adverse implications, gasping massive sighs under the burden of infinite responsibility. In the end he nodded gravely, being a fair man and not entirely without compassion however sternly hidden behind the mask of authoritative severity.

'I will see him,' he said formally, committing himself to neither a welcome nor a hasty rejection in view of the steadily dwindling Kuan population. Hegan's question was understood, her request partly and rather reluctantly granted - what else was there to be said? And consequently, nothing was said.

The moment of uneasy silence was broken by a man's voice calling from the byre with great urgency. Seconds later young

Patersen from the Kirk croft stood in the doorway, fighting hard for his breath. In his obvious distress he seemed hardly able to make sense even to himself.

'What is it, Godfrey? Why the haste on this holy morn?' Jan stood up with a groan of discomfort. 'Jesses and Mary,' he grumbled, 'there's much rain on the way; the weather is in my bones today.' He reached for the brandy and poured himself and the early visitor a drink.

Godfrey swallowed the much needed tonic in one noisy gulp and wiped large, shimmering droplets of perspiration from his brow. Fear and bewilderment glimmered in his usually calm, grey eyes, which now pleaded for help with unwarranted intensity. 'For the mercy of the gods, Midder Nielsen, Sanna's time has come!' he spluttered out rapidly as if to make up for the time lost in swallowing the drink. 'Pray, good woman,' lend your skills and help her coax the bairn into the world. She has laboured all night. I fear she is fading badly.'

'It's her first one, young man,' Josefa replied. 'She's bound to take time over it; it will come easier to her once she gets the hang of it, mark my word.' Her words of reassurance in her matter-of-fact manner were tainted by the grave concern her face could not hide. She stood up, crossed herself in the Christian way, reached with forced smile for her cape and her basket of medicinal herbs. 'I would she could wait till tomorrow,' she mumbled as if to herself, then expelled a huge volume of air followed by a deep intake of breath, making the whole thing sound like a back-to-front sigh. 'Be that as it may, I'll see what can be done. Hegan will look after the affairs here, though sooner or later she'll have to come with me to learn my skills; I shall not live forever - not that I wish to,' she added so by the way.

They had gone - the fretting expectant father in shabby grey smock and patched-up trousers tied with string around the waist, and the island's midwife, nurse and doctor, elected by the inhabitants without a vote being cast either for or against this good woman who knew better than any one how and when to use what herb and for which malady. The silent glances of those left behind adhered themselves to the byre door.

'A mortal child has no business to be born on Christmas day, no damn business at all,' Rory huffed his dismay and then fell silent again.

The fire seemed to have lost its warmth; the candles flickered as if under great agitation. A piece of peat fell from the grate, whined crackled, spit and then lay smouldering on the hard-trodden mud floor, soothsaying with noisy testimony the arrival of a visitor, whoever it may be.

'Nay, no good ever comes our way, it must be evil,' Maunsie offered with a sort of gloomy acceptance.

'Indeed not,' Siegund advised him. 'I dreamt of a beautiful stranger, indeed a god.'

'No, never though,' Krista interrupted her. 'Perhaps Erik is coming home.'

Hegan told all three of them to shut up and then fell into deep thought. Quite unintended she suddenly said: 'Might Sanna's child be a mere visitor, a traveller from the unknown, taking a temporary rest before returning to the unknown? The gods forbid it!'

Now she was told to shut up. Jan was at a loss whether to place the peat back onto the fire and thus bidding the visitor welcome, or to sink the smoking ember into a pail of water and bid him to keep away. He wrinkled his brow and closed his eyes in deep concentration. A moment later he returned the peat to the grate, hiding it discretely by a fresh piece, thus leaving the options open and placing the onus on the visitor to decide. To be on the safe side he chanted strange rhymes with even stranger voices and intonations; Jan knew rhymes for all occasions - for moments of fear, of joy, and of sadness. The family listened so intently, they almost fell into a trance.

'All is well,' Jan reassured his children at length, although his sombre face did not give away what he really thought. He saw the questioning eyes directed towards him, which prompted him to add in a somewhat easier tone: 'The celebrations tonight will instil courage and hope in us so that we may carry on the toil of life without complaint.'

# Chapter 2

Two figures, one tall and straight, the other small and crooked, were making their way to the Hawkledge croft to watch the annual Christmas spectacle. Siegund's chirpy song rang out into the winter air.

'Nay, it's not right that you should sing here,' Maunsie panted, pointing a thin finger in the direction of the graveyard way beyond the knoll. 'I hear them whisper and groan.' He shuddered, twitched and grinned embarrassed at his self-confessed cowardice.

'Blow me down, Maunsie, it's only the wind moaning across the moor,' she persuaded him, content to blame his lack of bravery on his dwarfish stature. 'The dead don't harm us. And even if old Swaalie's soul still wanders the hills, he must keep company with the creatures of the night; the day is for the living. Can't you walk faster? We're going to miss the game.' Then she reminded herself of his dreadful affliction and her eyes instantly filled with tears of compassion, but just as swiftly as the sadness had come it left her again, obliterated from her mind by other matters. They were approaching the Kirk croft where their mother was using her skills at this very moment. Siegund wanted to know where Midder coaxed all those bairns from; and why did she coax them into the world when so many of them did not stay?

'Nay, you'll know in good time,' Maunsie told her awkwardly, having no great knowledge of such matters either, and what he did know he would rather not explain. 'Yay, patience is a virtuous thi.....' His mouth slammed shut with a rattle at his sister's rumbustious hands as she pushed him hard against the hilldyke, the wall of stone and earth that surrounded all ten crofts to keep the crops safe from straying sheep.

Both on their knees now, they peered cautiously through a gap. By the rickety shed stood Godfrey, his back turned towards his troubles, drawing with the tip if his boots signs and symbols into the soft, wet ground. He was mumbling something to himself, his hands clasped over his ears, and there he stood, quite motionless now, unaware of being observed. They witnessed the man's disarrayed prayers, shared his moment of fear, of weakness. In silence they prayed with him. But they should not have intruded; emotions, anxiety, grief - they were private matters.

'Godfrey, you scoundrel,' Josefa called with mild aggravation. 'Can't you be at hand at a time like this? Your woman wants you. You have a fine daughter.' She shook her head impatiently and demanded his presence. And Godfrey, his senses instantly revived, raised his hands to heaven in gratitude. He left his signs and symbols, grinned from ear to ear and hurried after Josefa. A girl born on Yule day might be acceptable to folks; had it been a boy, well......

'Blow me down, the air is laden, indeed it is,' Siegund whispered full of guilt and secret excitement. Maunsie grinned a little sheepishly. His oscillating head on pivot neck prompted Siegund to fold up with laughter, and immediately she felt ashamed of her unkindness. As so often, her feelings suffered a severe identity crisis. She was not sure whether she ought to be happy or sad, but she rarely did things by half, indulging mostly in highly emotional extremities, and any uncertainties were short-lived. Already she skipped along the common path, piping a merry little tune, her philosophy being that, although singing did not solve problems, neither did it make them worse.

The path, stony in places and muddy in others, rose and fell like the sea, then ascended steeply to the Hawkledge. With severe expression Maunsie secretly envied his sister's agility. He was ashamed of his own weakness. Exertion tainted his bilious face not red but a kind of pale orange as he trudged along with wheezing breath. From the tip of his nose swung a tiny droplet from side to side; he had neither strength nor inclination to wipe it away. At the top of the hill he stopped and stood still for a long while, gallantly pretending to admire the view. And indeed, from this elevated spot the rolling landscape, despite its barren winter dress, deserved much admiration, though in Siegund's estimation the tiny plots of tilled fields were far less significant than the patches on Godfrey's trousers, to which Maunsie laughed his sheep-like baah-baah.

Far below them, clown-faced puffins skimmed low over foamy crests. Siegund remembered the falling ember. Her eyes began to search the vast stretch of ocean for the visitor. There was no sign of a boat. She shrugged away the disappointment. Cheers, laughter and the occasional groan came from the field nearby. Young men, some not so young, kicked a makeshift ball around - and the hell out of each other. They yelled to each other, at each other, tried to trip up a rival and tripped up themselves. Grimy faces glowed with excitement and exertion, mud-spattered legs in rolled up trousers chased after an inflated pig bladder covered in cow hide.

She longed to join the semi-controlled madness, longed to be free of imposed restrictions, even went as far as wanting to remain a child forever, though on this point she was in the habit of picking and choosing as it suited the moment. Bitterly she complained of unfair advantages and wished away her girlhood. Her self-pity quickly vanished under the renewed awareness of Maunsie's predicament, and once more her compassion burned fiercely for this crocked figure of a boy with flat, pasty face and ungainly gait. What were folks thinking of? They thought him fortunate and regarded him with great esteem on account of a cripple's good-luck influence. The crofters, especially when they turned their hand to becoming fishermen, appreciated his shrewdness when accidentally-on-purpose he crossed their path. He was their talisman; no rabbit's foot, no four-leafed clover could have provided such confidence.

Here, amongst the barren fields, Maunsie looked quite forlorn, his woolly hat pulled down to eyebrows that met on the bridge of his nose. Clad in dark grey, baggy trousers and equally baggy coat he resembled a tiny drowning man waiting for the last wave to come and swallow him up. His gentle, yet knowing eyes lacked the sparkle of youth and their almond shape seemed quite inappropriate in the square, broad face.

'Poor Maunsie, you will never be able to play with them,' she sighed.

'Nay, Siegund, I don't want your pity. I'm not unhappy - nay, not very much,' he told her.

'Indeed! Too much sadness is unwholesome for the liver.' She reflected briefly on the fiddler's inability to join the lads, being legless each Yule day somewhere on the Northstane. She got annoyed that the fiddler kept creeping into her head, brief though those moments were.

'Maunsie, I really did dream of a stranger with blond hair and skin of gold - indeed, a god. And he will come!'

'Nay, dreams mean nothing.' Maunsie cringed so that his shoulders met his ears. Sudden curiosity prompted his head to emerge again. A cautious scan across the swell revealed no boat.

She laughed her silver-bell laugh. The beautiful god was forgotten when she caught sight of mud-caked, mud-baked Malcolm Macalay, whose good looks had temporarily suffered great indignity. Glistening white teeth in a grimy face revealed his smile. His wind-tussled crop of hair resembled vaguely a fading harvest sun caught out by evening dusk; deep auburn - not at all the blazing redness of the old Macalay stock.

'Malkie, don't run yourself into the ground,' she called to him full of girlish glee. 'You'll not be able to dance if you're all done in. Remember, there's merriment in our barn tonight.'

A moment ago she had complained of her unfair lot, now she was glad to be a woman; she was in love with Malkie the harvest sun - redness or not, her heart knew best. Besides, what was good for the goose was good for the gander, and Hegan with her Duncan-fetish was definitely a goose. She cheered when Malcolm rushed off in a most gallant effort to display his worthiness. 'Blow me down, Maunsie, isn't it exciting?'

'What is?' he asked, far less impressed with life's fortunes and seriously urged his sister to a little more modesty. With downcast eyes he suddenly confessed: 'I wish you would never leave me, Siegund. How lonely I shall be.' Three death gasps followed, adding infinite gravity to his words as if his loneliness had already begun.

A sharp wind whistled across dead grass and sparse heather. Loose-fitting garments flapped and bulged like grand sails at high sea. There was no shelter from its blustery sting, and for all the heat of Siegund's young passion the cold ruffled her skin with menacing obstinacy.

'The tide is turning, let's go to the beach, Maunsie,' she suggested, and without waiting for an answer she cheerfully left passion and growing up for another day, gladly left the likes of Udo Patersen who was beset with more patches than his son Godfrey, and the likes of neatly-dressed Johannes the weaver who looked like the other's master, yet had no greater or lesser standing in the community, to their dreams of yester-year when they too had played the Yule-day game. She was Siegund the child again, a laughing, frolicking youngster, pitying briefly old Udo for not yet knowing of his granddaughter's arrival and pitying herself for not being able to tell him. She ran down the slope, kicking her whippet legs behind her. Her long blond hair streamed in the wind. She neither looked back nor doubted that Maunsie would follow.

From the lofty Hawkledge the tiny surrounding islands had seemed like scattered, floating pastures; down here, on the stony beach, amongst boulders and isolated patches of sand and shingle, there was no sign of another shore, no view of cottages and crofts - nothing but birds, stacks and skerries, and serrated rocks and slippery shelves rising out of endless, turbulent sea. Even Papa Kira, full of mysteries, a tiny island without beach, where people and boats had to be hoisted onto dry land, seemed now lost to the sea. In the solitude of this watery wilderness she forgot Malcolm and thought of the stranger again. A freakish piety overcame her, prompted her to kneel and pray. Vaguely she heard her brother's harsh wheezing and for a moment she looked at him with a rigid stare of incomprehension; concern for him demanded alertness to return.

Maunsie pointed to the skerries where a boat, partly hidden from view by the stony giants, precariously rode the surf in haphazard manner. It was hard to say whether it was coming or going, or intending to climb the rocks.

'Nay, nay, what lack of care,' he muttered. 'It's not even moored down.'

'Indeed not!' She replied. 'Can you tie ropes to the waves?'

The boat came rapidly closer and with a grating thud ran aground. The rolling breakers crashed against the marooned vessel. Through the clamour they heard a short eerie sound coming from what seemed no more than a bundle of rags. It may have been a moan, it may have been the wind, or perhaps they had not heard anything at all. The boat shuddered, unable to move either forward or back, but still, the sea refused to give it up, pushing and pulling, rocking the unsecured stern from side to side.

They stared at each other in hopeless indecision, but as always, resolution came swiftly to Siegund. Ignoring her brother's exasperated warnings she stepped into the foamy wetness, her dress and coat raised high above her knees. The icy water gushed into her laced up boots, saturated her woollen stockings and crept up to her thighs. Many a time had she clambered across this narrow stretch of stony terraces, worn smooth by a million flood-tides, but the tide had been out then. She waded alongside the boat. The icy water bit into her flesh, yet she hardly felt it. Maunsie lamented pitifully, all the while hopping this way and that, his arms flailing furiously inside sleeves that had fallen over his hands, and by all intent and purpose he seemed to be imitating a broken-winged albatross trying to get airborne.

For Siegund there existed only a boat, a ragged coat and a whispering voice inside her head. Her mouth agape, her deep-blue eyes large and round with astonishment she looked down at the tangle of hair - wet, greasy, unkempt, blonde hair. The god from her dream had come to her, lay helplessly, motionless to test her charity. His blistered lips twitched as if trying to form a word. A voice told her she must run to the stream of wisdom so that he might drink its healing powers. She looked around to know the speaker but saw only Maunsie whose wailing lamentations had no likeness to the voice she had heard.

'Blow me down, I don't know the stream, I'm not very wise!' she called out. It was her turn to lament now.

Maunsie had heard only the word *stream.* He was surprised at his sister's forgetfulness and tried to help her out by pointing to the white cascade gushing down from the cliff edge onto the beach. She nodded gratefully.

'Stay with him, Maunsie,' she told him. 'Don't let him go away.'

'Nay Siegund, he's in no fettle to go anywhere. Perhaps.... he never....will.'

Siegund was already hurrying away, had neither heard her brother's words, nor taken notice of the fiddle that lay at the stern of the boat. But Maunsie had seen it from the shore. He strained his neck to see it better.

'If the stranger were to die....' He struggled fiercely with his conscience; the tempter had come to him. How hard it was to resist the wicked thoughts. He wished his sister back and wished her away, then wished the stranger away, then himself. 'Nay, nay, it's not right, it's evil,' he muttered, fearful of his malevolent thoughts and words. 'But if the stranger were to perish....oh, great shame on me. Nay, it's damnable, it's sad; the longing is turning my heart wicked and I can't stop myself. But if he were to die...if only he would die!'

'Maunsie, how dare you say such dreadful things, how unworthy are your uncharitable thoughts, for indeed, he is a god.'

Maunsie seemed surprised at his sister's swift return, surprised even at her presence. His head gyrated, his face twitched, his bony finger pointed. 'Nay, he's no more a god than I am. Anyway, I think he's dead.' There was a hint of triumph in his voice.

'Blow me down, gods never die, indeed not.' She waded back into the foamy surf to offer the precious drink to the god for whose care she felt herself chosen. God or not, he would not have to mind drinking from her boot, which held the fresh water quite adequately. With her fingers tightly cupped she drew out a little of the life-giving fluid and released it onto his lips. A few drops trickled onto his stubbly chin. She carefully mopped them away with her skirt, uncertain whether such liberties as touching a god's face were forgivable. 'He feels so cold, so very, very cold,' she called through her own shattering teeth.

'Yay, that's because he's dead, so very, very dead,' Maunsie replied and wished him so. 'He is a dead mortal, who doesn't need a fiddle any more.'

'Maunsie, you'll be cursed forever for you blasphemy. Go, fetch Fadder and Midder. Hurry!'

He gladly left the beach with its unholy air; his unkind thoughts followed him and he began to sob.

'It's wicked, it's sad that my happiness should depend on death.' Clumsily he picked his way up the stony slope. For his sister's sake he must hasten, for his own he would tarry.

Siegund's mind filled with whimsical suppositions. She lacked time and space to know what was in her brother's heart; she was scarcely aware of what was in her own. An unknown voice, a magic force controlled her thoughts and movements, told her to climb into the boat, to crawl under the ragged coat - to lie beside the god. The sea roared, the blustery wind passed over her, whistling one moment and screeching the next. She lifted her hands to her mouth and felt the warmth of her breath.

'Gods need warmth too,' the voice inside her head said.

Willingly she shared her warm breath with him, placing her mouth close to his lips, not daring to touch them. Hard and prolonged she breathed into the sallow face, depriving her lungs of sufficient air so that her head began to spin. Entangled thoughts ebbed and flowed with the sounds of wind and sea which once more staged their furious concert, far more powerful than before - unnerving instead of enchanting, maddening instead of tantalizing. Gulls shrieked in chorus. Dream or wakefulness, god or mortal - it was not important; it was right to be here with this stranger, right that her body should be close to his, separated only by layers of wet clothing. -it was proper in its impropriety. If only he would open his eyes. Perhaps Maunsie was right, perhaps this was just a man - a dead man. The maddening, mind-corrupting music stopped abruptly, hurled her out of the quivering flight of fancy into momentary tearless bewilderment. She fled from his side, wanted to cry out but had no longer a voice. To abandon a god meant eternal wrath of all deities, but to lie with a corpse....

Trapped in this hopeless dilemma she commanded the doubts to leave her as if his survival depended on her belief in him. How dark and dismal the sky had grown. She felt the icy coldness of death creep to her heart; it numbed her trembling body into a kind of mortal rigour. Only her eyes and lips fought bravely her own death-like immobility.

'What does it mean? What must I do?' she managed to whisper. Her leaden eyes searched the heavens, but heaven withheld its answer. She dragged her glazed stare back to her charge. She thought she had seen a flicker of movement, then she was less sure, and then she was sure she had not seen anything at all. She shuffled a little closer to him. Her hand brushed stiffly over his coarse, lifeless hair. Beneath his closed eyelids his eyes began to move slowly. From his parting lips came a plea for water or it may have been no more than a sigh, but he was alive, that much was clear. If her breath had restored his life, now she drew new vitality from his apparent resurrection. Her chest heaved, her limbs trembled, her chin quivered, her teeth rattled, and all the while she tried to convince him and herself with the greatest tenacity of her unshakable faith in him. She lifted his head gently into her lap and held the boot to his lips. He flinched under the touch of the leather. Greedily he drew from the clear water.

'Not too much at once now,' she advised him. 'You'll throw up.' She wondered if gods really did throw up; she took the boot away just in case. Carefully she began to bathe the saline crust from his eyelids until he opened his eyes - gentle eyes, dark velvet stars dulled by immense suffering, but despite the dullness they shone deep into her soul and kindled a brilliant light, an eternal flame in her changeable heart. Blond hair and dark, dark eyes. She gazed at her god and beheld his strangeness with wonder.

'Who...are...you? I mean to say, what place is this?' the man whispered with great effort.

'Blow me, don't you know? I'm Siegund from the Harehill and this is Skerra Kua.' She reflected for a moment. 'I suppose you can't know everything.'

'Alas, no one knows everything.' He gave a harsh cough.

'Not even the gods?' she pursued the inquiry.'

'Not even the gods, I dare say. Knowledge goes far beyond infinity.'

'Blow me, does it indeed?' she asked, having no idea where infinity might be. The stranger lifted his head, glanced around nervously and fell back into her lap with ungodly heaviness.

'Can you keep a secret?' he asked and nodded at the same time as if he had no doubt of her loyalty. 'My name is Garwulf. Tell no one of me.'

'Maunsie knows of you.' Her hand flew to her mouth. 'He's gone to fetch my folks. What was I to do?'

'Then I must trust them too.' Awkwardly he wrested his hands from under his coat and held them close to her face. 'Untie them, sweet child.'

'Blow me, I didn't know, though I touched your hands.' She bit her lip. 'You didn't mind, did you? I mean, that I touched them.' To show her remorse, and to make good the trespass of others against him, she quickly offered him another sip of water, asking tearfully the circumstances of his plight.

'It is of little consequence. It was not malice, I dare say. Alas, fear and ignorance - these are powerful things that drive men and women to cruel, thoughtless acts. I have no hatred for them - hatred is as unprofitable as fear and ignorance.' His whispering voice added mystery to all he said.

He who could forgive his enemies so readily was indeed a god - to Siegund's way of thinking anyway. What did it matter that his face and hair were grimy, that his limbs had turned to ice, that his throat was ablaze with thirst, that his body was weaker than wilted grass? She believed in his power and greatness beyond those human frailties, and she told him so.

'If you also untie my feet I will make you my goddess,' he said, his eyes vaguely smiling since his lips were unable to do so.

'Blow me, do you mean it?' she gasped, though at the moment she would have preferred a warm bed to a heavenly star. 'But why were folks afraid? I'd never be afraid of you.'

'You ask many questions, child, and I am weary. Alas, my need of a friend is great, so I dare say, I must tell you. But it is our secret! You see, I was their scapegoat. They tied me up and set me afloat. I drifted, I know not how long, and when I thought that my hour had come, being quite beyond caring, I commended body and soul to the superior Beings of the sea.'

'But...but do gods have superiors, too?'

'You are a strange child. Well, yes, I dare say they have. No word to any one now; promise?'

The retreating sea had left the boat perched on the flat rock like a stranded dolphin. They heard muffled voices and hurried footsteps. With sudden alarm Siegund remembered the island's rules; to lie with a stranger was not one of them. She tried to estimate the gravity of her sin, if indeed it was a sin to tend to a god. With numbed hands and half frozen legs, one boot on and one boot off, she crawled on hands and knees over the stony terrace, calling her pledge of secrecy to the god who had no greater resilience to hardship than any mortal man.

# Chapter 3

The rescue had been swift and efficient, though not without a fair amount of chuntering; Jan and Rory had chuntered on account of the stranger's great height and weight; Josefa had chuntered because her daughter got herself chilled to the bone; Maunsie had grumbled because he had carried the fiddle that would never be his own; Hegan had grumbled because of the extra chores of preparing a bed of straw in the outhouse; Krista was unhappy because she was afraid of strangers and wanted nothing to do with him. As for Siegund - she had been in no state to chunter. She had been sent to bed. Now, as the weary day folded its grey shroud of approaching darkness around its shoulders, she woke from her unusual afternoon nap. Drowsily she squinted at the oil lamp above her head and propped herself up on the great driftwood pallet that was the girls' communal bed.

'Foolish girl,' she heard her mother say in the semi-darkness of the *ben*. 'There shall be no celebrations for you today. And you must blame yourself.'

'But I'm well, Midder, indeed I am,' Siegund insisted while her feverish skin tightened under crawling, cold showers; even her goose pimples had goose pimples and her headache had a headache, but she would rather die of the ague than of missing the festivities. She continued pleading immaculate health, blaming the beastly twilight for looking ghastly and - forgetting her place - rather hastily compared her mother's own paleness with that of a bedridden butterfly and immediately asked for forgiveness. She went further than that, she made the grand gesture of promising obedience and to work twice as hard from now on, to which Josefa shook her head, deeming it an improvement for her to work hard just once; besides, children were not to barter with their peers, but in the end Josefa, much against her better judgement and quite out of character, gave in.

In the *but* Hegan was busy with needle and thread. She rolled her ice-blue eyes upwards in disbelief at her sister's appearance so that they looked like tiny snowballs in her cold face. Jan shook his head, but had nothing to say. Rory frowned and furiously poked the ever-burning peat fire, producing a lively shower of sparks that bombarded the old, smoky hearthstone.

'Will the stranger live?' Siegund ventured to ask. 'He was dead, indeed he was.'

'Holy Midder, what nonsense you talk, child,' Josefa muttered. Her tongue produced a whole string of disapproving clacks. 'He'll live, mark my word! You may take some broth to him; a little and often is the rule in a case as his. Take Maunsie with you - for decency's sake.'

Siegund hugged her mother, kissed her lined forehead, praised her cleverness with unreserved generosity and secretly longed for her affection. But Josefa pushed her away - she always pushed her away. Josefa sternly denied cleverness, but allowed herself humbly the attribute of common sense and urged her daughter to try using her head for more useful things, too. As far as Siegund saw it, it was not so much the trying - the results just were inadequate, disappointing even to her, which in turn reduced the merit in trying.

All the while Maunsie had looked on with an unprecedented see-if-I-care manner, and now, with the same mute disinterest he headed for the byre, opened and closed the doors for his sister as a matter of duty and carried the light that guided them across the yard. His angular face was as grim as that of a hangman's assistant who had opted to hang himself instead of the condemned.

'What's griping you, Maunsie,' Siegund asked and quite inappropriately added that his face was as long as short man's legging, to which Maunsie had no reply.

In the duskiness of the outhouse the grey blankets blotted out Garwulf's form. His head seemed the only part left of him. The faint glow of the lamp above him shone like a halo either just in the making or about to extinguish. Unreality returned; it whispered in wordless, motionless worship and hung sullenly in the shadows of the low beams. Amongst the shadows quivered the dark reflections of contrasting human figures. Two outstretched arms offered food to a god. At any moment the three people, neither united nor apart in destiny, might slip into irreversible suspended animation.

'Nay, Siegund, if you don't look sharp, you'll spill the boiling stuff all over him,' Maunsie piped, determined not to be drawn into his sister's fantasy world again. 'You'll frizzle your god to a frazzle once and for all.'

Startled out of his sleep Garwulf rose with a sudden jerk and shielded his eyes against the light with a violent sweep of the hand as if to fend off an assailant. The tangled hair framed his stubbly face, a face too drawn and pallid to pass as handsome. The borrowed shirt stretched tightly across his chest and the shortness of the sleeves exposed a strong arm; not that Jan, whose clothes he wore, lacked in stature. Siegund saw only beauty, saw benevolence in his gentle eyes, saw forgiveness in his distorting lips that suggested a smile, saw generosity in his large hands, saw redemption in his broad shoulders.

'Lo! My goddess Freyja and St. Maunsie! I am in good hands,' Garwulf said with a soft, baritone voice not yet entirely restored. All the same, he managed to speak elaborate words of appreciation with a good deal of sincerity. To Maunsie, with an axe twice his own size to grind, they smacked of falsity, of cheap flattery.

'Nay, nay, you need not bother. Do not mock us so,' he replied stiffly, imitating annoyed the stranger's formal way of speaking. Maunsie was not moody by nature and generally thought moderation in all things far safer than his sister's extremities, but he disliked the pompous wreck of a man who had no intention to die. The fancy words of gratitude, of being indebted to them until the end of time, and his promise of reward one day, fuelled his anger.

Siegund's fierce kick, directed towards her brother's shin, stunned him into a speechless stare. It instantly adhered the flow of further regrettable words to his lips. She took it upon herself to invite Garwulf to the celebrations that were to commence shortly, but he declined on account of his present unfortunate infirmity, of the need to reflect on past events and of the necessity to think of the future.

'That's just as well,' Maunsie replied. His unprecedented anger confused and frightened him and hampered him in contemplating the right course of action to take. He wanted to put an end to his sister's unworthy pleading. In his lack of regular strenuous mental exercises he was seldom blessed with instantaneous inspirations, but now the demons of envy and jealousy overwhelmed the once so gentle heart.

'Play for us, stranger,' he demanded. 'Or can't you play?'

'I play as well as most, and better than some. Alas, not today, no, not today. No worthwhile music can flow from hands devoured by cold. Perhaps tomorrow. Yes, if the gods will it, I shall play for you tomorrow.'

'Tomorrow, tomorrow!' Maunsie aped. Gratitude, my eye! Nay, it's all fancy talk. Reward us now if your gratitude is so great. Give me your fiddle.' In his bitterness he had broken a sacred rule by asking a reward for a life saved; a reward might be received, but never asked for. Josefa came into the outhouse not a moment too soon and with her no-nonsense voice prevented Maunsie from sinning further. She left as swiftly as she had arrived.

Maunsie took Siegund's hand and pulled her outside. The wind cooled their glowing cheeks. At the far end of the yard the barn stood in brooding silence, oblivious of the merriment to come. Skilfully they negotiated the stepping-stones, which paved the way from barn to byre and from byre to outhouses and sties across a sea of squelching mud and slurry. One slip could mean anything from washing feet to the whole blessed treatment with sandy soap and lukewarm water.

Through the slightly open byre door peered Krista cautiously into the early night. In her hand trembled two lights, one to guide her, and the other to grace the barn. She was to help with the final preparations to make the barn presentable for the guests, but she refused to venture out into the dark. With a multiple of facial contortions she pushed the lamps into Siegund's hand while lisping something about bedtime, then hurried back to seek the safety of the *ben.*

Siegund shrugged her shoulder's, preferring not to figure out her sister's lack of spirit when her own heart was brimming with an enthusiasm that left neither room nor time for psycho-analysis had she known the meaning of it, or indeed, the word itself. To and fro she ran, fetching, carrying, dashing this way and that. And all the while Maunsie's mute shadow bobbed up behind her at every turn, every corner and every door. 'Spy or chaperon?' she wondered and wished he would fall into the slurry.

At last all was ready. The barn in its discerning stillness seemed to hold its breath. Herbs, rushes, heather and roots hung from crooked driftwood beams and lend their unobtrusive decor to the dignified plainness. The dried vegetation constituted Josefa's dispensary and were meant to save lives; now they added their scent to the aroma of fresh oatmeal cakes, mutton and roasted chicken.

On the common path flickered specks of light, which announced the approach of the guests. The blustery night brought them rapidly closer. Friends, neighbours, the not-so-friendly, they all came, bringing with them goodwill and gifts of food to be shared by all. Their lamps would be left burning through-out the night so that with each new arrival the barn became a little brighter.

Now that the hustle and bustle of preparations was over, Siegund felt the sickening ague creep back, intensified by the pungent odour of the burning fish oil that stifled the air. She shuddered. The goose pimples had come to the dance after all. Her body ached; her head seemed lighter than air, her face burned more intensely than all the puny lamps combined. With feverish eyes she searched for Garwulf. Disappointment pulled her throat tighter.

'Nay, Siegund, he'll not be coming, and it's just as well.' Maunsie reminded her with semi-controlled irritation of her folly. 'Nay, don't pretend. I know of your foolish fancies. You had your eyes on Malcolm this morn; yay, and for all the redness, he is a better fellow than the wreck in the shed, of whom you know nothing.'

'Blow me down, Maunsie, how can you compare a boy with a god?' she whispered. 'You don't understand!'

'Nay, I don't. But it's wrong, it's sad,' he muttered. As always, his sadness made him look comical as much as pitiful. His dark head swayed so that his pudding-bowl haircut orbited like a moon in total eclipse.

'Blow me, you cluck like a hen with toothache, Maunsie. Leave your clucking to Hegan and Krista; it suits them better. Anyway, what's keeping the fiddler? I want to dance.' Her watchful eyes registered every new arrival. Garwulf or Malcolm - she would dance.

Roland Mulvoen stalked into the barn, his black hat a little battered, his coat a little creased, but his body none the worse for his earlier indulgence. He shook himself as if to shake the wind out of his clothes, then bowed to the cries for music and to the thunderous applause he accepted as his due.

'Aye, aye, good people; music you shall have, that you shall, but first I need a drop of brandy - medicinal reason, you'll understand.'

Jan Nielsen was an excellent host and a man of good humour when humour was appropriate. He obliged with a knowing smile, praised the healing power of the good brew and commiserated with an exaggerated wink the musician's regular Sunday malady, to which Roland bowed again. There was nobleness in the fiddler's gesture, which almost gave the alleged malady credibility, though it was clear from the first cords he struck that the music did not do justice to the expertly stilled mountain dew, but neither where there mountains on the island, nor any great musical expectations.

The young folk danced; Duncan with Hegan, Rory with Ingeborg Johansen, Sven Klaasen with Adelika - yes, pretty Adelika Macalay with flame-red hair, ivory skin and a rainbow of freckles across the bridge of her nose. In her gentle smile lurked doubt and sadness. Perhaps at this very moment she thought of poor Bridie who had never been a bride. But time, the proverbial healer of everything, had weakened the barrier and taken the dread away from the young generation; time had also brought forth the very first Macalay bairn with near black hair. This miracle-child, Ethel's eight year old daughter Nellie, was adored by her family as a symbol of salvation, of unity, of hope; she would be remembered and talked about long after Nellie and her contemporaries were no more.

Nevertheless, even today when struggle and strife were pushed far from folk's minds, the elders were still wary of matrimonial alliance with the redness. They looked on, at a loss at what should be done - and did nothing except keep discreet vigil over them as over all the young folks. There were weds and unweds on Skerra Kua - never lovers. Stern glances would soon remind any over-enthusiastic admirer to keep affection hidden within the throbbing heart; they would impress upon the careless offender that displayed emotions were unworthy of the children of the Norsemen. They talked of those absent - the sick, the very young and the very old - but avoided talk of those who were no more; today was a day of joy. And amongst all those smiling faces there was scarcely one that could have matched Malcolm Macalay's if charm had been in question - his hair ruffled by the wind, his hazel eyes beaming.

'Och, Maunsie, will ye fergive me fer taking yer faverit sister from yer,' he asked with impish smile.

'Nay, what do I care for dancing? I'd rather watch Roland's fingers move over the strings, yay, but I wish he wouldn't try to strangle the fiddle. He has no ear for a good tune.'

'That's a fact,' Malcolm, at heart a true native, replied in his peculiar Kuan-Scottish Macalay dialect. 'Our pigs were sheer scared out of their bacon this morn, ye ken.'

Siegund scarcely heard his words. She looked at him with blank eyes while her mind saw Garwulf's image. Familiar faces seemed like strange masks, homely voices came to her like plaintive mutters. Roland's fiddle cried its wooden heart out. The music seemed like the distant roar of the ocean. It came closer, louder, grew to a thunderous clamour in her paining ears. For the third time this day the wild orchestra staged its formidable concert - three, a good number, the Kuan's sacred number. She allowed it to posses her, to control her, had no choice in the matter anyway; it urged her on, drove her naturally high spirits beyond the threshold of propriety. Dignity! She remembered her mother's much repeated demand. What did dignity mean? Hiding the truth, by all accounts. How could dignity be proper when lies were not? Dignity! Dignity!

The word echoed inside her head and then was swallowed up by the maddening intermezzo. Dark-skinned girls with scented flowers in black hair beckoned to her, invited her to dance with them, showed her how to move gracefully and whispered of seduction; they did not tell her what the word meant. The music played faster and wilder; it linked sadistically with the pain in her limbs and drove her into deeper frenzy. Her wiry body, clad in unflattering grey dress, swayed. She glowed with fever as much as with exhilaration, unaware of the aching and breaking hearts around her. Against all principles, the young men, blinded by her beauty and spurred by her fiery temperament, became contaminated and almost started a brawl over whose turn it should be next to dance with her, though they did not know her way of dancing. Malcolm had withdrawn into the shadowy background, his pride damaged, his hopes for the future shattered.

Maunsie looked on with awe. His sister was untamed like storm and ocean and would be in immeasurable danger if her wildness could not be harnessed. He saw the frozen stares of incredulity on the elders' faces, saw Roland's devilish delight; either he too was possessed, or he was the devil himself.

'Nay, nay, it's wrong, it's wicked,' the boy cried and pummelled feebly the fiddler's arm. 'Stop it! Can't you see what you're doing to her?' But the fiddler in Puritan dress and less pure at heart ignored his pleading.

'Take a break, Fiddler,' Jan at last scowled, looking stern and resentful. 'We are all in need of a rest.'

The music stopped abruptly. All feet stood still, all talking ceased. There was only painful, embarrassing silence now. The door gently creaked; someone had left the barn, unnoticed by any one. Jan pushed his daughter to one side. His hand struck her face, which stunned her out of her frenzy.

'Go to your bed at once,' he growled. You bring disrepute and bad fortune on this house. Go, so that your Midder and I may be spared more shame.'

'Fadder, what have I done?' Siegund asked bewildered. Scores of glaring eyes focused on hers and looked away as soon as they made contact. She shuddered at their coldness. How much hatred there burned in them, how much hostility, how remote their forgiveness seemed! She did not understand their anger, remembered nothing of what had gone on before, only that she had looked into dark eyes, black as the night. Sometimes they had been gentle, sometimes dominating. The music had carried her into an unknown existence, to heaven perhaps, but she had fallen from the sky, mortally injured; her heart was bleeding, her spirit broken. She stumbled out of the barn, humiliated before the entire township. Garwulf stood no longer by the door; perhaps he had never been there at all. Maunsie too, seemed to have abandoned her, though he managed a sad smile as she passed him.

'Nay, nay, why did you do it?' Maunsie questioned the fiddler. His almond eyes struggled to become round with outrage. 'Why did you play the way you did and make her lose her mind?'

'Was I not asked to play? Am I to blame if the mood takes me? Nor did it transport the other girls into madness. But tell me, was my music not to your liking?'

'Yay, for once you played well, I grant you that,' Maunsie reflected, and quickly forgetting his outrage he asked: 'Will you teach me to play, Fiddler?' His head sank between his hunched shoulders. He was ashamed of his selfishness and disloyalty, ashamed that his devotion to his sister was tainted by a longing that could no longer be kept in its bounds.

'You? Play the fiddle? You'll understand - it's a gift not all possess and an art not all can learn, aye, that it is.' The statement was more than apt in the fiddler's own case, though tonight had been an exception.

'But I feel the music in my hands and in my head, and my heart shall never know a greater love,' Maunsie insisted stubbornly.

'And if I consent - what can you pay me for my efforts?'

'Nay, nay, I've nothing to give. I could look for driftwood on the beach each day for you.'

'Driftwood?' Roland shook his head and laughed. 'No, not that. But I will teach you, aye, that I will, if...,' He bent down to Maunsie and whispered, '...if Siegund will show me her favours.'

'Nay, it's not right, it's wicked. Siegund is still a child.'

'That, she is no more. She has fired the blood of many young men tonight, aye, that she has - and of a few old ones, if you ask me. No child does that.'

Maunsie's face became pale orange with fury. For Siegund's and for decency's sake he must sacrifice his own happiness a second time. And again, temptation struggled fiercely with propriety. Bitter resentment ran like poison through this throbbing temples; resentment against Siegund who needed protection, resentment against his father who was too poor to buy him a fiddle, resentment against his mother who had given him a crippled body and a life of misery. He gave an enormous triple sigh. 'Nay, Fiddler, then I shall never learn to play.'

'It's entirely up to you, aye, that it is. I have given you my price; I can take no less. It costs you nothing, nothing at all.'

'How can you bargain in such degrading manner? Does honour mean nothing to you, fiddler?'

'Many a yearning heart resorts to reprehensible ways, aye, but for all that, my intentions are honourable. And, Maunsie, when you are ready for your first lesson, I'll be waiting, aye, that I will.'

'I bid you good night Fiddler.' With those words Maunsie stole out of the barn. The gusty wind met him head-on and almost blew him off his feet into the mire. He would not have minded too much had the slurry been deep enough to drown him and his misery.

The solitude of the *ben* kindled a gnawing presentiment of tragedy ahead. Already it lurked in the dark shadows. He knew not when it would strike and in what manner, but it would come, quite unlike the sleep he longed for. The three box beds, mere wooden pallets raised two feet from the floor, each in its own wooden enclosure for warmth and privacy, now seemed like graves to him. The straw mattress seemed hard and cold like solid rock. How different it had been when Grandfadder had shared the box with the boys, when Gunther and Jakob had livened bedtimes with their jollity, when Grandmidder, forgetful in her old age, had sometimes come to the wrong box and had been hauled amongst the lads; she had played merry-hell with them. Crowded like puppy dogs they had lain, warm and secure with the narrow box door closed. Except for Rory and Erik they had all gone now, passed over to another plane. Maunsie lay quietly, trying to ignore the harsh, chesty cough coming from the adjoining box. He tried to persuade himself that Siegund deserved her punishment, but he was incapable of sustained unkindness. Through another violent fit of coughing he heard his mother's matter-of-fact voice.

'Holy Midder, you're sheer burning up. It's the error of your ways, child, mark my word,' she told Siegund. Babbled prayers mingled with the clattering of a chain against a pan. Josefa was brewing a tea for Siegund. Then she returned to the girls' box and thrust a cup of steaming herbal tea into her daughter's hand. Krista was fast asleep, or perhaps she only pretended to be to avoid involvement. 'Come child, drink this,' Josefa demanded. 'It will make you feel better.'

'But it's too hot, Midder, and it tastes ghastly.'

'Penitence is bitter, child.'

Siegund forced down the bitter-sweet brew as if it were a poisoned potion. Her head fell back onto the pillow. 'What are my sins?' she pondered as her mother cooled her feverish brow with a cold, wet cloth. She felt herself drift away. Ah, Garwulf's icy hand is taking away the ague. Before her closed eyes she saw her god. She heard him promise to make her his goddess. 'I should like that,' she whispered. Then he had gone. She tried to open her eyes again. A cold fear crept to her heart, the same fear of death she had felt in the boat. 'I breathed life into you, Garwulf; am I now to die?' Far, far away she heard Maunsie sob. 'Poor Maunsie...how lonely you shall be.' But Maunsie, loneliness and fear drifted away and were lost in dark silence.

# Chapter 4

Timidly, as if afraid of intruding on the silence of the dying night, a new day took its first breath. It eased away the nocturnal air of gloom that hung menacingly over the island. Uneasiness had come to Skerra Kua.

'I know of no stranger, no never though.' Krista was adamant. Sullenly she cast her small, mousy eyes down to her chubby hands and screwed her cherub face up like a marginally wilting pumpkin. She refused to say any more on the matter to Siegund. And no, she would not take a walk while she was busy knitting socks - which in her case meant never. Josefa came in from the byre, stood for a moment in the doorway, propping one hand into her back for support. Through pursed lips she gave her noisy back-to-front sigh.

'Take some eggs to Midder Macalay,' she said, giving Siegund a searching look. 'The air will do you good. And on the way home, call on Claire and see if she is in want of anything; times are hard for her - having no folks of her own. A husband, three grown sons and two daughters - all claimed by the sea, the cliffs and the mortal pox.' She sighed again, yet her words had been bereft of any great sympathy; she had merely made a statement.

A lively breeze embraced Siegund, played in her hair and caressed her face. Her air-starved chest, after four weeks of illness and herbal potions, expelled a somewhat stunted squeal of joy. Against the dilapidated wood shed leaned Maunsie. From his crooked stance it was hard to tell whether the shed propped him up or whether he propped up the shed. The sagging door swayed in the wind like an indecisive ombudsman. Maunsie's tiny, amber hands clutched a piece of driftwood, a pitiful remnant of a once noble ship perhaps, now doomed to end its days as a soup bowl. But such thought - any thought at all - seemed far from his mind. In his present state of physical and mental inertia there was a vague similarity between the wood and the boy's square face, a hint of relativity, of consanguinity in which his fixed almond eyes resembled two elongated wood knots.

'Blow me down, Maunsie, 'driftwood to driftwood, sawdust to sawdust, I do declare! Old Mackerel-Face is too busy to take a breath of air. Krista shall be wed to a sheep one day; she cares more for wool than anything else. Are you too betrothed to some mindless thing, Maunsie?'

'Betrothed?' Maunsie was slowly coming to his senses. 'Nay, I shall never be wed; who'd have me?'

'Emilie Klaasen likes you, indeed, she does.'

'Nay, nay, Siegund, you talk like a duck's rear end.' His head rolled from side to side, his arms flailed furiously at such absurdity, and quite out of character his unhappiness manifested itself in a severe bout of staggering rudeness.

'Listen Maunsie, I have something frightfully important to tell you.' Basket of eggs in one hand she pulled him by his sleeves, hurried him through the gate out onto the common path. He allowed himself to be dragged with no more enthusiasm than a puppy dog that feels collar and lead for the first time. 'Listen,' she began again, 'when I was dying - well, nearly dying - I had a dream. Indeed, you may smirk, but listen anyway. A trowie woman promised me to cure your... your hump and make you tall and handsome if....'

'Nay, nay, why are you mocking me so, Siegund?' he cut her short. His grin had vanished. Deep hurt distorted his ill-shapen face.

'Blow me, I'd never wish to pain you; I really dreamt it. We must bring her a bird - not dead and not alive.'

'How can that be?' He stood still for a moment, finding it too hard to struggle with reasoning and walk at the same time. He loathed talking of his affliction, even now when temptation was whispering of a miracle cure. His soberness quickly smothered all credibility of what his sister had just said, but as he hobbled after her, temptation and reasoning were holding their own private battle inside him.

'We must try, Maunsie.

'It can never work, Siegund, nor should we tangle with the creatures of the night.' The lack of breath mutilated even his attempted triple sigh, which only added to his frustration. Anger, shame, the fanciful possibility of ultimate liberation, more anger, hopelessness - they sapped all his strength from him. He fought back the tears; that too took strength; everything he did was awkward and required much effort. Oh, how he would like to be tall and straight, to have a chest large enough for his lungs to expand.

'But the trowie woman promised.'

'Oh Siegund, if only it could be!' he gasped. In a desperate do-or-die attitude he made up his mind there and then to take his chance with the trolls, grave though the risk might be. 'What else do we have to do?' he asked with quivering voice.

'We must find the stone she held in her lap and roll it over the cliff. When it hits the sea below, your hump will be gone.'

'And nothing else is asked of us?'

'Nothing! Only the bird and the stone. Her husband has a mad craving for a bird, but being of great age - three hundred years or more - he can't catch one himself.'

'But what has the stone to do with it?'

'Blow me, Maunsie, how should I know? We must never tell the grown-ups of this.'

'Nay, where could such bird be found?'

'It's easy.' Siegund held one of the eggs before his eyes. 'Eggs turn into birds. Not dead and not alive, don't you see?' She even went as far as to attribute a semi-occult quality to the Macalay hen's for delaying their reproductive activity. Dreams, messages, imagination - who could prove or disprove the validity of premonitions? How smart to believe in the useful bits and discard the others. And Siegund was smart.

'Nay, Siegund, it's wicked to steal,' he winced.

'It's only one egg. And how can we steal that which belongs no longer to Midder and does not yet belong to Midder Macalay? 'Don't you see, it was all meant to be?' '

He saw the logic in what she said, but still, he would rather ask Malcolm to catch a bird for him; after all, Malcolm was renown for his skill in scaling the cliffs, and his courage was said to be nothing short of foolhardiness - being a Macalay there was always a point to be proven.

The north cliff with its great sheerness, its jagged projections and smooth ledges had claimed lives before and would, no doubt, do so again. Her face dropped at the thought that Malcolm might come to harm. It lit up like a sunray after a thunderstorm when she saw the youth with hair of a deeper red than the Volkers' rooster. The dashing harvest sun had lost none of his charm in his present occupation of tethering squealing pigs near the Northstane.

'Greetings, Malkie,' she chirped. 'What a good morning it is!'

'That's a fact, though it might change either way, ye ken,' he replied, halting his struggle with the muddy creatures. Are ye well again now, Siegund?

'Indeed, very well! We're going to the hills shortly to check the sheep,' she lied. 'Would you like to come with us, Malkie?'

'I would, but I have werk te de, ye ken. Later I hope te catch a few puffins on the Kilcairn ledge.'

'Yay, Malcolm, that would be grand,' Maunsie joined the conversation. Catch one for us, if you will; mind you don't kill it.' He grinned embarrassed and point-blank refused to give a reason for his request.

Midder Macalay appeared by the door at that moment. Ethel was a tall, slender woman. With vaguely accommodating gesture she invited the visitors into the *but.* It was the same hazy den as all the Kuan homes, with food and clutter stacked on the shelves, yet somehow it was different - it had a different smell, a different air, a different history. Next to the cow skull stood a wooden cross that refused to be overshadowed by its bony counterpart. Spread across two rafters under the roof, and exposed to the preserving smoke, hung half a pig, its squealing days well and truly over.

Ethel was Robert's Highland wife, and like all the Macalay wives before her, was secretly regarded with a sort of nervous esteem by the Kuans. With Mona-Lisa-features and black Rapunzel-hair she was something of a mystery in her own right, wearing the grey and black, almost uniform Kuan garb with the serenity of an abbess. She had few words for folks outside her family and not all that many for those within, but her solemn, steel-grey eyes spoke volumes to any sensitive listener. In all she did utter, there lay wisdom, truth and unprejudiced honesty. Folks took heed of her, which prompted Siegund to broach the matter of old Claire, asking if it was safe to go to the Girse croft, for Claire - so Siegund implied - had the looks of a witch and the shiftiness of a hunted animal.

'Wee lass, not all are blessed with beauty; have ye not yet learned that?' Ethel replied without reproof. Her eyes came to rest briefly on Maunsie. She took the eggs from the basket and replaced them with two rolls of her fine cheese. 'Tell yer Midder

I thank her,' she said and then turned her attention to the fire, a clear signal that Siegund and Maunsie were dismissed.

They hurried along the path that led to the Girse croft. As soon as the Northstane was out of view they left the path again and strayed towards the hills in search of the trolls - Claire would have to wait; after all, she seemed to have lived at the Girse since time immemorial - she would still be there on their way back; it was this other matter that could not wait. The steadily growing incline made their progress painstakingly slow. There was no path at all now, only sheep tracks that led everywhere and nowhere. With each deep breath Siegund took, her shabby coat popped open. She soon gave up the futile task of fastening it. She wore Hegan's cast-offs - with two years grace to grow into and two years grace to grow out of - if they stood the strain - with the refinement of a lesser spotted woodpecker condemned to wear a moulting peacock's plumage. The dress was at the early growing-in stage, the coat at the latter stages of the growing-out phase. The spasmodic handover of such unflattering garb had severely stunted her vanity. With vanity out of the way there was plenty of room in her heart for uncomplicated affection, full-blooded compassion and calculated generosity.

Occasionally they stopped to catch their breath. Around them was little else but rugged terrain, stones, scanty heather, wilted grass, isolated shrubs and rabbit warrens. Massive boulders clung precariously to the bleak hillside like stony giants suspended in eternal immobility, yet, looking vulnerable as if one gust of wind might hurtle them down into the valley. Despite Maunsie's affliction and Siegund's temporary lack of energy they soldiered on without complaint until the climb became a pilgrimage of pain and weariness, as any pilgrimage should be. It was a small price to pay in return for Maunsie's health. He just wanted to be like other boys, and she wanted that for him too. Out of weariness grew hope, out of pain - belief. But even hope and belief could not give them the strength they needed. Trembling with exertion they sank limply to the ground for a rest, pressing their hot faces against the side of a rock. Specks of moss, which seemed to share their struggle for survival in the lofty wilderness, adhered themselves to their faces like minute flakes of minced spinach. Maunsie, the tiny man who had stood at the Hawkledge waiting for the last wave to swallow him up, seemed finally to have drowned.

In the valley the weather had been fine, especially for early February; up here in the hills the air was moister and colder. The mist was coming back, or perhaps it had never cleared at all. How eerie solitude could be. Far below them opened out the agitated ocean. Against the greying sky line the white wings of the birds seemed whiter and the dark wings darker; they seemed mere flashes of light or fleeting shadows darting over the water.

'I wish he'd come back, indeed I do,' Siegund sighed. She was feeling quite sleepy.

There was no need for Maunsie to ask who *he* might be. His eyes, so often lacking lustre in dejected resignation now glimmered with reviving resentment and his boyish voice rose to a high pitch, as was the norm when he was riled.

'Folks said the stranger brought bad fortune, though now they don't speak of him. Nay, he was not for you, Siegund. He has left. That much I will say, not a word more. Fadder has forbidden us to speak of him.

'Blow me, Maunsie, he was my friend; he told me so. It's not the way of friends to part without a word, indeed not. Why will no one tell me what has happened to him or even what happened on Yule day?'

Maunsie looked away. How was he to decide where his loyalty should lie - with his father, his sister, or even with the stranger who had wrested a pledge from him? In the end his reaction was as predictable as day follows night.

'Nay,' he began cautiously, 'Johannes Johansen from the Blue Bane fell off a ladder.' Maunsie paused as if the statement explained everything. He, too, was tired and wanted to sleep.

'Blow me, Maunsie, you must tell me everything.'

'Old Tobias Klaasen's sores are festering badly, and Godfrey's bairn took a fit. Yay, folks talked. They blamed the stranger. Johannes and the bairn are well again, but Tobias...' Maunsie shoulder met his left ear. 'Tobias is not well at all. One morning a mob of angry folks came to our croft, but the stranger had gone - boat, fiddle and all.'

'You warned him, Maunsie? Then you too must have felt his greatness.'

'Nay, greatness was not on my mind, but a fellow must be given a fair chance.' His hand delved into his pocket. 'He left this for you. Yay, and you are to take good care of it.'

A green stone with a multitude of glittering edges, yet smooth to the touch like a tide-worn pebble, lay in the palm of her hand. She held it up against the grey sky. A cluster of dancing lights glistened as if enshrined in its almost transparent centre lay last summer's precious sun-rays

'It's the eye of a god after shedding his human form. Look Maunsie!' She rested her head against her brother's shoulder. 'Now, Garwulf will always be near me.'

They did not speak again. As if agreed upon, their thoughts went to the trolls. No Kuan alive had ever seen the little people, but their presence was often felt and every one had heard of someone who in turn had heard of someone who had encountered them.

The youngsters listened to the rustling wind - and fell asleep. Knee-high, three-eyed creatures entered Siegund's dream. Their flat faces grinned impishly as they invited her into their home to share their food, and all the while telling her of their loathing of human intruders. A thousand and one tiny Maunsies, all identical, all wearing the same over-long clothes, limped to and fro. They squeaked and laughed, danced around a basket of eggs and spoke of a good-luck token they had left at the Harehill. Fiddles played happy tunes that would have made Siegund dance had she been able to dance; they played melancholy tunes that would have made her cry had she been able to cry. For three days and three nights they frolicked until they flopped exhausted to the ground, each closing two of their three eyes; one thousand and one eyes in as many foreheads kept vigil and watched her leave. She squirmed in sorrow and pain at her rapid aging and at the sight of her withering hands. A youth lost, young adulthood never experienced, a life wasted, for three nights and three days in the trolls' life meant seventy-five years in human terms. She wailed with pitiful voice as a frail old woman might.

'Nay, Siegund, wake up; you're dreaming.' Maunsie shook her frantically.

She stared into his face, then stared at her hands and whistled relieved through her teeth.

'Indeed, only a dream! But it might have been real.'

A flock of sheep made their way in mindless follow-your-leader conformity down to the beach; their various high and low bleats drifted across the hills like the sound of a distant orchestra tuning up before a concert. At every winter ebb tide they came to feed on the seaweed and ambled back to the barren hills when the tide turned again.

'Have ye counted them all?' Malcolm, who seemed to have appeared from nowhere, called to them. His hearty laugh drowned the distant ovine orchestra.

'Blow me down, Malkie, decent folks don't creep around,' she yelled at him, throwing her head round.

Malcolm's tanned face beamed with amusement to the point of flagrant smugness. His face was clean shaven; it was the custom with all unwed lads - not that he intended to remain unwed. He was twenty now, of fair height, wiry like a fox and blessed with great charm and quick wit. At the sight of Siegund's baffled expression, which mirrored suspicion with a hint of coquetry, he once more burst into laughter.

'Ye are a sight fer the gods te see, Siegund Nielsen. That's a fact. Yer face bears mere dirt than a freshly tilled field, ye ken.'

'And you are a Macalay,' she cut him short, implying, without blinking, that even with a dirty face she was at an advantage over a Macalay. 'Be off with you, I'll not be slighted by a pig-man's son, indeed not.'

'A pig-man's son, eh? He slapped his thighs and laughed louder. 'I think ye want yer hide tanned fer yer uncivil tongue.'

'Indeed not. Children you beat - women you do not. And I am a woman.' She turned to Maunsie for his vote on the matter of child or woman. Maunsie was adamant that she was a child. To settle the argument once and for all she took her brother's hand and guided it to her chest.

'You see, I am, indeed, a woman.'

Maunsie pulled his hand away as if the touch had burned him. He stumbled backwards, shocked at her liberality. Malcolm stumbled forwards, his hand reached out, begging permission for the privilege Maunsie had rejected. He looked into heavenly blue eyes. He saw not exactly an angel's face but the face of a woman child, a face no longer entirely innocent, yet sweet and beautiful despite the muddy streaks and mossy specks, a face that combined virtue and seduction in clownish manner. Propriety lost its way, as occasionally it will do. She met his hand and led it to her bosom. The lights of passion burned in Malcolm's eyes, not mysterious eyes like Roland's or velvety like Garwulf's; they were honest eyes with their message easily read, but at this moment Malcolm was Garwulf and Garwulf was Roland, all so different and yet the same somehow.

'Nay, Siegund, it's wicked, it's wrong, it's sad,' came her brother's shrill cry. 'And you, Malcolm Macalay, have you no honour? If Fadder knew....'

The spell was broken. Her logic returned; punishment was no fun. But liberty ranking high above her questionable concept of pride and dignity she was seldom plagued by scruples. In her estimate the acceptance of a beating from her father amounted to a neat piece of heroism.

She remembered her business with the trolls and without further ado sent her Romeo on his way. Malcolm, blaming himself for overstepping the line, had entirely forgotten what he had come for and disappeared down the hill from whence he had come. Brother and sister were alone again.

'Can you hear the silence, Siegund?' Maunsie shuddered.

'Indeed!'

The air seemed not air at all but quivering feelings. Hand in hand they walked deeper into the hills. Fitful conversations started and failed; their talking seemed too loud, their silence too silent. The Northstane, hemmed in by a crescent of coastline to north and west and by barren hills to the south, seemed far away. Flimsy wisps of mist, like gigantic cobwebs, spread out before them, invisible eyes seemed to lurk everywhere, watching, probing while their own eyes could barely see the crown of the hill.

'Nay, Siegund, let's go home. This place scares me,' Maunsie whispered.

'It scares me too,' she professed without pretence, but her belief in premonitions and destiny were greater than fear; she was willing to take the risk - and run like hell if things should get out of hand. They began to quarrel over the issues of egg or bird, fate or coincident. And who could say whether it was fate or coincident that placed a broken-winged sparrow right in front of their feet that very minute. The tattered little creature, too weak to escape its captors, lay warm and light like a breath in Maunsie's cupped hands. Not dead, yet not alive! It opened its stout beak as if to call for mercy, yet it remained mute. A tiny life was ebbing away, sacrificed to bring new life to a crippled boy.

They hurried along with their gift, praying and hoping on the way that the troll man might be partial to sparrows, and he could still have the egg. The ill-reputed place, the alleged home of the trolls, lay before them and their hearts began to beat a drum roll for the occasion. Here the hillside levelled out to a narrow plateau before rising again. A singular gust of wind rushed with hollow whistle through an isolated, retarded gorse bush and hurtled deeper into the hills as if it, too, were on some important mission. On a flat stone, as close to the dreaded cave as they dared go, they presented their offering with profound solemnity, bowing their heads in awe and respect for the much feared little folks. The sparrow lay still, its beak open as if in mute astonishment; perhaps, like its captors, it too was holding its breath.

'Siegund! The stone! Nay, how can we know which one to choose when there are so many?' His eyes burned with impatience while his hands clasped one of the smaller rocks.

'No, not that one, Maunsie.' Her eyes searched amongst the rocks. 'There, I think that's the one, indeed, that's the stone I saw in my dream.'

'Nay, you must be mistaken; no trowie could hold such weight in her lap. We shall never be able to move it. It's wicked, it's wrong. She has tricked us,' he cried, seeing his hope of salvation disappearing.

They pushed and pulled, pulled and pushed, puffed, blew and even cursed. Exhausted and near tears they relented their fruitless endeavour. Perhaps the trowie did not care for a sparrow - a dead sparrow by the look of things. They remembered the egg and placed it beside the bird. For good measure and determined not to let the chance go by, Maunsie decided to offer a little cheese too. He dug his fingertips deep into one of Midder Macalay's savoury rolls to prise it into two halves. But cheese can be much as other things in life; a share may be ample or next to nothing. The trolls were offered the ample piece.

They felt a new magic in the air; good or evil - they could not say. Maunsie closed his eyes. His arms stretched out, the palms of his hands turned up towards the sky. He waited to receive the precious gift so that his crippled body might be healed. His strained face was of exaggerated bilious colour, much like Ethel's cheese. It became more angular under tremendous concentration. His sincerity absolute, he opened his heart to the trolls, summoned them to listen, to hear his complaint, his humble petition.

'We've brought you the gifts willingly and in good faith and bear you no malice. I ask you to keep your part of the bargain for honour's sake - and for mine; yay, especially for mine. It's a sin to break a promise, don't you know? Nay, I hate the way I am; I hate my affliction. I don't mean to be disrespectful, but I really don't want to look like you. It may be handsome for a trowie, not so for humans.'

His emotive pleas, his unprecedented admission of unhappiness, his bitter words of resentment shattered the stillness and rebounded from the cave. Again he tried to roll the stone. The magic had gone - reality was cruel. To assume the old indifference again and accept his lot seemed now as impossible as moving the boulder. He would have been free if...if.... Hope born out of a dream lay shattered like a ship on the ocean bed. This was just a place like every other. There were no trolls here, or if they were, they were asleep.

Siegund folded her arm around his shoulders and rested her cheeks against his face. She had never accepted his deformity as being part of him but as some gross thing that had attached itself to him. For his sake she had been prepared to face the trolls, she had never meant to cause him pain; now she must suffer this pain with him forever.

'Perhaps tomorrow....' she began.

'What good is their tomorrow when my life will be wasted?' In a final half-hearted attempt to appeal to the trolls the tiny, insignificant man with nothing to lose and perhaps nothing to gain, prepared himself for a compromise.

'If you can't give me health....I'll settle for a fiddle, so that I may play my sadness away. Yay, a fiddle would ease my pain.'

They listened and waited to learn the effect of his plea. Then they knew that their mission had failed. A fine drizzle of rain began to fall; it fell on them like a sprinkling of holy water and mingled with their tears. They knelt on the ground, not to pray, but to allow their emotions to subside. And when their hearts beat calmer and threatened to stop altogether, they thought they must be dying, for, as the pain slowly oozed away, life too seemed to drain from them.

'Maunsie! Maunsie Nielsen!' A deep voice echoed from the cave.

Bravery collapsed in a heap. Forgetting miracle cure and disappointment the only sensible manoeuvre would have been to scarper. Instead they froze in rigid embrace.

The mighty voice spoke again, and with it the magic returned once more. 'Maunsie, do not pursue your futile dream. Why ask for the impossible? Have you not wealth and good fortune around you? Think on it. You have your father's protection, your mother's care, your sister's devotion and your neighbours' esteem. Are you thus not blessed with riches far more valuable than a sleek body? Maunsie, why those tears? Why your sister's tears? Do not fret so. The shape of your body is of little importance, only your heart and soul matter; and with that consideration you are the richest boy on the island. Never try to barter for a straight body again. Will you promise me?'

Maunsie nodded and did not know why and to whom.

'And Siegund, never come to the cave again. The consequences would be grave if you were thought to have dealings with unearthly creatures. Will you promise?'

'I promise,' she said. 'But...who are you?'

'It matters not. Go home, and tell no one.'

Slowly they walked away.

'Maunsie,' came the voice once more, 'I too will make a promise. Before the next harvest is done you shall have a fiddle.'

The boy's head emerged from between his shoulders. With convulsive jerks he tried to straighten his back, his whole body writhed in desperate struggle to force a new Maunsie out of the deformed shell. His eyes were blinded with tears, yet he saw the path that was his to walk until the end of his days. 'Yay, a fiddle will do. I'll be content; and I thank you.'

'Go then, and remember your promises well.'

It had stopped drizzling. A fine sheet of mist rolled over the cave and obscured its rocky contours. They wondered if it had been there at all. Who was to say what was real and what was not? A feeling of emptiness, of being eternally trapped between fantasy and reality, mingled with curious soberness. They felt grown-up somehow, as if years had passed by, and silently they mourned the loss of a dream and the loss of childhood.

With Siegund's arm around Maunsie's shoulder they walked away. The singular gust of wind that had rushed into the hills earlier seemed to have returned with its numerous comrades, whistling past their faces and sweeping with boisterous breath the low-hanging clouds far beyond the hills. The horizon began to expand into a vast milky white sheet with tiny patches of pale-blue sky peering through. High above them circled an eagle, watchful, graceful - solitary. Perhaps it was her god keeping vigil over them, Siegund pondered. He would know of their plight. But he would also know of her brief moment of sinful bliss with Malcolm. Shame and guilt began to colour her cheeks; perhaps she really was as bad as Midder always seemed to think? But how was she to cope with the temptations that made her forget propriety? How difficult it was to know one's own heart when even the heart was uncertain! Maunsie's foot became entangled in the straggly undergrowth. The flowerless heather pulled him down and embraced him. If the hills could laugh - Siegund could have sworn she heard them laugh now. Ah, but hills do not laugh.

# Chapter 5

Calling on Claire had been a sobering business for Siegund and Maunsie. The old woman had neither made them welcome nor chased them away. She had just sat there in her squalor - gaunt, cold and distant. Now and then she had muttered something to herself as if unaware of her visitors. There had been neither wood nor peat in the shed to light a fire, and no food on the shelf.

They met Duncan Macalay on the way home. Duncan had at last plucked up courage to confront Jan, which was just as well, because Josefa, agitated by her children's lengthy absence, was waiting for them by the gate.

'Greetings, Midder Nielsen. Is yer man at heme? I would speak with him, ye ken,' Duncan said. His voice, robust at the onset, swayed towards a kind of resolute indecision, then ebbed away in uncertainty.

'Come in, lad, you'll find him mending a net,' she replied. They all followed Josefa in single file across the stepping-stones.

'Duncan, how is it with you,' Jan asked a little too stiffly to make it a welcome. He knew why the young man had come.

'I am well, I thank ye,' the other replied, still standing under the low frame of the doorway, which forced him to stoop.

'Sit down, Duncan. There's no point in standing there.' Jan's invitation was no warmer than the interest in his health had been.

Duncan pretended not to notice the cool reception - he had expected no other - and sat down by the table. He was a stocky young man with an almost chinless face. The effects of the brisk walk and the delicate matter of the heart intensified the colour in his naturally ruddy face. He doffed his woolly hat and revealed two equally ruddy ears. In his nervousness he forgot what to say next, which did not matter all that much anyway; words were not necessary. He did not seem to notice Hegan, who looked up from her sewing and immediately bowed her head low again, pushing the needle through a threadbare hem with exaggerated haste. Duncan promptly drew an earthenware bottle from under his coat and placed it on the table. There! The proposal was made. All he could do now was to wait for the equally wordless reply.

Jan paced up and down and mumbled something that no one understood. Great sighs, more mumbling. In the end he fetched two wooden cups, poured some of Duncan's brandy and sat opposite his guest. Rory entered the *but* that moment and rubbed his hands over the fire with ridiculous vigour and duration while testing the general attitudes. With one of his infrequent broad grins he joined the two men. They talked of the weather, of beast and poultry, of fishing and boats without making a single reference to the gift of brandy or its purpose. Jan sipped the brew as if he had been forced to sip Macalay blood. He seemed to have difficulty with swallowing and made absurd grunting noises, but each sip of the rich golden liquid lifted his anxiety a fraction until by and by the black clouds seemed washed clean from his mind. His blessing was manifest in no more and no less than a strong smell of brandy in the air.

The men drank and talked - it was their privilege; the woman carried on with their work - it was their duty. Krista whispered something about a husband of her own. A husband instead of a sheep? The unexpected revelation of her sister's normal feminine ambition stunned Siegund into silence. She wondered if Krista had already someone in mind, and could not imagine who it could possibly be. Hegan, whom the whole matter concerned most, displayed amazing disinterest. Before Bogle day she would be wed to her man. She was content. Maunsie, who felt that he belonged neither to the men nor to the women, had no opinion on the matter either way. Josefa smiled without conviction. The smile faded altogether when she learned of Claire's unhappy state. It was not entirely charity that urged her to call on the old woman there and then and take Siegund with her; she needed an outlet for her dismay.

'But I'm to go to the Klaasens shortly, have you forgotten, Midder?'

Josefa had not forgotten. A moment later, on the way to the Girse, she could no longer hold back her dismay.

'Child, I'm grieved with your careless attitude, with your wilfulness, your...waywardness. Abandon your childish games and dreams. Holy Midder, reality is harsh, I know, and growing up means there are lessons to be learned. You may turn the heads of the lads now, but, mark my word, they want no plaything to settle down with. Mend your ways, show humility and dignity. Take Hegan as your example.' She stopped abruptly, reflecting on the validity of her words. Her body, which had temporarily lost its lean appearance, trembled a little. She placed her hand on the plainly visible bulge beneath her apron as if to reassure the unborn child that all was well, but her hand trembled too. She pulled her shawl a little tighter around her shoulders. After an enormous back-to-front sigh and a noisy gulp she became calm again as if she had swallowed all anxiety.

Why did Midder not try sighing the other way round, Siegund mused. And Hegan the righteous, Hegan the virtuous, Hegan the miracle worker! She was annoyed at her mother's reluctance to criticise her sister. She knew that she could never compare with such apparent perfection, nor did she intend to imitate her sister's insipid docility. But one day - indeed, one day she would show them her own worth.

'I'm not wicked at heart, Midder; I try to be a good daughter, indeed I do.' She was not even sure what she had meant by *a good daughter* since she had never considered herself a bad one.

They walked in silence, neither of them willing to pursue a matter they were not likely to agree upon.

It had been a reasonably bright afternoon with a pale sun making a timid appearance, which in turn had postponed the hour of darkness; now, the dusk came rolling down from the moors, descending on the two lone figures and blending them into the scene like gliding shadows. The faint lights of their lamps were neither noticeable nor yet quite necessary, but darkness had a habit of descending on folks rather suddenly and it was better to be safe than sorry.

'Why do folks speak of Claire the way they do, Midder?' Siegund asked out of the blue and knew instantly that her mother's grim look of determination meant that she knew, but would not say. 'Blow me down, she looks so hungry.'

'Holy Midder, something has to be done,' Josefa said and left it at that.

Another long silence ensued. They walked a little faster. Siegund's thoughts went from Claire's poverty to her mother's talk of mending ways. It vexed her so. She quickly abandoned the unsettling topics and thought of the hours to come. Tonight she would see her friends again at the Klaasens. Malcolm would be there too; tonight and every night for a whole week - wool-combing and spinning at day time, music and dance in the evening. Dance! The idea made her feel uncomfortable, the word had a sinister sound to it now - she did not know why; she had no recollection of the Yule day dance, and that, too, vexed her.

In the duskiness of the fading day the Girse cottage appeared like a mere heap of stone, a relic perhaps from the time of the first Norsemen on Skerra Kua. Doorless empty sties and outhouses stared with silent accusations at the two approaching visitors and impressed upon them the Kuans' shameful neglect of one of their neighbours. A morbid smell of stagnant finality hung in the darkness of byre and *but*, a smell that seemed to imply the end of Claire's path, yet not quite the end of her wanderings, though judging by the moans that came from the wooden bench, it seemed that this end was not far away either.

'Holy Midder,' Josefa exclaimed and clacked her tongue. 'Come child, shine your light over here; two lights are better than one. Don't stand there like a corpse. Take her legs; they'll not bite you. Can't you see the woman is sick?'

Claire was still sitting in the same place and apparently in the same position as she had done a few hours ago when Siegund and Maunsie had called on her. Siegund giggled. She thought that her mother's commonsense had gone astray; not even Claire's toothless mouth would have been able to bite anyone, let alone her spidery legs which, to Siegund's surprise, remained firmly attached to Claire's frail body when she got hold of them.; that too made her giggle.

Shocked out of her stupor by the sudden man-handling Claire squeaked cascades of verbal unwholesomeness. With feeble, ancient voice she ranted and raved her protest against the trolls' rough treatment of her. Claire was confused, cold, dirty and inebriated, but through the brandy trickled a truth that spoke of loneliness and abandonment.

Josefa the benevolent, the guardian of health, mumbled words of self-reproach, though she had far less to reproach herself for than most of her neighbours. Had Claire asked for help Josefa would not have refused it, but she had no time to run after folks, nor was it in her nature to dwell on things; right now Claire was in need of a good wash, a warm bed and a soothing medicinal tea. She set about it immediately, much to the annoyance of the struggling old woman.

At last Claire lay neatly propped against her straw pillow, looking vaguely human again, yet to Siegund's mind, also repulsive - the ashen face with its deep lines criss-crossing the loose skin, the fleshless body sprawled under shabby blankets on a straw-starved mattress. Old age itself repulsed Siegund. She remembered the dream that had shown her her own old age and the pain it had caused her. Topsy-turvy emotions, from fading repulsion to burning compassion, set her heart in uproar. She felt Claire's pain - one day it would come to her, too. She vowed to make an effort to like Claire, to never again scramble over a wall or hide behind a shed to avoid her, and all the while Claire's amazingly florid vocabulary coloured the air. It shocked Josefa who had never known how to swear, and who had long forgotten how to laugh or even cry. Josefa was always too busy for compassion and never too distraught for dignity. She sternly reminded Claire of her manners.

'Manners; the devil take them! Should I care for manners when the rest of the Kuans have none?' came her slurred reply. 'Ha-yee, now they come, reluctant still, trusting me none the better - not even now. I've done no harm to no one. For Marnie I cannot speak, and Marnie speaks no more.'

'Be that as it may.' Josefa replied, her lips pressed tightly together into a single thin line. She was not prepared to speak of it and swiftly removed herself and her daughter from the *ben*.

'Light a fire, child, this place is as cold as a grave.' Josefa picked up a broken stool which, like the rest of the cottage's contents, was fit for no more than fuel for the fire. Claire obviously had come to the same conclusion some time ago. Debris seemed all that was left of her past.

'Midder, who was Marnie?' Siegund asked.

Josefa gave no reply. Grim-faced she shone her light up to the shelf. It had partly suffered the same fate as the rest of the furniture. What need was there for a shelf anyway when there was nothing left to store except the great cow skull - and the next-to-nothing share of the Macalay cheese, which was no smaller now than on its arrival. They heard Claire moan.

'Holy Midder, no wonder she has colic and unsavoury visions - not that the brandy made matters better,' Josefa exclaimed, examining the remnant of cheese from all sides as if it were some incredibly mysterious object.

'A purge, that's what she needs to clear her inners.'

'But...but, blow me down, it was only...I...we...Maunsie...'

'Why are you stammering when you can speak properly? Speak up, child.'

'I...I didn't say anything, Midder.'

Josefa delved into the basket that went where ever she went. She drew out a small bundle of roots and selected further ingredients for the remedy in what seemed an artful eenie-meenie-mo fashion. She plunged them into a pan of water and hung it over the fire. Over the quickly discolouring brew - folks said it was potent enough to move boulders - she murmured rhythmical Nordic verses. Her eyes were closed one moment and wide open the next. Steam momentarily obscured her face. She chanted, stirred and talked of cheese. How sad when intended benevolence, when those who seek to do good, only bring pain. Siegund, too, had meant well in leaving the remnant of the roll of cheese, although it had also meant avoiding awkward questions. Claire would surely get land-slide gripes if she took the remedy she did not need, to rid herself of cheese she had not eaten. As a humble gesture of her penitence Siegund followed into the *ben* to witness the forthcoming catastrophe.

'Blow me down...,' she mumbled at the brink of confessing, but she deemed it better to remain silent. She watched Claire's uncoordinating hands reach for the wooden cup, watched her take a slurping sip, which was followed by a moment of utter astonishment on the old woman's face. The black liquid sprayed from her pursed lips in one grand shower.

'Are you intent on poisoning me, Josefa Nielsen? Ha-yee, this is what it has come to! Cheese! The devil take it! You babble of cheese, woman. Have you been at the brandy, too? I've eaten no cheese.'

'I say you have! And an unwholesome lot of it, mark my word!'

'Maybe I have, maybe I haven't; I can't recall, though I remember how the brandy comforted me.' She leaned towards the splintery opening where the box door had once been. The remainder of the brew gushed onto the mud floor. 'There, that's what I think of that!'

'I see you don't want my help, Claire. You are a foolish woman if you think that brandy brings contentment.' Josefa was deeply hurt by such ingratitude, but dignity kept her anger at bay. She merely said: 'I bid you farewell, Claire.' Claire's reply was a high-pitched, feeble laugh filled with bitterness. She too had clung to dignity until dignity had made a mockery of her.

'Ha-yee, can't you bear to be slighted even for such short moment? How does it compare to years of mistrust? Was I to blame for a young girl's waywardness, for her unholy bairn? No, I was not! The devil take it, why do I speak of it? Do stay a while, few visitors come this way, and those who come are in great hurry to leave.' She met Siegund's eyes briefly while her cyanosed lips distorted to a vague smile.

The mentioning of Marnie had yet again been met by Josefa with the remoteness of a deaf-mute hermit. She quickly diverted the talk to Claire's quitting the croft sooner rather than later. Claire, remarkably sober now, and far less slatey in colour, would rather make it later. To be at the Kuans' mercy, to stay a few weeks here, a few weeks there, whoever cared to give her food and shelter, had little appeal to her. She swayed the conversation to the trolls. Josefa agreed that the little people had been quite active of late; they had taking things from the crofts, though they had left no token of appreciation behind them.

'Be that as it may.' Josefa turned to Siegund to remind her, quite unnecessarily, of her hire to the Klaasens at the Heather croft. 'It's getting late, child, don't dally; go straight there. Tell Katrine that Hegan has work to do at home, and that Krista is....'

'....Afraid of the night?' Siegund helped her out.

'That's not what you tell her, child.'

It was dark already, not the sullen murkiness of the cottage's obscure interior but an exciting darkness. The moon played its game of hide and seek amongst gliding clouds; glittering silver stars looked on. The cool air smelled of all things grand to Siegund, of magnificence, of purity, of peace, of liberty. Perhaps this was infinity of which Garwulf had spoken. She felt free of her mother's tired, reprimanding face, free of commands and demands, free of Maunsie's persistent shadow, free of repulsion, guilt and compassion, free of wayward Marnie of whom folks occasionally whispered but never really spoke and whose name turned Midder temporarily deaf. A peculiar feeling of uniqueness, of belonging to the sky, made her skin crawl a little. Distorted, shadowy outlines of familiar scenes conjured up in her heart brand-new fantasies and brand-new emotions. She was not sure whether she ought to be afraid or joyful, and with scrupulous honesty admitted to both. Sinking into spasmodic flights of fancy she forgot her promise to make haste until a hand suddenly touched her shoulder and chased all fanciful illusions right out of her head.

'Ah, fair Siegund, it's an evening for the deities, aye, that it is!' The fiddler stood beside her and grinned. Draped around his shoulders was a purple cloak. His purple leggings, with countless pea-sized holes through which the bare flesh peeped, looked much like a starry sky. She thought of asking him there and then how he had come by his ridiculous garb. But she did not ask. Somehow, his strangely colourful clothes, obtained from obscure sources, gave him distinction, charisma - mystique.

Roland Mulvoen, neither obese nor flimsy, was taller than Malcolm and shorter than Garwulf. No longer young but still without a woman he could not make up his mind to which category he ought to belong - the bearded elders or the clean-shaven unweds. Hence, he regularly alternated between the two, so that more often than not a bristly growth crowded his chin like fungus; only the black, bushy moustache covering his full upper lip had permanence. In the silvery moonlight his eyes seemed to hold all his various daytime moods in one single glance - gentleness, sullen obstinacy, jollity, strength of will, and always that look of secret knowledge.

'Tell me, fair Siegund, will you show us your talents again tonight?' he asked, keeping close to her side with annoying familiarity. 'Ah, perhaps not; the stranger has gone, aye, that he has - and perhaps he has not,' he added as an afterthought. 'But why do you draw away from me? Do I frighten you so?'

'Why should you frighten me?' She gave an unnatural little laugh.

In his melodic voice, which never quite lost its softness whatever the mood, he spoke her name as no one else did, full of flattery and mischief. They walked together; his arm occasionally brushed against her shoulder. The contact made her heart flutter like a trapped bird and immediately her unworthy response angered her, as did the fiddler's forwardness and flippancy.

'Why indeed?' he asked after a pause, then paused again. 'Maunsie seeks to learn the art of fiddling, aye, that he does; but the price - the price he will not agree upon.'

'What is your price, Fiddler? Maunsie has nothing to give you, indeed not.'

'I ask nothing of him.' His face came close to hers. 'The price is your heart.'

'Blow me down,' she cried out and pushed him from her. 'I thank you to keep your distance as is proper. You talk in riddles.'

'Is that so?' He grabbed her arm and held her with iron grip. 'You must understand, I....'

She shook herself free, fled from him and her own feelings. What was it with her that Malcolm, Garwulf and Roland had all aroused such obscure sensations within her? She decided to tell Katrine Klaasen of Roland's creepy manners, but by the time she reached the Heather croft she was not sure what there was to tell.

Katrine welcomed her with motherly smile. She was one of those jolly, energetic creatures for whom nothing was too much trouble and who could always find time for a friendly word. Wed to Hanno at seventeen and, blessed with five children, all living and thriving, she had not allowed the burdens of life, of which most folks seemed to complain, to break her lively spirits. She was a tall woman with massive bosom, fleshy arms and well-padded hips and carried her maternal plumpness graciously with an air of great achievement. Her dark brown hair was streaked with tiny strands of grey, which stood in stark contrast to her still youthful complexion.

'I trust you are well, Siegund? Have you brought your wool comb and plenty of goodwill with you?' she asked, laying a dimpled hand on the girl's shoulder.

'Indeed Katrine. And I'll do my share.'

'Which is no more and no less than I expect of everyone, but this evening we shall be merry.'

Katrine's fawn eyes twinkled as she looked across the congregation of young men and woman. Roland stalked into the barn at that very moment. Smug in the knowledge of his importance he held up fiddle and bow as passport to join the young folks. He was more than thirty and less than forty; people conveniently lost count when the years on their backs were best forgotten. Artfully he drew back his cloak and graciously accepted the hail of applause with a deep bow. The cheers belonged as much to his red and purple pantaloons as to the promise of music and dance. There was a calculated method in the way he chose his place on the wooden platform; not that it mattered whether he sat a little this way or that, but the prolonged attention he received gave his self-esteem a massive boost.

Numerous feet in laced up boots hopped and skipped, leaving traces of mud where they had been. Amongst the assembly of prudent girls and marginally less prudent lads the degree of happiness varied somewhat; the Yule-day affair was still fresh in everyone's minds, everyone's except Siegund's. Some of the girls safeguarded their future prospects by keeping as close to their partners as decency would allow. Now and then they looked in Siegund's direction with a fair deal of mistrust. The lads might have been less reserved had they not been aware of Katrine's eagle-eyed vigil over them.

And Siegund - she stood alone and looked on, bewildered at her friends' neglect of her. She tried to recall that disastrous evening, wished that Malcolm would come, or Maunsie, or even Rory - anyone - to rescue her from her embarrassment. How lonely one could be even in a crowd! She sensed Roland's piercing eyes on her, forcing her to look his way. Once more this day she felt repulsion, this time not in conflict with compassion but with the fiddler's strange magnetism.

'I will not look at you, I...will...n...ot'. The words died on her lips. She turned her face slowly towards him, expecting to see him grin. The light of an oil lamp flickered above his head, sending dancing shadows and sprinkles of yellow flashes across his calm face. He was not as beautiful as her god, nor even as handsome as Malcolm, but his jet-black eyes that beckoned to be noticed overshadowed all blemishes. 'Curse those eyes!' she gasped under her breath; for those eyes held gentle pleas one moment and made stormy demands the next, they carried a burning fire that scorched her face and parched her throat; they willed her to know the unknown, they told her everything and yet told her nothing. She winced under sinful fancies incompatible with an innocent heart.

'Siegund,' came a voice as if from afar, 'Siegund, will ye dance with me?'

'Blow me down, Malkie,' she gasped relieved despite his late arrival. 'I...I've been waiting for you this past hour.'

'Is that a fact!' Yer eyes were elsewhere for twice that time. I thought ye liked me - I'm not sure these days. Yer heart is like a butterfly, ye ken; it flirts and trifles and will not settle. What is it with ye that ye play such dangerous games? How can a man live with that?' Malcolm swallowed hard, his Adam's apple almost jumped to his cleft chin and then slid down his throat again. He was hurt by what he had just witnessed, but as soon as he had made his complaint a smile of forced forgiveness brightened his face. He held her hand as if he were loathed to ever let go of it again.

Roland played and the young folks danced. Judging by the fiddler's play he clearly tried to equal his recent musical performance. With closed eyes he coaxed the fiddle, demanded it to obey. Somehow, the Yule day magic would not come. However, his frenzied efforts brought one result; Siegund began to remember the wild orchestra, the grass skirts - the humiliation.

'Blow me down, Malkie, I don't want to dance any more. I'm all done in,' she told Malcolm, who opened his mouth in disbelief and kept it open far longer than was becoming to him. Katrine's grating voice and her unambiguous hand signal saved the awkward situation. Music and dancing halted at once.

'Enough of your music for today, Fiddler! The girls have to make an early start in the morning and I need them fresh and able to do a good day's work. There is plenty of straw in the barn, blankets too, for those who wish to stay the night. Bed down immediately - and remember what's proper; we are decent folks here.

It may be judged a strange arrangement on an island where lovers were only allowed to be 'good friends'. The Kuans' strict rules - and punishments - curbed temptation. It was all a matter of trust. Woe to him or her who betrayed that trust; the islanders knew no forgiveness. With that in mind the youngsters settled down on the deep bed of straw. There was ample room in the barn to keep proper distance even if togetherness may have been preferred. Still, they thought themselves privileged to lie near the one they liked best.

'Sleep well,' Malcolm whispered, reaching for Siegund's hand.

'Sleep well, Malkie,' she whispered back.

Boyish whispers and girlish giggles, sighs of tiredness, sighs of secret desires, of someone's disappointment mingled with the straw-dusty air. Already, here and there the even breathing of the first sleepers was audible. Malcolm too, seemed to belong to the instant capitulators of consciousness, his desire snuffed out like a candle. Somewhere amongst them lay Katrine who had probably by now slipped beyond the border of wakefulness herself, leaving the guardianship over decency to the good fairies. And the fiddler - he was there too, somewhere.

Siegund wondered if Roland, like the trolls, slept with one eye open, not to miss anything. As for herself, sleep was as far away as the land of everlasting ice or that of eternal summer. She listened to the even breathing as it progressed to a tuneless song of snoring and tooth-grinding. The air stifled her; it seemed that all the whirled up straw dust had settled entirely on her alone, clogging her throat and suffocating her. By the door glowed a solitary oil lamp. It marked the exit rather than give light. She sat up and listened to the whispering wind. It whispered and beckoned, invited her to come out of doors into the cold night. She stood up, wrapped the blanket tightly around her and began to carefully step over a row of curled-up bodies. Her foot caught an out-stretched hand. It drew away; the body attached to it grunted and turned over.

A clear crisp night greeted her and forced a cough from her dry throat. She hastened away into the night lest she might be heard. A confusion of thoughts of what was pleasant and what was proper, of what was freedom and what was obedience, occupied her mind. She frowned at herself. How was she ever to please her mother when she liked all the wrong things? Now and then she glanced back. No one was following. She hurried along as if carried on a cloud, careless of time and distance, and was surprised how quickly the Northstane had come into sight. She could not say why she had come this way - nor did she care. A pale full moon looked down on Malcolm's home. But Malkie was fast asleep in the barn beyond the little stream.

'Blow me, I should fear the night; other folks do; yet, I'm not afraid,' she mused and eased her pace. How peaceful it was to walk under a starry sky, to tread through the cool solitude with nowhere to go to, no destiny, no duty. There was a silence that was yet not entirely silent; the heather rustled in the light breeze, the sleepless sea sang its tuneless song. She thought she had heard someone call to her - not with a voice or even a sound - it was just a feeling. She turned her head. There was no one there. Before her rose the gloomy hills that were doomed to sullenness until the end of time. Perhaps their listless souls were summoning her. She remembered her promise to the voice in the cave, but the hills kept on calling. They called stronger now, more urgently. She was a little afraid after all.

Once more she turned her head. A shadow moved on the lower slope and disappeared behind a boulder.

'It must have been a sheep,' she tried to persuade herself. 'Perhaps, I saw nothing at all.' She stood still for a moment, straining her ears to listen. It was not footsteps she heard, nor even the call of the hills now; it was a soft, melancholy sound of a fiddle. 'The trowies!' She gasped, hardly finding the breath to utter the dreaded word. The little people were said to be superb it the art of fiddling, they were also renowned, amongst many other things, to kidnap young maidens. She tried to turn and flee to the safety of the barn. She could not turn, could only walk towards the music that charmed her into sublime forgetfulness.

At length the music stopped and her heart threatened to follow suit. Before her, in the silvery moonlight, leaning against the cave, stood the tall, motionless figure of a man - so great was his inertia he might have been an extension of the rock face, or he may have been Vidar the silent god, carved into the stony wall. Inertia overcame her, too, and held her in its debilitating grip.

'Blow me down...is it really you...Garwulf?' she stammered at last. Oh, do tell me. I'm not sure whether I'm awake or asleep.'

'Come, give me your hand and you shall know that I am flesh and blood.' Garwulf replied, stepping forward. His questioning eyes showed neither approval nor disapproval.

'You've come back to me. I feared I should never see you again.' She flung herself into his arms. What had propriety to do with her? Rules were made in the valley; that is where they should stay. Here by the cave was a different world, her very own secret world. Lower down on the slope they heard a twig snap.

'A fox, I dare say, or a rabbit,' Garwulf said, then turned his head back to her and smiled. 'I never left the island, sweet child. How could I depart without a farewell? The cave makes a secure enough home. As for food - well, Kuan larders hold enough to feed an extra mouth. Alas, a man has to eat.' He shrugged his shoulders in apology for his ignoble activity.

'Blow me, how lonely you must be!'

'Not so! The hills and the wind, the sea and the sky are noble companions.' His eyes wandered across the shimmering stretch of moon-drenched water as if to trace back the way he had come. There was almost a helplessness about this gentle giant and a strange sadness in his borrowed, badly fitting clothes that yet defied all pity. 'Solitude is good for the soul,' he added. 'It helps me to look inwards so that I may get to know myself better.'

'I don't understand. Don't you know who you are? Blow me down, I know who I am.'

'Do you? I mean to say, do you really know yourself?' He chuckled, bent forward a little and kissed her hair. 'And do you now what brought you here in the depth of the night when you ought to be asleep in your bed, sweet child?'

'I...I'm not sure.'

'Then I will tell you. You see, I willed you here and you answered my call.'

'Can you really do such things?'

'Anyone can do it; you too. All that is needed is solitude, a clear mind and a perceptive heart to hear you. To wipe everything else from your mind is the hardest part of it.'

Siegund knew at once that her lack of sustained concentration disqualified her from ever achieving such feat; he ought to know it too. She thought she was still dreaming, but they were real - Siegund, Garwulf, the cave and a million twinkling stars. Real too were the spectacular Northern Lights which in great splendour now draped their red veils, edged with splashes of green and blue, across the northern sky. Like Roland's eyes they demanded to be noticed and feared. The present shape and colour of the veils bore a warning of raging storms to come, but neither Garwulf nor Siegund would concern themselves with that now.

'Is night not also magnificent?' Garwulf asked. 'Why not behold with joy the grandeur of the shadowy side of creation? Those lights, those pretty dancers - are they not superior in grace and beauty to the sun?' He stopped to reflect. At length he suggested with a smile that she might give the dancers a fair contest.

'Do you mean it?' Blow me down!'

'I never say things I do not mean,' he replied earnestly.

'Do gods always tell the truth? I tell fibs sometimes. I think that one white lie a day is forgivable; it gets me out of trouble. Midder doesn't believe me anyway; indeed, not even she can tell truth from lies. Besides, folks prefer to believe the lies; it makes everything look neat and tidy.'

'Granted, the truth is often harder to speak and to accept than lies. As to the honesty of the gods - I really cannot say.'

Despite his refusal to admit any connection with the noble entities she was still convinced of his godly status. But god or man, his presence and the magic of the starry night forced her overfull heart to surrender much of the affection she had reserved for Malcolm. She wanted to tell him so, but to speak now would have seemed a transgression against holiness, although unfortunately, sins came her way far too easily. She questioned him about the voice in the cave.

'Sweet child, it was not in my mind to frighten you. Alas, your brother is what he is; no one can change him. False hopes frequently end in bitter disappointment. He shall have his fiddle, I gave him my word. As for calling you tonight - I have no excuse to offer except that beneath the glistening stars I longed to see you, speak with you and share with you the beauty of heaven and earth. In my selfishness I forgot the danger and your tender age. Forgive me. And if you hear me call again you must ignore it. Soon I shall be gone from here.'

'Then my heart will break, indeed it will,' she insisted.

'Not so. Your hunger for life will see you through. Come, time is passing. Make haste before your folks miss you. I should surely weep until the end of time if I were to be the cause of sorrow to you.'

A shooting star, brilliant in its final moments, emerged from the veils, hurried across the sky and was lost somewhere on the vast horizon, and with it her new-found world seemed lost too. He was sending her away and she could do no other than obey. She hesitated a moment, wanted to speak, but Garwulf shook his head.

'Alas, you are a mere child and I am an outcast, a humble man driven from his home and wished to hell by his fellow men. Your future is with your folks; it holds nothing for you and me save a few memories. Go now.' He pushed her away gently yet with an authority that permitted no objections.

To flee from him made no sense at all to her, but flee she did. In speedy descent she scurried into the waning night, her sporadic sobs audible only to herself and to the hills. This very morning the hills had witnessed the loss of a crippled boy's dream and now they looked upon her own loss with the same indifference. She ran without stopping, wondering for the first time whether Katrine might be awake already. She opened the barn door just wide enough to squeeze through and stood still for a moment to allow her eyes to adjust to the darkness within and to estimate where her place had been. Once more she stepped over the sleeping bodies. Someone grabbed her ankle. She fell forward onto the straw.

'Let go,' she hissed, getting back onto her knees.

'It's a fine night, that it is,' Roland whispered. 'I know many secrets, aye, that I do.'

'What do you mean?' she whispered back.

'Just that! No more, no less.'

Malcolm was still asleep. With the troubled conscience of a traitor she lay beside him while she promised her heart now and forever entirely to Garwulf. Silently she called upon the shooting star to hear her testimony. Too tired to stay awake and too troubled to fall asleep she floated into semi-awareness. Katrine stirred noisily, got up, yawned loudly and coughed even louder in an attempt to sabotage her guests' unprofitable idleness, opened the byre door, clapped her hands together as if to applaud the sleepers.

'Wake up, you lazy heap of mutton,' her voice grated. 'There's much work to be done.'

The temporary residents knew better than to displease Katrine and risk exclusion from the evening's dance. Malcolm, with straw still in his hair and dust clinging to his strongly curved eyebrows, playfully pulled her apron stings.

'Too much unused energy, that's the length and breadth of it,' Katrine scolded him. 'You young folk haven't tasted the burdens of life yet.' Then she smiled. 'On my soul, I don't begrudge you your youth - it's but short-lived, though now we must concern ourselves with wool.  Be on your way, lads, and let the girls get to work.' Katrine was a good woman, but work was work and play was play.

The girls began the task for which they had been hired, the reward being no more than the chance to be away from home, to socialize, to gossip and make merry. Soon the idle talk was exchanged for songs of love and happiness, of death and sadness, of fishermen and stormy seas and of heroic Norsemen. High and low voices, some in and some out of tune, mingled in a somewhat disarrayed medley that tempted the occasional passer-by to steal a glimpse of the fair maidens and observe their industrious attitudes, but such distraction was not discouraged by Katrine.

Ingeborg Johansen from the Blue Bane, the weaver's daughter, with permanent smile and bubbly as the Blue Bane brook, had brightened her grey dress with red piping, which she had either begged, stolen or borrowed from her father's rare colourful merchandise intended for some fine lady on the mainland. She always tried to make a favourable impression, especially on the Nielsens in whom she saw, quite prematurely, her future in-laws. It was true that Josefa favoured her as Rory's future wife; she had even lent her treadle spinning-wheel, a gift from Erik and probably the only modern gadget on Skerra Kua.

'Wool, Potty, more wool!' Ingeborg called to Pattie Volker with a kind of tolerant impatience. And rotund, red-faced Pattie with rotund blue eyes and white dandelion-clock hair hastened along, if haste could be ascribed to her. Still, the simple-minded girl from the wind-swept Hawkledge croft, the ragweed amongst wild roses, was always eager to please.

A second wheel was turning, not by treadle power but by a blind girl's hands under Adelika Macalay's gentle instructions. Hedda Volker usually relied on simple Pattie to guide her, which was generally regarded as more tragic than her blindness. Hedda too liked to please. The simple task of turning the wheel left Adelika's hands free to transform large tufts of well prepared fleece into even, chunky threads. Adelika's expression was that of cautious meditation and permanent sadness; she was neither of the ragweed nor the showy kind of flower but a rare orchid. Not far from Adelika, Siegund had settled to the task of combing and preparing wool for her. She liked Adelika, partly because she pitied her and partly because she liked her brother Malcolm. Poor Malkie, how he had laughed and joked this morning, quite unaware of Siegund's disloyalty!

'Oh Malkie, what's to become of us?' she thought. 'I can't be yours. You'll be ever so unhappy. But I'm unhappy too, indeed I am.' From poor Malkie her thought went to poor Adelika. Siegund's volatile imagination instantly reincarnated the unfortunate, unmentionable Marnie - of whom she knew nothing - and embodied her within the pale Adelika.

By the time the lads arrived at the end of the day, when aching backs yearned for relief from their crouched positions, when tired hands put aside combs, spindles and whorls, Siegund's extravagant mind had travelled through the most tragic of all tragedies on the matter of Marnie-com-Adelika. Exhausted by so much hypothetical suffering and lack of sleep she found herself in a state of severe apathy. Malcolm's chin dropped when she told him she was not staying the night. How easily his confidence was shaken, how quickly the harvest sun lost its glow, she mused troubled. They had all noticed it but said nothing. Pattie scratched her dandelion head, Adelika sighed, Sven Klaasen frowned, and the fiddler - he just gave her a knowing glance.

'I'll walk ye heme, Siegund,' Malcolm offered despite the fact that such chivalry was not acceptable for decency's sake, but neither ought she be walking alone at this late hour. 'We're in fer a proper downpour, ye ken, and there's a mean sterm brewing up.'

Maunsie came into the barn, or rather - was blown in by a gust of wind. He seemed to consist merely of legs and hair until his whole head emerged from deep out of his coat. He announced that Rory was still out of sorts with runny eyes and nose and would not be coming. The advice was given to all and to no one in particular.

'Walk me home, Maunsie,' Siegund demanded in a rare bout of selfishness.

'Nay, why?' Maunsie asked.

'Because I'm tired, that's why.'

'Shall we see ye temorrow?' Malcolm enquired.

'Blow me down, do I know what tomorrow brings?' she replied with an unkindness quite alien to her.

Her dramatic exit puzzled everyone, most of all Maunsie who found himself man-handled out of doors without even a chance to pretend he had volunteered. They battled against the wind that caught their clothing and stung their faces, it whistled and roared through the darkness and seemed to become ever more riled at the night-wanderers' defiance. Through the deafening clamour she screeched into his ears: 'The hills are calling me.'

'Nay Siegund, it's wicked, it's sad. Your mind is addled. You make no sense at all. Midder must brew you a potion to heal the madness in you,' he screeched back

'Addled? Indeed not. My mind is clear and I know what I know. Go back to the Klaasens, before the storm breaks loose good and proper and carries you away. Keep out of sight for a while; hide in an outhouse until a fair time has passed. I'll have no one call you a coward for letting me walk alone. She kissed his forehead that looked like wood, yet, was as cold as stone.

'Nay, nay, where is it you're going?'

'I can't tell you, Maunsie. Don't fret, I'll be safe. But if I don't return - remember I'll be happy.' She pointed the stunned little man towards the Heather croft, gave him a gentle push to sent him on his way, then she stalked off so fast in the opposite direction that his efforts to catch up with her proved hopeless. Faintly she heard his voice call to her. She turned her head and shouted into the wind: 'Remember I'll be happy.' His tiny light flickered in the blustery darkness for a while and then vanished from her view. She lifted her eyes to the cloud-laden sky. Heavy drops of rain began to pelt her face. She started to run. Tonight she had a destiny. Her lamp flickered, grew dull and eventually went out altogether. The vague outline of the Northstane told her that she was walking in the right direction.

'Forgive me Malkie,' she said half-loud. 'I'm not meant for you nor for Skerra Kua. Perhaps you'll wed Potty Pattie; she'll make you a good wife.'

She cursed the weather. Her numbed fingers buttoned up the battle-scarred coat with an automatic spontaneity that comes with repetitive exercise. She was determined not to turn back. The wind drove icy sheets of rain into her face. Bravely she climbed uphill, bearing a little to the right as she thought appropriate. In the merciless downpour all landmarks had lost their identity. Old Swaalie had lost his way in the hills on a night like this and had perished. She would not lose her way, she knew the hills well and the hills knew her, but that in itself now caused her anxiety. Was the thunderous roar inside her head the madness of which Maunsie had spoken? With both hands she covered her ears to muffle the maddening sound and instantly realized that the rowdy commotion was nothing more than the howling wind in fierce competition with the crashing breakers far below, vying for the title of supreme champion. The tempestuous darkness had disorientated her and had brought her close to the cliff's edge. She staggered away in horror from the menacing sound of the broiling sea, her body bent forward like a wind-swept willow with little more resistance to the onslaught of the storm than a sapling.

She was not sure where she was now. Folks said that only the mad and the wicked went into the hills at night. She longed for a rest - just to rest, or perhaps to sleep a little and forget anxiety and coldness; in the morning she would wake up and find it had just been a bad dream. The sodden ground provided a surprisingly comfortable mattress. She did not feel the cold any more. Her battered mind set out on a journey through fading, monochrome memories while her body became strangely detached. Wipe everything from your mind, Garwulf had said. Her eyelids fluttered. The image of a god carved into the cave wall appeared before her closed eyes, his stony arms reaching out to her. Briefly her reasoning returned.

'Garwulf,' she cried with a feeble voice that might well have come from near deflated bellows. It was swallowed by the howling wind. Rain fell into her open mouth and moistened her parched throat. She scrambled onto her knees. With her hands shaped into a funnel around her mouth to carry the sound she forced an earth-shattering shriek from her chest. She tried to get to her feet, but her legs had lost all feeling. She fell back, buried her face in heather and, expecting to join old Swaalie very soon, she cried bitterly, mourning her untimely end. Then she prayed - for herself and for all those she knew, even for the fiddler, and then cried again.

'What on earth...what has possessed you to come out here on a night like this? Have I not told you to keep distance?' came a voice that sounded like a clap of thunder to her numbed brain. Garwulf lifted her into his arms and carried her away as if she weighed no more than a feather. She rested her head against his chest; the dull, steady beat of his heart seemed to promise the continuation of her life.

'I thought I was going to die,' she sobbed against his drenched shirt.

'You might well have done. Now we are even; I owe you nothing,' he said with a harshness that abruptly halted the flow of her tears. A moment later he pushed her through the narrow entrance of the cave. Her first thought was to turn and flee; gods and trolls might live together – she, however, was a mere human. But there were no trolls, no dancing, squeaking, fiddling trowies - only the glow of a fire. Her great relief was followed by an illogical sense of disappointment; what story she might have been able to tell folks if she had been the first on the island to see them! She knelt by the small circle of stones that kept the fire in its bounds and held her hands over the glow to speed long the thawing-out process.

'Where has all the clutter come from?' she asked, pointing to a disarray of pans and tools on the floor. 'A matter of interest, no other reason,' she added and then wished she had not reminded him of his plight. And no, she did not want him to return them to their rightful owners; she wanted him to live in the cave forever.

'That cannot be, sweet child. It s hardly a life for a man to hide away like a leper and survive by thieving.'

He took off his wet shirt and spread it over the clutter to dry, then squatted down opposite her. Huddled there on the floor, united, yet kept apart by the glow of the fire, they talked of nothing grander than the weather, a topic that kept Siegund shivering.

'You shall never dry out like this, soaked to the skin as you are. Take off your wet coat - and the rest. Here, wrap this around yourself afterwards.' he suddenly exclaimed, handing her a blanket without the blink of an eye.'

'Blow me, you mean...?' The idea of undressing made her shiver all the more.

'Why yes, that is precisely what I mean.'

Siegund rarely took all her clothes off, and never in front of men folk. Was he not aware that she was a woman? She wished he would not keep calling her a sweet child. But her dress being baggy and her coat forever agape she forgave him this oversight. In the darkest corner of the cave she wrestled with her wet clothes because her fingers were savagely tortured by more pins and needles than Hegan carried in her sewing basket. Garwulf had turned his back to her and busied himself with brewing a tea. She was grateful for his discretion, yet in her controversial nature she also felt slighted by his apparent indifference.

'And what shall it be for supper?' he chuckled. 'Cheese, an egg or a dead sparrow?'

'I'm not hungry, only cold and tired.'

He ignored the mentioning of tiredness, but decided that a more radical remedy than tea alone was needed to warm her up. He offered her a glazed stone bottle and told her to take a sip.

'Brandy? she asked. 'Isn't that for special occasions? Mind you, Claire and Roland....blow me.' She bit her lip for thinking of the fiddler.

'Every day of our live is a special occasion, sweet child.'

A couple of sips proved to be far more effective than any peat fire could be; peat fires baked one's front and left one's back to fend for itself. Whichever homestead the devil's brew might have come from it spread its glow evenly though her body. More than that - it awakened tiny demons inside her head which prompted her to take two rather more generous sips.

'Too much of a good thing soon turns to a bad one,' Garwulf advised her and took the bottle from her lips.

He reached for his fiddle and began to play a sweet, celestial tune. It spoke to the enchanted listener of pain and love, of loneliness, of solitude, of joy and peace, and of all things that an open and mildly intoxicated soul might be willing to perceive. She rose to her feet like a snake charmed out of its basket. A slender arm emerged from beneath the blanket that draped her nudity. Her body began to sway in rhythmic motion, her bare feet stepped delicately this way and that. Garwulf's eyes were closed, though now and then he looked up and nodded his approval. Once more the world of magic beckoned to Siegund. Up, up she soared to a breathtaking height; high above the clouds she danced and swayed and glided from star to star. But once again she fell from the sky. The music had stopped. In the glow of the fire she looked confused down on her nakedness. The blanket lay like a discarded snake's skin on the floor. She snatched the blanket to cover herself while stammering explanations and apologies. Garwulf stared silently into the fire, holding his head in both hands. She backed away from him, away from his hurtful muteness and from her shame until she made contact with the pile of straw that was his bed, flung herself onto the straw, buried her face in it and wept.

'Why do you fret so? What harm has been done?' Garwulf's voice trembled.

'You despise me, and indeed, I understand your disgust.'

'Should I despise grace and beauty? And who am I to judge you?'

'Then sit by my side so that I may know I haven't offended you.'

'I think not,' he replied, his eyes distant and troubled. 'How can I explain? You would not understand. You are a woman in body and a child at heart, but your mind is neither one nor the other - yet it is both. Are you surprised then that temptation runs hot in my veins while decency urges restraint?'

She did not understand his resistance and was in no mind to relent her plea, which in the end brought him reluctantly to her side.

'I'm so dreadfully tired.'

'Sleep then. I'll wake you when your clothes are fit for wear again.' He prepared to get up.

'Don't leave me,' she begged. God or man - I don't care. Don't ever leave me; I couldn't bear it.' She caught his hand and drew him close. He did not speak. Outside howled the wind. Weariness got the better of her. She closed her eyes and fell asleep, unaware of his struggle with his desires and his respect for decency. Alas, Garwulf the god was human with all the weaknesses of men.

# Chapter 6

Evening darkness once more wrapped the homesteads into morose cocoons and isolated the night-shy folks from their neighbours. The Nielsens sat by the fire, each member engaged in some useful craft while listening to the menacing wind that hauled across the Harehill yard; it rattled a badly secured shed door and robbed a sty bit by bit of its peaty roof. Such nights meant all things to the folks inside their snug den. To Krista it meant security; to Jan endless toil; to Josefa humility; to Rory a longing to sail the stormy seas; to Hegan rebuke for loving a Macalay; to Maunsie it emphasised his own insignificance, to Siegund it meant rebellion. She smiled to herself, remembering the days at the Klaasens where new romances had started and old ones discreetly been reaffirmed or shattered. Pattie's efforts to comfort Malkie had gone sour right from the onset.

But whatever their thoughts might be, folks kept faith with the gods and trusted in their own good workmanship, confident that the cottages would withstand the onslaught of the storms. These tiny fortresses, forlorn and vulnerable in appearance, were firmly anchored to Mother Earth by a rocky outcrop, which occupied the corner of the *but* and was hallowed as an altar that turned plain water from the brook into Holy Water.

'Bed,' Josefa said, addressing Siegund, Krista and Maunsie. 'And don't forget to put a clean bowl of water by the fire in case a trowie woman wants to come and bathe her baby. And hang your clothes up properly; the little people loathe untidiness and may cast a spell on us if we offend them,' she ended her instructions. Jan nodded his agreement. Siegund grumbled her resentment against the three-eyed little cheats - where ever they might be - but she completed her task with care, as she did every night before she crawled into bed.

Krista, too, grumbled, when her sister's icy toe poked her calf. 'Darn your blunder-bungled socks will you though,' she lisped, her tongue making far too much contact with her fleshy lips.

'If you darn them for me, Krista, I'll tell you a secret, indeed I will.'

'Secrets mean trouble. I want to hear of no secrets, no, never though.' But Krista was told anyway.

'We've lain together, properly I mean - like weds,' she whispered her unmentionable secret into the darkness, pausing now and then to give her voluntary confession the impact she thought it deserved. 'That's why we belong together for ever. He'll have gone by now, but he'll be back. He said so.'

The blatant confidence plunged Krista into a state of shock, which left her rigid like a corpse for a moment, preventing her from lisping the words of horror that came into her mind, or even from pulling faces. She was devastated by her sister's shameful talk, tried to cross herself and forgot the right order of it, not being entirely used to the Christian ways.

'Shame on you, Siegund, shame, shame,' the mousy girl cried at last, which in turn devastated Siegund, who swiftly pressed a pillow over the shrieking voice.

'If you tell on me, I'll gouge your eyes out, and you'll never know night from day again,' Siegund yelled, still holding the pillow tightly over her struggling sister's face. Jan's fist hammering against the wooden partition came none too soon; the consequences might have been regrettable. As it stood, Siegund thought that apologies and denials would put matters right again. 'Blow me, Krista, forgive me. I never meant to squeeze the life out of you. But why, why did you howl so when all I told you were ghastly lies?'

Coughing, sneezing, sobbing Krista buried her distress under the blankets, accepting neither apologies nor explanations. Siegund realized how foolish she had been and vowed never to speak of Garwulf again, not to any one; indeed, she would not speak at all until he came back. Somewhere, an owl hooted its eerie call into the night. She called upon the creature to witness her pledge. The wind had eased a little. Tiredness crept over her eyelids. She welcomed the approaching sleep that took away anxiety. Between wakefulness and slumber she gave her mind free reins to wander across the picturesque plains of fantasy. The image of a lone man crossing the swell in single-handed battle appeared before her closed eyes. Vivid illusions transported her right into his arms where a hazy glow of shimmering lights embraced them both, isolated them from all else and carried them away.

She was woken by an unearthly clamour. In the *but* Maunsie was trying to play a fiddle. He struck the cords at random in the most undesirable combinations. Through the screeching concert came his excited squeaks and laughs.

'Yay, Siegund, yay,' he piped. 'He has kept his word. Bless him who heard my plea.' In his joy he seemed to have lost all control over his jerking neck, but there was a sparkle in his eyes that had seemed absent all his life. Josefa stood behind him, her bosom heaving with outrage, her brows drawn close together.

'What do you know of this, Siegund? He keeps babbling of some promise. Speak, child.'

Josefa searched her daughter's face for the truth.

'Blow me, I...I think...yes, that's it - he must have had a dream,' Siegund replied, despite her vow of silence.

'Nothing comes from dreams,' Josefa cut her short. It's not natural that things should appear over night, not natural at all, mark my word! Unless the trowies...,' she reflected briefly. 'Be that as it may...' She said no more, but began to search shelves, byre and barn to see what the trolls may have taken in return.

'How stupid of you to speak of...of him, Maunsie,' Siegund hissed. 'We gave him our word not to tell.'

'I don't know what made me say it, nay, I don't even know who or what he is, but he's not evil, that I do know.'

Rather than tell Maunsie the truth, or lie to him, Siegund conveniently renewed her vow of silence, and in this silence her awareness of being different from her folks was re-enforced.

She had lain with a god, had tasted the pleasure of the flesh before her wedding day. Folks called it sin, but their rules could no longer be her rules, their destiny no longer hers. Present, past and future - in her world they were one. Perhaps Marnie belonged to this world since she had no place elsewhere. Maunsie's unsavoury fiddling, Josefa's harping-on about what was natural and what was not, Hegan's rolling snowball-eyes, Krista's sullen muteness, even her own occupation of flicking a feather duster over tools, cow skull and cheese - all those things seemed neither particularly real nor important; she seemed merely a spectator looking on at a vaguely familiar scene. She saw Nellie Macalay weep by the door, saw Midder patting the girl's dark head, saw them hasten outside.

Siegund followed them to the byre door. Josefa was hurrying along the path with Nellie clinging to her skirt. Men with ropes, blankets and wooden stakes ran past the gate and with every loping stride seemed to loose substance in the dull misty air. Dazed, Siegund followed them. They made their way to the Kilcairn ledge, whistling a distress signal as they passed each cottage. Why had Krista run in the opposite direction? Siegund wondered. Like a belated echo, Nellie's words entered her mind. Bewildered she brushed a hand over her eyes as if that might make her mind clearer. 'Not Malkie, indeed, not Malkie,' she told herself.

High above the ledge, rescuers were securing ropes around a massive boulder. They had all come, the Nielsens, the Mulvoens, the Volkers, the Bidebergs, the Johansens - some had brought their entire families as if to some grand show.

Duncan Macalay and Roland Mulvoen carefully checked the lifelines around their chests. They gave the signal to be lowered down to the ledge that had saved Malcolm from falling into the foamy depth where jagged rocks and swirling breakers did their constant battle and from where no one had ever returned.

Amongst the onlooker's stood Ethel who, like her neighbours, seemed to have grown roots, so still did she stand. No one knew how badly Malcolm was hurt, no one asked; no whispers could be heard, no lamentations. If prayers were said, they were spoken within the heart; if encouragement or sympathy was expressed, only their eyes conveyed the message. In the respectful hush the commands of the rescuers, who knew what to do, seemed twice amplified.

'Heave,' came the order. Eager hands reached out to the driftwood-stretcher as it appeared at the edge of the cliff with Duncan alongside it. They lifted Malcolm swiftly and expertly to safety. Ethel knelt beside her son who lay motionless as if life had already left him. A flicker of emotion quivered across her white Madonna-face. She cast her eyes to heaven and prayed that the Holy Midder and Josefa Nielsen might heal his shattered body.

Josefa was already making her matter-of-fact assessment of the youth's condition. With Duncan and Robert Macalay's assistance, surrounded by a crescent of mute bystanders, she carefully tied Malcolm's legs together. In Siegund's estimation it was the dumbest thing her mother had ever done. Did she think he would get up and jump back over the cliff again? As she reflected on the absurdity of it she suddenly thought it less absurd; perhaps he had been heart-broken and had really tried to end his life. Her vow of silence once more collapsed.

'Blow me down, Malkie, why?' she asked. 'Forgive me, I never meant to hurt you, indeed not.' Her voice trembled a little. As she spoke he opened his eyes. His lips moved, but he could not speak. Pain distorted an attempted smile to a grimace. From the corner of his mouth ran a thin trickle of blood.

'Take him home, men. Don't you see he is in need of warmth and rest? Mark my word, no good can come from wasting precious time,' Josefa said rather quickly and just as sharp, knowing well what the gasps of sudden horror and the suppressed murmurs meant. Her daughter had made a grave error by openly speaking of her remorse; the blood oozing from his mouth as she spoke to him would be interpreted as a further sign of her guilt.

Ethel's priority lay with Malcolm rather than with fixing blame. Bred from marginally less superstitious stock she was, however, not entirely persuaded of the girl's innocence, but she needed Josefa's help to save Malcolm's life, and besides, the Nielsens were shortly to become their kinsfolk. To show her good faith in them she laid a hand on Siegund's shoulder as she passed her. The gesture did little to reassure the others. Helter-skelter and with flailing fists they fled, disappearing swiftly into the mist. Only the Nielsens, the Klaasens and the Macalays trod carefully down the slope with their fragile charge, and with them was Roland Mulvoen.

'Blow me down!' was all Siegund could utter at the sight of the fleeing Kuans.

'See what you have done? They think you a witch,' some one said beside her.

'Hegan! I...I didn't know you were here,' Siegund stammered.

'That's hardly surprising, my girl. Your head is lacking some vital matter. One of these days you'll come a cropper, to be sure, and it might happen sooner than you think. What exactly have you done that made you speak of regret?' Hegan's icy eyes allowed no evasion.

'I can't tell you. Blow me down...'

'So you have something to hide! I might have known,' Hegan said coldly. Her black shawl, insufficient to warm her icy nature, gave her the appearance of someone in mourning - quite superficially - a death that had not yet occurred. 'Call yourself lucky that Midder and Ethel reacted the way they did. Folks might well have driven you over the cliff edge there and then, my girl,' she continued, waving a pointed finger at her sister. Her thin, tightly closed lips and the pinched nostrils exaggerated the severity of her expression. 'For your own sake, take heed; as for Duncan and me - goddamn it, need I say more?'

A sense of doom hung in the smoky semi-darkness of the Harehill cottage as if there were no escape. However, the thick stone walls offered a welcome anonymity. Siegund longed to be with Garwulf; he knew the pain of being despised by one's own people, he would know her pain too; perhaps this very moment he was weeping for her - he said he would, until the end of time. From one of the outhouses came the wildly disjointed notes from Maunsie's fiddle; they almost sounded like laughs and cries. For all its unwholesome sound it brought a degree of comfort, and like the fiddle Siegund, too, began to laugh and cry while Hegan was preaching humility, manners and work that was to be done, although she, herself, seemed to have forgotten what that work was. Rory tramped into the *but,* dragging Maunsie and his fiddle with him. Rory, too, seemed to be looking for an occupation and could not make up his mind what to do, and meanwhile paced up and down and did nothing. Only Krista sat quietly, her head over her knitting. She tried her best to suppress her sobs by swallowing them, and all that could be heard was an occasional little cluck. When at last Josefa returned from the Northstane her report on Malcolm's condition was short and matter-of-fact.

'One leg is shattered. But that isn't all, mark my word! I have done my best, I'm no physician. Fadder, Duncan and Konrad Mulvoen are rowing to the mainland to fetch a medical man. It'll cost the Macalays a pig and a half to settle the fees.'

'What's a goddamn pig compared with the lad's life?' For the second time Hegan, who hated strong language, blasphemed. Red-faced she apologized for her temporary lack of control on account of the bad business getting to her.

'Be that as it may, I have no doubt that the fault lies with the fiddle. No good will come of it, mark my word!' Josefa was wringing her hands now. 'It's not natural, not natural at all, the way it came here. It's not the trowie's method to part with their fiddles.' She paused for a moment. 'We must destroy it, burn it to ashes at the break of dawn when a crow flies over the graveyard, so that all evil shall be taken from us like a corpse.' With amazing swiftness she snatched fiddle and bow from Maunsie's hands and, holding them between thumbs and index fingers as if she were handling some monstrous tool, she headed for the byre.

'Nay, Midder,' Maunsie yelled, grasping Siegund's hand in despair. They both ran after their mother. 'Nay, Midder, don't take my joy from me,' he cried. 'I'm playing well, and I shall play better; it's all I've ever longed for. If you take it away from me I have nothing.'

The byre door slammed shut before their faces. Siegund's attempted words of reassurance fizzled out into a pathetic stammer. Josefa was already returning, closing the door with more gusto than was her usual way. She wiped her empty hands on her apron as if to remove any stains the fiddle might have left. Maunsie tried to push past her; Josefa held him back.

'Will you disobey me, even you, Maunsie? Holy Midder, what's happening to us?'

'What indeed?' Siegund shrieked at her. 'You'll take his life from him, don't you see? Don't you know how he has fretted? Don't you see his tears? Blow me, even if you did see them - you would be too busy to wipe them away.' As she spoke those bitter words her mother's solid hand struck her face. It momentarily blurred her vision and made her ears ring. She barely flinched, as if the hurt of her recent rejection had raised her above all physical pain. For the first time she thought herself wiser than her mother and older than her brother whose head seemed to have forgotten how to sway and whose whole body seemed to have fossilized; the lights that had shone all too briefly in his eyes had gone out again.

Siegund folded her arm around him. Under her firm touch it was as if all tension and anxiety was beginning to flow from his rigid body across to hers. He seemed to be shrinking in her arms while the acute curve of his spine grew sharper. She thought he was dying, leaving a shell without a mind and soul. Under promises she could only keep at her own peril she led him to the *but* and lifted him onto the cushionless driftwood bench. There he sat, no more than a tiny dark speck, a blemish on the freshly scrubbed wood, looking with blank eyes at the sliver of wood and the knife which Josefa thrust into his hands.

Josefa never attempted to heal broken hearts, she had no liking for weakness of the spirit, and she made no exception now. Instead, she plunged herself into her work at the spinning wheel with a vivacity alien even to the likes of her, so that it hummed like a swarm of bees on a hot summer's day; the quantity of wool accumulating on the spindle was nothing short of amazing and the quality disastrous. No one would have thought her capable of such carelessness, but neither the stilted Rory nor the prudish Hegan dared to intervene. It was just as well that at last the endless thread of knots, joined by hair-fine fibres, snapped and the humming stopped. A massive back-to-front sigh seemed to suggest that for the first time since the commencement of her frantic occupation she allowed herself to take breath.

'I think I'll go to the Northstane and take another look at the lad,' she said, and without waiting for a reply she rushed out of the cottage, armed with the inevitable basket of herbs. On this murky late February day, evening had followed morning without giving noon much of a chance, now the mist was turning to fog. Rory, knowing that he could not stop his mother, went after her to make sure she was safe.

'And where do you think you're going, Siegund?' Hegan snarled, taking her glacier eyes from the pan of stew over the fire and fixing them firmly on her sister. 'Have you not caused enough trouble?'

'I've done nothing wrong, indeed not.' Siegund stamped her foot hard on the ground. 'Blow me, what's the use; you've condemned me already. But even a sinner has to go for a ....'

'Hold your tongue, girl, we'll have no foul language here,' Hegan cut in. 'Go, I count to ten. You'd better be back by then.'

'Blow me, I never said I had the runs. Make it twice ten, will you?'

'Your flippancy is ill-advised, my girl. Be gone with you. One - two -'

The stew began to bubble over into the fire and called Hegan to more pressing duties. Outside, the fog settled in Siegund's hair and gathered on her long, silky eyelashes. The yard seemed a stage of rigid shadows. Her hand groped over the muddy elevation where the slurry had not yet reached. It stood to reason that her mother would have chosen the place for the fiddle with care; soggy wood would not burn cleanly. The sea sounded far away now; the mist muffled its usual roar. Her hand made contact with fiddle and bow that only a few days ago had sung to her of pain and joy, but there was no time to waste on dreams of yesterday or even tomorrow. Probing the ground with the bow for the stepping stones she fumbled her way along the path to hide her treasure amongst the driftwood in the shed. She praised the gods for their goodness and felt quite good herself until Hegan called and spoiled it all.

Josefa and Rory returned quite late. Josefa reported that Malcolm was neither worse nor better, while Rory doubted that any physician could be persuaded to make the journey from the mainland tonight, nor that the men, despite Konrad's legendary strength, ought to risk the crossing themselves; after all, belated men were more use than drowned ones. That was all that was said. The gloom settled in the *but* - cold, distant, unnerving.

Siegund whispered to Maunsie that his fiddle was safe. He did not seem to hear or even notice her. She closed her eyes. How easily the world of dreams came to her. It was just as well; her own family now treated her as if she did not exist, as if her name had already been erased from their memories. Indeed, she could dream, but she could not choose her dreamland companions. This very moment the ghostly figures of Marnie, Bridie and old Swaalie beckoned to her, inviting her with outstretched arms to abandon her folks and join their ranks. Cold sweat began to trickle down her back. She was afraid of them and afraid of her folks; most of all she was afraid of herself, believing that she was surely going mad. She ran out into the byre, out into the yard, into the fog.

'I am not wicked,' she shrieked. 'I've harmed no one.'

She was dragged back and propped up beside Maunsie, who remained quite unaffected by the commotion. A bowl of stew and a spoon was pushed into her shaking hands. Confused she began to slurp the hot soup. If food could not settle the turmoil in her heart, at least it might ease the emptiness deep in the pit of her stomach. With vulgar haste she emptied the bowl, scarcely aware that Hegan was pulling Maunsie onto his feet and, under despairing cries, was brushing the steaming contents of his bowl from his hands and legs.

'Goddamn, goddamn, he doesn't even flinch; he feels no pain,' Hegan cried, nothing short of being hysterical now. 'I can't take any more.'

No remedy on earth could have revitalized Siegund more than her sister's total loss of self-control. Capable, sensible, righteous Hegan, the know-all and dare nothing apart from falling for a Macalay, Hegan, whose virtues were quoted as an example to others, was weak after all. What revelation! In her sister's short-comings Siegund found comfort and felt almost a sense of deliverance from misery.

The Harehill lay asleep; Josefa's chanted prayers for Malcolm and for her absent man had at last ceased. A beam in the roof creaked, relaxing under the burden of another day passed. Only Siegund lay awake, listening to the sounds of the night. Time dragged its immortal feet. At length she crept into the byre, dress, coat and boots in one hand, an oil lamp in the other. The sleepy cattle acknowledged her with a gentle low as she passed them; the door creaked its 'Good Luck' behind her, or it may have been a 'Farewell'.

The fog obscured outhouses and flagstones and her lamp was little use. She slithered forward to the shed; its rough wood grazed her outstretched hand. Anxiously she groped along the drift wood, unaware of the host of tiny splinters that buried themselves into her skin. But search as she might, the fiddle was no longer where she had left it.

'Indeed,' she whispered, 'you know what has happened, Garwulf. You have taken it back. Then you also know of my troubles. You must take me with you, take me away from here. You see, I'm in great danger, but you'll know that too.' She glanced back at the cottage. There was nothing but solid greyness. She stumbled through the gate and along the common path, guided only by her need to see her god and by the faithful hilldyke that would take her at least as far as the Northstane. Now and then the fog lifted a little and then her progress became a little less tedious until she was swallowed by another patch of the swirling vapours. Through a stretch of solid nothingness the Northstane seemed to grow out of the ground, a dull grey mass against a dull grey horizon, shades and shadows rather than colour and form. And somewhere amongst the shadows lay Malcolm, his youthful body shattered. A stone, dislodged from the hilldyke, caught her shin. She rubbed her hurt and felt the stickiness of blood on her hand.

'You see, Malkie, I'm bleeding too. Blow me, we're both smashed up - you mostly in body, I mostly in soul. You have your family watching over you - I have no one. Still, I'll pray for you, for if you die then I must die too; such is folk's sentiment. You believe me, don't you? I have no power to harm you, nor would I wish to if I had such wicked talents.' With one finger she drew a large circle in the air and within the circle she drew a cross. She raised her arms upwards, the open palms of her hands facing the cottage. 'I will you to live, Malcolm Macalay,' she whispered. Her hands sank by her side again. Silently she lamented her human inadequacy. 'If I am never to see you again, I bid you farewell, Malkie. Perhaps we'll meet in Valhalla amongst the warriors, for you and I must fight hard for our lives now, but first I must fight for Maunsie.'

Baffled and frightened she turned away in sudden flight. Garwulf had been right, she did not know herself; she did not understand her own words and actions, if indeed they were her own. The wind began to stir from its short nap, sighed sleepily, then moaned disgruntled on its way to the hills as if to clear a path to the cave for her. She followed the wind, trusting its sense of direction more than her own on a night like this. The ocean droned its warning to keep distance.

With pounding heart she peered into the hollow blackness of the cave. No sound came from within, no glimmer of light to bid her welcome. If Garwulf had left the island - then what of the fiddle? She tried to make sense of the situation. Who had taken it? Perhaps her god had just gone to the crofts for food; perhaps he was asleep - or even sick. A whole string of possibilities came to her mind as she squeezed through the narrow entrance. The cold, dark shelter felt abandoned, yet somehow not entirely bereft of a tenant.

'Blow me down, Garwulf, why do you frighten me so?' her voice quivered. The darkness stared at her with unsavoury indifference. When no answer came she probed along the moist wall - a long, long wall it seemed now, and a long, long crawl. She knelt down on the straw that had been her wedding bed. Her hand made contact with something solid. At once she recognised the smooth, finely shaped wood of the fiddle. 'I don't understand,' she whimpered, cradling the fiddle in her arms. 'How did it get here when you are gone? What does it mean, Garwulf?'

'It means that he will never come back to you, fair Siegund. I know many secrets, aye that I do.'

'Fiddler...blow me down...what right have you....?' Panic choked her words. Her heart beat furiously one moment, threatened to stop the next, then raced away again, leaving her precarious reasoning for a frightfully long time behind. And when she found Roland sitting beside her and talking in his soft sing-song voice of loneliness, of always being the provider of music and merriment but never the participant, she was still more confused. He was speaking of his old mother who sat all day mumbling to herself, waiting for her final day to come. He spoke of his colossal brother Konrad with his colossal spitting-habit that had earned him the name of Fulmar Kon. He spoke of Arlene and the young fulmars; he talked of all things, even of his Irish ancestors. Siegund wondered what his kinsfolk might have to do with her; she thought she must have asked him about them.

'I'll take good care of you,' she heard him say, feeling his arm around her shoulders. 'I'll treat you well, aye, that I will.'

Her need of kindness after the day's events temporarily retarded her wariness of him. In greatly delayed reaction she pushed him away.

'You are lying, Fiddler. You never spoke with him at all. He will be back, indeed, he will. He told me so.'

'The truth is the truth, aye, that it is, Siegund. But tell me, why do you turn your nose up at me? Do I revolt you so?'

'You...you muddle my senses, that's all. I don't understand your ways.'

'And he did not muddle you? I say he did. You allowed him unspeakable liberties. You see, I know. Not many a man would have you now. And what if you are with child?'

'That's absurd, Fiddler. Married women have bairns, never the unwed.'

'Is that so? One day you might find out differently, Siegund, aye, and when you do, remember me. And when all have forsaken you, I'll stand by you, aye, that I will.'

'You are devious, Fiddler. You made all this happen so that you can preach to me of shame. But he will be back; he promised.'

'Many a false word is spoken by a man whose heart is filled with desires. The truth is - he has a woman waiting yonder those shores, and bairns too.'

'Liar, liar!' she yelled and pummelled his chest with her fists, refusing to belief what the fiddler was telling her, but the first seeds of doubt had been sown all the same. Her single, long-drawn howl echoed hollow through the cave; it was the Kuan women's way to vent sorrow while wails and lengthy lamentations were deemed undignified. Siegund had not yet learned to keep dignity in sorrow, nor in other matters, come to that; all the stress broke free in the most un-Kuan capacity while Roland, not always a strict observer of pride and dignity himself, rocked her in his arms.

'Aye, that's right, weep away your sorrows. Love can be cruel, aye, that it can,' he told her, brushing a tress of hair out of her face and drying her eyes with the tip of his tunic. From his pocket he drew a small bottle from which he, for his standards, took a surprisingly small sip. 'Take a drink, Siegund, aye, it will make you feel easier,' he said. 'That's right; take another one. Aye, aye, is that not better already?'

The potent drink with its distinct bitter-sweet undertone worked like a tonic. It gave warmth and comfort; it compensated for the absence of light and fire and chased away the heartache. Someone was holding her; someone liked her instead of despising her. It was not Garwulf - no, not Garwulf; perhaps he was lost forever, perhaps this very moment he was with his woman. With every sip she took, his alleged disloyalty became a little more tolerable. The drink set her face aglow and her body aflame. She could not see Roland's burning eyes on her, could only feel them. Gently he eased her into the straw. She offered no resistance. Nothing mattered any more. Roland was kind, quite unlike the cynical fiddler... but Roland was the fiddler...oh, how confused she was. She felt his breath on her face. Dignity, sorrow, reality - they all merged into the twilight of semi-awareness. The straw smelled musty, the blankets were damp, even Roland smelled musty. It did not matter. Warm lips smothered her face, her mouth, her neck; trembling, caressing hands explored her nakedness. Garwulf, Roland, attraction, repulsion - they seemed one and the same.

It was not until the fire of passion subsided that Siegund sobered sufficiently to the gravity of her immoral act. If Garwulf had cheated on her - now she had cheated too; their pure, gentle love had been sullied by Roland's tempestuous seduction. For a moment she contemplated ending her life, not out of duty but out of shame. The laced drink was still clouding her judgement, which accounted for her thinking the episode too benign for such drastic action; she went to sleep instead. Her thoughts drifted away like feathery seeds in a summer breeze.

The shrieks of a frightened bird woke her. Her head was aching. With painful clarity her conscience reminded her of her sins, but it would not tell her why she had allowed the fiddler to lie with her. His intimate closeness now sickened her. To dress and flee from him was not exactly salvation, but it seemed the next best thing. Roland stirred, stretched himself leisurely and gave a self-satisfied yawn. With almost instinctive swiftness he grabbed her ankle.

'Don't go down to the valley, Siegund,' he begged earnestly. 'You know the folk's sentiment, aye, that you do. Stay here where you are safe, no one dares enter the cave. I'll light a fire for you, aye, and bring you food and news of Malcolm.'

'You are the devil's whelp, Fiddler. If the whole wretched world were after my hide, I would not stay with you.'

'I say it again; I'll take good care of you, aye. I want you to be my wedded woman - on Skerra Kua or elsewhere. I will admit that I have long waited for you.'

'And will you also admit that you tricked me? That you doped me with brandy and herbal extracts? I belong to him. To him I came willingly, to you I did not.'

'Yet your heart flutters when you look into my eyes, though you will not let it speak. You have lain with me; I claim you as my own, aye, that's my right and duty, for you are vulnerable and he has gone. '

'I shall tell Fadder of you,' she hissed.

'That you will not, no more than you will speak of the other one, nor of any matter you are not yet supposed to know of.'

'Blow me, you're a serpent, Fiddler, false and slimy. I've often wondered why you're not wed. Now I know. Who'd have a snake for a husband?'

'I might have been wed, aye, a long time ago.' In the lengthy pause that followed lay a hint of mystery, or at least, a reluctance to speak of it. 'But I shall be wed; I've made my choice. It's just a matter of time, aye, that it is.' He let go of her, made no further attempts to hold her back as if quite sure of her now; secretly he relied on his rival's lesser tolerance to infidelity, should he come back.

She stamped her foot at the fiddler's impertinence, rushed out of the cave and fled. The fog had almost gone. The cold air made her eyes water and blurred her vision, which prompted her to lift a hand close to her eyes to rule out impending blindness - a punishment too harsh even for her sins. She wondered what poor Hedda Volker might have done to deserve blindness. She glanced up at the clouds for an answer, though reliable answers rarely came from the sky and were as unsatisfactory as those of her folk.

Through the pre-dawn stillness, when night creatures have already returned to their dens and the day creatures have not yet woken, she hastened along. The ski was beginning to grow a little lighter. On the white-crested sea below bobbed a tiny boat, too unclear and insubstantial to seem real amongst the jagged cliffs that rose sullenly out of the waves like sombre giants.

The valley greeted her with sleepy nonchalance despite her shame. Less indifferent was Hegan who chuntered annoyed that some folks had to work hard during the day and needed their rest at night, but she drifted instantly into sleep again, her gentle snore rolling over her lips like the purrs of a cat. Josefa left her box bed with unusually noisy activity, which meant that she had had a bad night.

Hard-working Hegan, who had obedience and submission written all over her face, knew what was expected of her and needed no time to gather her thoughts. She asked no questions but immediately rose to the sound of the fire being stoked. She seemed not to have noticed her sister's absence during the night, or perhaps did not care. Siegund, too, slid out of bed, although she had only just got into it. Rory sat at the table, expecting with blank demeanour to be waited on by the womenfolk. Josefa stormed out of the cottage, her mind set on the destruction of the fiddle. As fast as she had made her exit so equally fast did she storm back, her face pale as chalk.

'It's not natural, not natural at all. It appears one night from nowhere and disappears another in the same fashion. It's not na....'

Before she could finish her much repeated words Jan stalked into the *but,* groaning a little and rubbing his hands over the fire after rubbing his aching back. He complained of the physician's reluctance to make the crossing. Before dawn, colossal Fulmar Kon had made his mind up for him and had swiftly man-handled him into the boat.

'Let's pray and hope he's not too late,' Josefa said, crossing herself. 'I'll go and see for myself; and if anything needs to be done, the medical man can show me the way to do it.'

Jan had no doubt that it was the other way round, that Josefa could show the doc a thing or two. His brief smile of confidence in her craft waned when he heard of Maunsie's state of health and of the likely cause. He rushed into the ben, rushed out again perplexed.

Josefa had already left for the Northstane. Rory ran in and out of the cottage with no apparent purpose; Krista sat with downcast eyes over one of her mother's threadbare dresses, doing her best to salvage it from being reduced to rags. Occasionally she swallowed hard, emitting a cluck or two. Hegan flitted between byre and but in her efficient, industrious manner while Jan kept up his excursions to Maunsie's bedside with maddening frequency. Occasionally he gave Siegund a searching glance, but chose not to speak. In their maddening industry, where nothing seemed to get done, no one had a single word for Siegund; no one cared to ask how she might feel. Roland had been right - she would not tell.

Josefa returned from the Northstane. The family fidgeted around her with uneasy expectancy. Josefa took her time to allow the sudden manic pace at the Harehill to slow down so that sanity might have a chance. Solemn-eyed she glanced up at the tiny glimmer of light that tried to find its way through the whirl of smoke under the roof. Five pairs of eyes followed hers.

'Praise the gods,' she said at last. 'The lad is going to live. He is in full presence of mind and vouches for Siegund's innocence. He has demanded that the vicious talk against her be halted at once - it was an accident, nothing more.'

Jan gave a sigh of relief. The rest of the family followed his example, each sighing at a different moment with different intensity according to the length of time each one needed for the tidings to sink in.

'I could have told you so,' Siegund said calmly, flashing glances of triumph at Rory, Hegan and Krista.'

They, in turn, cast their eyes down and looked quite sheepishly with their airs and graces dispersed like a puff of smoke and their righteousness ridiculed. She felt high above them now, powerful even, all-knowing and all-daring in her restoration. She wanted to make more of the unique moment, but instead, she begged humbly for permission to see Maunsie. Her triumph was tarnished when in the meagre light she saw Maunsie's lifeless body, looking more like wood than ever before. It seemed he had slipped into the dark shelter of unconsciousness where no one could reach him, where no pain could cross the threshold of his safe haven.

'Wake up, Maunsie, come back to me,' she whispered. 'Your fiddle is safe. Tell me what you want me to do and I'll do it, but you must help me; I can't do it alone.'

The will to live must come from within, mark my word,' came her mother's disturbingly cool observation from behind her. 'If he will not fight, there's nothing any one can do, not even the medical man. There's no point in fetching him - and waste our preciously few resources.'

As might be expected of Josefa's sort, she tried to steer the family back to normality in her matter-of-fact way. Jan put her trust in her, Hegan preferred to trust the gods, Rory seemed to trust no one, and Krista did not know what trust meant. The days passed in a false normality, carefully guarded by Josefa. In her harshness lay strength and wisdom, for, with each dying day a little sorrow died too, so that each new day began with a little more hope. And the days passed by.

Candlemas had come round once more, though celebration was scarcely on the Nielsens' minds. Siegund was sent to the Girse with a basket of eggs, a jug of milk, two small fish and a small piece of pork. If Maunsie's persistent shadow had occasionally irritated her, now its absence made her feel uncomfortable. She threw her head back in defiance. Scavenging gulls pierced the air with their aggressive shrieks. A slender-winged skua turned sharply in its flight and with rapid powerful strokes, descended on one of its smaller cousins and robbed it of its breakfast.

'So, you have your struggles too,' Siegund mused, 'using and being used, eager to take and reluctant to give, sharing by fair or foul means what the gods provide.' She wondered which way up she might find Claire. As it happened, the old woman was the right way up and in a better state than on their previous meeting. With no more than a nod Claire accepted the basket and immediately stuck her thin, red nose into it as if it were easier for her to smell the goods than to see them, though the fish hardly warranted such close olfactory inspection.

'Ha-yee,' she remarked, 'it reminds me of my man - the gods rest his bones.'

It was not clear whether it was the food in general or just the fish that had brought back Claire's memory of her husband. Her mind appeared to have momentarily wandered across to the other side of life to meet him, her watery eyes locked in the past with all its joys and miseries. Yet, she seemed content. Her nightcap sat perched on the top of her head as if it had dropped there by accident. She wore it day and night. It might well equal her great age, though while her wispy grey hair had become white, her white cap had grown grey. The tattered dress hung loosely around her emaciated body and seemed to be held together only by her stained apron.

'Where shall you live when the laird takes your croft from you?' Siegund ventured to ask, making a genuine effort to be sociable.

'Ha-yee, where shall I live!' She shrugged her frail shoulders. 'A few days here, a few days there; where ever folks will have me. I'm too weary to toil in the fields, but I have a good way with bairns whose minds have not yet been filled with nonsense. I'll earn my keep.'

'I...I should like you to live with us, indeed, I'll ask Midder this very day.' Siegund said generously, but cringed as soon as Claire's bony hand touched her face. How difficult it was to shake off old fears even when the intentions were good.

'But how are things with you, Siegund?' Claire's voice came wispy - everything about her was wispy. 'I heard much sinister talk - not that I believe any of it. The devil take it; tongues wag quickly, and before you know it, you're branded for life. They don't forget, you know.' She tugged a little absentmindedly on the bristly hair that grew out of a wart on her chin.

'Malcolm has cleared my name and all is well now.'

'Ha-yee, all is well until they need a scapegoat again. They don't forget. Always beware of them.' As she said those words she gave her visitor a wispy hug.

It took Siegund quite by surprise; Midder never hugged her - she used to do, a long time ago. And here was Claire, not even her kin, showing her that it was alright to have heart and emotions.

'I'm not worried for myself, it's Maunsie I fear for. He has neither eaten, nor moved, nor even spoken a single word these past days. Death is sitting by his side, ready to snatch him from us.' She was wrestling for the right words to explain the matter of the fiddle without giving too much away. Claire did not pry, she only listened; Claire understood her as no one had ever done before.

'Blow me down, what am I to do?'

'You must do what's right in your heart, Siegund. I can say no more. Kuans don't readily understand compassion -

your Midder, a Papa Kiran, even less so; it interferes with their sodding pride. I can help you no further, but remember now and forever - they don't forget.'

'I'll remember, Claire, but I will do what's right in my heart. And whatever happens, I am grateful to you.' Siegund rushed to the door, then rushed back, hugged the old woman and planted a kiss on the wrinkly cheek. 'How stupid I was to be afraid of you, but now I love you; now and for ever more.'

Like a bird in flight she hurried to the cave. Who was to stop her, who to catch her? She was in league with the wind; it carried her along and she carried the wind in her streaming hair. The hill seemed to level out before her feet, to bow down to her, eager to hasten her progress. Wind and hill offered their friendship, made her their equal; even the cave, the place of joy and humiliation, its mouth agape as if in astonishment, was waiting to receive her.

How different the cave looked with a shaft of daylight falling in, but somehow it looked even less welcoming than at night. She did not tarry, grasped fiddle and bow and rushed out again. Specks of mould had settled on the fine wood. She wiped them away with the hem of her dress. She raced downhill, hiding the fiddle inside her coat as best as she could, hoping that her folks would be busy around the croft and not notice her. Krista was in the *but,* bent over her knitting, but Krista did not matter.

'Wake up, Maunsie, I've brought your fiddle back,' she told him excited. She plucked a few strings, then took his hand and placed it on the wood to show him it was real, but Maunsie seemed not to hear her. Josefa had followed Siegund into the ben. She wrung her hands and shouted that it was not natural for the fiddle to reappear. She tried to reach out for it, take the evil thing from Maunsie. Siegund barred her way and had both cheeks slapped for it. They screamed at each other now, forgetting Maunsie altogether for a moment and then remembering him again. From under his closed eyelids trickled tears. He opened his almond eyes and tried to speak, but Josefa's voice came loud and matter-of-fact.

'Tonight, on our pilgrimage, the holy lights will tell us what to do, tonight when our hearts are filled with piety we shall know what is right, though our church is in ruins and we have no preacher man. Be that as it may, Robert Macalay does his best to preach the gospel when it is asked of him.' She left it that, secretly relieved that the fate of the fiddle might be decided at a later time.

'The boats are coming back, the boats - they are coming back,' came the cries from a bunch of lads running past the Harehill in the already fading daylight; they called eagerly, yet without regard whether or not the news had been received.

Hegan took off her apron. With painstaking correctness she folded an enormous white shawl around her shoulders and picked up her basket. Her stance was that of someone dreadfully important, her face sombre with reverence. Without a word she left the cottage to go to the beach, to meet the boats and receive the holy lights. Siegund and Rory followed their sister at the respectful distance befitting someone who had been entrusted with such high office; only virtuous young maidens were worthy of taking the holy flame to the church at the edge of the moor and prepare the altar for the midnight ritual - pure maidens, unsullied by the sins of the flesh.

Siegund reflected on her own worthiness. Folks, though ignorant of her adult experience, would never nominate her, not after the Yule day and Malcolm Macalay affair; and even if they chose her, she would have to refuse. The fiddler had made her unclean and she would never sully the altar with her impurity, she was not a cheat, even though Midder seemed to think so.

Three boats, each manned by a crew of three, brought back from Maalie Voe three burning candles safely carried within three cow-bladder lanterns. Maalie Voe was a tiny barren island incapable of supporting a community. A godly man, inspired by a visitation from the Holy Virgin, was said to have built the church; to this day it bore the holy flame of protection. Three young maidens were waiting to receive the lights. Three - a good number, a sacred number. But there was a more sober reason for sending three boats when one might have sufficed. In the changeable season, when winter and spring held their battles for supremacy, and when the sea sided more often with the former than the latter, the journey was wrought with danger. If at least one flame arrived safely on Skerra Kua unforetold hardships, sickness and poverty would be averted, such was its powers said to be. Sending three boats was a triple insurance.

Hegan Nielsen, Ingeborg Johansen and Adelika Macalay stood apart from the crowd like apparitions in the dying daylight, silent, motionless, each draped in a white shawl from head to hips. Men pulled the boats onto the pebbly shore, dragging them far away from the lapping waters and keeping all noises as low as such a manoeuvre would allow. Three elders took charge of the lanterns, stepped purposefully out to hand them to the three ghost-like figures. Johannes Johansen kept his enormous pride hidden beneath his great white beard. Tilo Volker lifted his cap and brushed his hand over the smooth, tanned surface of his bald head that had far more presence than the scanty moon above them. Udo Patersen, his mind and body thankfully in better state than his patched-up trousers, bowed respectfully. Robert Macalay, in his present role of spiritual leader, cleared his throat noisily as signal that he was about to speak. He had been taught the Christian ways first by his Highland mother and later by his Highland wife and knew more about the gospel than his neighbours, and what he had forgotten he supplemented in his own way; one miracle more or less - where was the harm?

'Take the lights of the Holy Virgin,' he commenced, 'the lights that have burned for three hundred years. Let our church shine in her glory so that our folks might be safe throughout the year.' His voice rolled like thunder in the worshipful air that had silenced even the rowdiest children. His fire-red hair fluttered in the wind like lapping flames. As he stood there, arms raised in blessing, he might have been Moses himself, parting the Red Sea or giving his ten commandments on Mount Sinai.

'Three hundred years - and the flame is still burning? Blow me, how big is the candle?' Siegund whispered to Rory who did not reply. Her eyes followed the maidens as they began their lone walk to the church, protected against the darkness by the holy flames. The rest of the people, their voices barely raised to a murmur, prepared to go to their homesteads. Rory took Siegund by the hand to lead her home; Rory, with his mother's dark hair and humourless attitude attempted to make good his previous harshness towards his sister. Gentleness was quite alien to him, just as it was a rarity for him to hold her hand. It was not easy to understand why the laughing, joyful Ingeborg secretly adored him. But now Siegund liked him too, for he seemed to like her after all.

Such were indeed the powers of the sacred lights; they brought peace and forgiveness even if it did not always last. She might even forgive the fiddler on this day of benevolence when Claire had become her friend, when Midder had allowed the fiddle to stay, at least for now, and when Maunsie had come back to her. It was no wonder that with so much good fortune her belief in Garwulf revived, and with it her loathing for the fiddler returned, despite the lights.

She wondered if this loathing had brought on the slight nausea she had felt this morning, but being still in benevolent mood, opted to blame it on the growing-up process. With a glimmer of sadness she doubted that she would ever have the makings of a useful adult, her commitment being what it was. Growing up was a painful business for her; it was as if two souls were fighting for one body. Siegund the child refused to let go and die with dignity. She giggled at the thought, threw her head back and wrought all her feelings into fitful melodic recitation.

Throughout the evening Rory's temporary, agreeable manner enhanced the tranquillity in the Harehill cottage. It was a time to reflect for those capable of intense thought, a time to idle for those who were not. At last, the moment of the pilgrimage drew near. Jan was concerned that the long walk might prove too much for Josefa in her present condition; the determined wave of her hand answered his question.

Out there in the cold night tiny lights speckled the path to the sullen foothills like fireflies. Men, women and children, with a burning oil lamp in one hand and a lifeless lantern in the other, made their way to the church; one lantern per person present, one lantern per person absent - for those at sea, for the sick, the very young, the very old and the very scared such as Krista who could not be persuaded to join them. Each family made their way in their own time and at their own speed, all hoping to receive the holy light before the hour of midnight, when the lights that guided them now would be extinguished.

The mute, dark figures gathered by the church. Some had already entered it, others waited patiently outside. Years ago this humble house of the Christian God had accommodated all the Kuans at once. With a large part of the coarse building collapsed it was reduced to less than half its size and the ritual had to be performed in stages. The Nielsens, the Klaasens, the Volkers and the Mulvoens were the last to enter, the order having been predetermined according to rule. Last year the groups had been made up differently and next year it would be different again; it had something to do with fairness. Such systematic arrangements had resulted from decades of closest relationship and precarious self-rule.

A large rock represented the altar. Its once rounded top had been painstakingly chipped away by generations of island folk to achieve the flat, if rather crude, surface now hidden by a red drape. The numerous white tassels set off the sides of grey stone. The solidness of the altar was a symbol of strength and stability, though the walls, once squarely built around it, had lost their air of continuity. On the altar burned the three sacred candles, stumpy, brown products that forfeited elegance for durability. The formula of their consistency was known only to the Bidebergs who profited by their secret knowledge mainly in that it improved the Kuans' estimation of their worth, but tonight the question of worthiness was not on the agenda. A wooden crucifix among pagan relics lay encircled by a chain of stone runes, laid down at random by the three maidens who knew only their individual meanings. It was for the elders to interpret the runic formation as a whole.

A few suppressed groans of displeasure could be heard. The runes were foretelling bad times ahead. Folks kneeled down to pray to the gods for leniency. Amongst the kneeling worshippers walked the three maidens silently like spirits, and with their pure white, flickering tapers they lit the kneeling worshipers' lanterns. In the presence of such reverence Siegund thought her sister Hegan quite impressive. And how was it that jolly Ingeborg could be so profoundly serene? But Siegund's greatest admiration belonged to the gloriously angelic Adelika whose hair seemed to burst into flames whenever the candlelight caught it. If kin could be exchanged as easy as folks exchanged a piglet for a lamb, Siegund would gladly have bartered for Adelika as her sister.

Remembering the purpose of their midnight endeavour Siegund tore her stare of admiration away from Adelika and directed it to the crucifix. She wondered who might have carved the knotty Jesus on it. And why had men nailed Him to the cross? He reminded her of Garwulf, which in turn reminded her of the green pebble in her pocket. Shimmering stars looked down through the open space where the roof had once been. Folks were pleading for the Almighty's blessing, for a good harvest, for health, and for eventual eternal rest; high voices, low voices rose and fell, swelled one moment to a flood tide of sounds and eased into unintelligible murmurs the next in staggered sequences. Josefa prayed for Erik's safety, Tilo Volker prayed for his sick cow, Katrine Klaasen for an end to old Tobias' festering sores, and Roland Mulvoen - he prayed for time to pass; time would see him right.

For all the variations of volume and pitch the droned prayers took possession of conscious thought and made the worshippers forgetful of the discomfort of kneeling, or at least, furthered their willingness to suffer discomfort as token of their faith. If sober folks could be so influenced by the chants and murmurs, what chance did the dreamers have? Siegund's head filled with the sound of a heavenly choir, gentle as a breeze, tender as spring blossoms, and through it she heard the thunderous voice of the Almighty Himself.

'Siegund of Skerra Kua, bride of a god and seducer of men,' she heard him scowl, 'grave are your sins. Repent! Build me a church; build it for the sake of the Holy Virgin, for the sake of your people and for charity. In return I will grant you redemption. Leave me a token of your pledge, so that I might know your true intention.'

'I...I...blow me, all I have is the green stone. I would rather not give it away,' she mumbled through clenched teeth. 'To part with it means giving the memory of Garwulf away.' All the same, afraid to risk damnation, she shuffled on her knees to the altar and lay the glistening stone beneath Jesus' feet. Folks saw it sparkle in the blessed lights, dared not remove it, nor did they know whether to deem Siegund's gift as innocent, presumptuous, divine or evil.

The wind carried a faint sound of church bells from the mainland. It announced the hour of midnight, the time for the walk home. If the folks had arrived in family groups, now the whole community returned together in one slow, purposeful procession so that the pilgrimage might last a respectable time. Their sacred lights illuminated the path, their chanting and citing of Nordic verses filled the air, and as so often, the Christian faith lost itself within the pagan beliefs. For all that, there was sincerity and deep conviction in their hearts and no one could, with honesty, have suggested sacrilege. Their faith could be no other; it served them well throughout their struggles.

And again, order had been observed without noticeable procedure. The Macalays formed the rear, because they were the first to part company. No one acknowledged their departure from the ranks, no one bade them good night. With every croft they reached, the procession dwindled. Each family, one by one, returned to their home as they came upon it. Not once was the solemn worship broken until the last lights vanished, leaving the rest of the night to the trolls, the ogres and suchlike.

# Chapter 7

March with its gales and driving rain had come and gone. Jan thought it best to get the business of the wedding out of the way; there would be no time for lengthy celebrations once the work in the fields began. Niggling disagreements about the wisdom of the union had not quite come to rest; only time would tell who had been right. Right or wrong, today was Hegan's day, which meant a rare trip to the mainland, rare for the women anyway. Despite apprehension the whole island community followed the wedding party to the beach and under chants and prayers for a safe return they sent them on their way.

Three boats, each one rowed by three pairs of capable hands, manoeuvred eastwards into the hazy sun to honour the Nordic gods; only when they were truly on the swell did they change direction and headed for the mainland. The men, being quite used to this see-saw excursion, took great pains to reassure their female charges. But a swell is a swell; and when at last they set foot on firm land again it took some stomachs a fair while to settle into their proper places.

Konrad Mulvoen had merely been invited on account of his strong rowing arms. Once on the mainland he opted to go his own way, much to the secret relief of the rest of the party who detested his indelicate spitting habit.

'Lead the way, Roland,' Jan gave the order. 'We have business to attend.'

The fiddler in Puritan dress bowed, stuck the fiddle under his chin and stalked away. The others followed two by two according to rule and strict order of importance for the occasion. The first in line were Jan and Josefa. Josefa was now heavy with child. Jan had protested against her risking the journey, but she had come anyway.

Then followed Hegan in plain, useful dress, with Candlemas shawl and pink sea-shell brooch. With her starchy dignity and sturdy matronly figure she looked refined rather than pretty, insipid rather than sweet - an ice-queen had it not been for her ruddy complexion. This ruddiness seemed the only thing she had in common with her man to be. Beside her walked her brother Rory, equally starchy; his gentler mood had perished with Candlemas day. Next came Robert Macalay, his hair spasmodically aglow as if a lamp was being turned on and off each time a scanty sun-ray broke through the clouds. Beside him walked his good woman Ethel. Both seemed equally impatient to get their son wed. What a unique day! The first Macalay to wed a local! Behind them walked the groom in plain grey tunic, looking no more important than the rest of them and perhaps a little afraid. His sister Adelika beside him was afraid too - of her own future. Then followed the two witnesses - the patched up Godfrey Patersen and Johannes Johansen who with his eagle-eyes and white beard looked like a marginally younger version of Father Abraham. The last place of importance fell to the youngest sister of the bride and the youngest brother of the groom - Krista Nielsen and Malcolm Macalay, young Thomas being a mere babe in arms. Malcolm's damaged leg was still in the process of healing. Supported by his somewhat asymmetric driftwood crutches he hopped on one leg along the cobbled street while Krista, solemn, prim, a sheep in Sunday dress, tried to keep as close to him as possible and as distant as was proper. Siegund and Maunsie had no role to play; they had merely been given the doubtful honour of tagging along. Roland's sombre tunes and the almost uniformly clad party gave the whole thing an air of a funeral cortege with only the coffin missing, or at best, of a mission that had to be accomplished, come what may. They received little more than a fleeting glance or a smile and a nod here and there from the busy mainland folks.

The mainland, though in truth only an island itself, was a strange world to them, exciting yet repulsive with its stale smells, its narrow streets and its houses huddled close together as if for warmth and support. The air seemed to become staler by the minute. When at last a large open square opened out before them the entire congregation took a deep breath as if by appointment. Set back from the other buildings stood the church, its grey walls imposing rather than welcoming, its mighty spire swaying in the sky.

Maunsie tugged at Siegund's sleeve and urged her to go into the church with him; it had already swallowed the rest of the party. No one had looked back even once lest some one might lose heart. She told him to go by himself. Triple-sighing he reluctantly obeyed. She watched him enter the church, her compassion for him once more burning brightly. Her interest in the square with its market stalls was just too tempting. Market traders offered garments, fruit, oil lamps and fish in random display. Eels dangled in the strong breeze to dry. Those black sleekies reminded her of serpents - the fiddler was a serpent. Shiny beads demanded her attention - blue ones, red ones, white ones; they tempted and tantalized.

'Pretty, aren't they, young missie!' A stout woman with protruding eyes smiled at her, displaying unabashed a brown quarry of decaying teeth. She pulled one of the red necklaces across her open palm and then held it up to Siegund for inspection. 'As dainty as your face, and that's the truth,' she commented, not in the slightest perturbed by her own lack of daintiness.

'But...but...' Siegund shook her head.

'Only a bawbee and a plack to you; where else would you find such a bargain.'

'I...I have no money,' Siegund confessed.

'No money - no ware! My generosity has limits.' Immediately the woman lost interest in her dainty customer.

The wind was gathering strength. Siegund tried to bunch up inside her outgrown coat. The coat bunched up with her and popped its buttons open. At the corner of one of the shabby houses stood a young girl, wearing little else than an enormous shawl and a sleepy couldn't-care-less attitude.

'What's ya gaping at?' the girl asked sharply, rearranging her scanty attire with stiff, bluish-red hands.

'I thought you might be lost. Not that I know my way around, myself, indeed not.' Siegund confessed.

From a nearby building came unruly singing and laughter. A man stepped out, looked about him for a moment and reeled towards the two girls. His cap hung precariously on one side of his head, bound to drop off at the next teetering step. He anchored his feet to the ground while his upper body swayed a full turn. With outlandish accent and clumsy drawl of advanced intoxication he asked the girl with the shawl her price.

'Eight bawbees,' the girl replied in business-like manner. 'Three for me and five for my sick mother.'

'That is mighty much money.' The sailor gave a whistle of surprise through his yellow teeth. He had difficulty in pronouncing the words or even finding them; it did not hamper the negotiations. The man nodded, pivoting yet another round-trip through the air while his feet remained cemented to the ground.

Siegund watched them go. She had taken everything in and understood nothing. If she had one bawbee and one plack she would be able to buy the beautiful red necklace, she mused. She stood and dreamt of the beads, scarcely aware of the comings and goings around her.

'One bawbee and one plack,' she thought aloud when someone tapped on her shoulder and told her it was mighty cheapish or sheepish. She swung around, her mouth agape, as she stared surprised at the stranger. The red beads were tempting and testing her dignity - and won the day. She had never intended to ask anyone for money, but now that it was said she did not feel so bad.

'Indeed, one bawbee and one plack,' she confirmed with a big smile. 'One plack for me and one bawbee for my sick mother.'

The sailor handed her the money and immediately regarded her as his property. He raked her close to him and leaned heavily against his purchase, then tottered away with her; and all she could do was to totter with him. It seemed wrong to go with him and wrong to yell for help; she had made a deal, but she was ignorant of its nature. Together they staggered through a maze of narrow alleys littered with rotting waste. High walls of back-to-back houses drew ever closer to each other, blotting out air and daylight. Stench, filth and the babbling, reeking sailor suddenly shocked her into soberness and out of the soberness rose panic, and when the panic truly struck her, she in turn struck the sailor. The burly lover, whose bandy legs were controlled by rum rather than his brain, fell cursing to the ground. His head hit the stone wall on his way down. It silenced him instantly. She fled from the scene of crime, dared not look back in case she had killed him. In the end her conscience forced her to stop briefly and glance back. The sailor was not dead, probably not even dying, though each time he got to his knees his rum-laden head pulled him down again.

The market square felt clean and friendly after the stench and squalor of the alleys. Siegund opened her fist to release the coins. To keep them was a sin. But was it not also a sin to throw away such scarcity? Whatever she decided to do she would be guilty of transgression against honesty and decency. And since she dared not return the money to its rightful owner she might at least have the beads for carrying her sins through life. She considered it a reasonable deal. The woman at the stall still called her a dainty missie, but she did not know of the dainty missie's sins.

From the church came the unmelodious clanging of a single bell; for the rich three bells would have rung. Its monotonous sound demanded discipline and piety and, only so by the way, announced the end of the wedding ceremony. The fiddler, emerging from the dusky inners of the church, was followed by Duncan and Hegan. Duncan looked vaguely triumphant, Hegan vaguely nervous, and both were equally red-faced. The rest of the congregation stepped silently into the daylight as if reflecting on what they had just witnessed. Jan looked concerned at the darkening sky. To folks who go looking for omens - good or otherwise - they come remarkably easy. Heavy clouds were gathering. Jan urged the party to hasten to the harbour without delay, irrespective of order. And when they saw their moored boats rear up like frisky horses they knew at once it would be a rocky ride home.

'You are quite safe with us, aye, that you are.' The fiddler gave his lop-sided smile and offered his hand to Siegund to help her into the boat. She drew back from him and refused his help.

'Go to hell, Roland Mulvoen,' she gasped hardly audible. 'If I must be rowed by the devil I will not take his hand.' Like a rag queen she perched herself next to Maunsie on a wooden box, proud, defiant, showing the fiddler that she was not afraid of anything. The men took the oars. There was no specific order in which the boats left. Just to get moving, just to get through the swell was the only consideration now. Johannes' great, white beard bobbed up and down with every stroke; he looked more than ever like Father Abraham, Godfrey soon dripped droplets of perspiration all over his patched-up trousers while Roland pulled the oars seemingly effortlessly in perfect rhythm with the others, yet the strain soon became apparent in his face. His great hat, weighed down by a metal hook lest the wind take it, lay by his feet.

The cross-swell flung the boats to and fro like flimsy toys. The rowers laboured hard, constantly correcting their course and trying to row into the swell instead of being carried away by it. All land seemed to have been swallowed up by the sea with neither the mainland nor Skerra Kua spared. Maunsie and Siegund linked arms for moral support while their free hands clung to whatever offered a handhold. Icy showers of spray covered crew and passengers alike. There was nothing but sea. Huge waves rolled towards them, grew in size and towered high above them, their crests curled towards them. Siegund and Maunsie slid off their wooden perch as if by common agreement and huddled in the bottom of the boat where a pool of water was collecting. The boats were lifted upward until for one blink of the eye they seemed to ride the foamy crest only to plunge down into the gurgling depth again. The black sky turned day into night. Lightning flashed across the sky, followed by a deafening clap of thunder that made the boat shudder. Siegund cast her eyes upwards to plead with the gods for mercy, but her plea was answered by yet another brilliant flash, spectacular, awesome, a burning bush with fiery, jagged branches.

'Blow me down, mighty Thor, why do you tear the heavens apart?' she whimpered. 'Is it my sins that make you so angry? I gladly feed the red beads to the sleekies; I care nothing for them, not very much anyway. Do you want my life for so small a sin? Though I have sinned most of my life and for that I am sorry.'

She tried to loosen her grip to take the beads from her pocket, but her hands had a will of their own and would not let go. Another fiery reverberation, another boisterous see-sawing trip from the depth to the crest and into the depth again. She looked to her companions for counsel, but they looked quite insignificant themselves. Their hair streamed in the wind one moment and was flattened to their heads the next as the heavy sea spray passed over them. There could be no counsel from them. Hard-faced and tight-lipped they were fighting for their own survival. And Poor Maunsie seemed to have turned into a piece of driftwood altogether and was way beyond giving or even receiving counsel. And where were the other boats? Had they all perished? Hegan and Duncan on their wedding day? Why did Hegan have to fall for a Macalay? Siegund wanted to cross herself, but her hands were locked in an iron grip. And Krista - she was with Malkie. If Siegund had to go down to the bottom of the ocean she would prefer to go down with Malkie rather than Roland.

A jagged rock loomed up beside them, a dark, cold finger pointing accusingly to the sky. The Puritan hat rose from the bottom of the boat and flew towards the rock like a big black bird; the fiddler's curses followed the hat. Churning nausea cramped Siegund's stomach and twisted her inners into a painful mangle. The thunder seemed further away now. Her head filled with the sound of swirling water. She thought herself on her way to the other world with the devil riding beside her, an endless journey to the kingdom of evil. It seemed as if time stood still, had neither existence nor relevance - distance and direction had no meaning. She gave Roland a weak smile and did not know why. The nausea overwhelmed her. With an impressive projectile eruption of breakfast and bile - like a grand finale to a memorable drama - she showered the amazed fiddler who had no choice but to carry on rowing despite it all.

When her stomach stopped heaving and her eyes managed to focus again the shore of Skerra Kua lay close before them. Folks were waiting on the beach, praying and urging them home. As if by a miracle all three boats reached the shore within minutes of each other. They were safe - everyone was safe if somewhat battered. Hands reached out and backs were patted. Rory slung Maunsie over his shoulder and stalked away without delay. Everyone was in a great hurry to get home. Siegund looked for Malcolm, but he was busy comforting Krista.

'Your prayers served us well, fair Siegund,' Roland grinned.

'Indeed I prayed. I prayed for the devil to take you,' she snapped.

'That's uncharitable, aye, that it is. But you must understand that, had I gone down, I would have taken you with me. We belong together, in hell, heaven or on earth; I don't mind which.'

'Leave me be, fiddler,' she hissed and hastened away from him as fast as her still shaky legs would carry her.

The wedding feast was a grand affair despite the soberness of the barn and lingering apprehension. A Macalay pig roasted over the fire. There was mutton too and the inevitable barley-this and barley-that. Old Claire, who had been persuaded to join the celebrations, chomped tediously on a piece of pork, having only two incisors and two molars left in her mouth, and even those were in unrelated positions and no help to each other. Big Fulmar Kon, goofy like a rabbit, had no difficulty at all, spitting fragments of cartilage and small bones as far as they would go. Martha Bideberg went into instant economy overdrive, urging her young brood to cram as much as they could into their rotund bellies, so that she might not have to feed them for the next three days.

After the feast Roland, helped along by Jan's splendid medicinal brandy, played his fiddle. He took regular breaks for further treatment as he was want to say. It gave Maunsie a chance to demonstrate his newly acquired skill of playing the fiddle. He played a lively tune, his eyes gleaming the way folks had never seen them gleam before. His performance procured gasps of surprise and appreciation, tinged with a hint of yet more apprehension. According to Josefa, the fiddle had come to the Harehill as token from the trolls in remuneration for a blanket they had taken. Some folks believed her adamant claim, some doubted her, and some were simply envious.

Bruno Bideberg grumbled that things had gone missing from his place too, but no reward had been left for him. The fiddler smirked and unhurriedly searched for Siegund's eyes, confident he would find them looking his way.

'Aye, we know the truth, that we do, but we shall not tell,' those dark eyes told her and, as so often before, they burned massive holes into her soul. She felt sick again; each time she saw him she felt sick, and each morning when he was not near her she felt worse. Perhaps tomorrow she would ask her Midder for a remedy to take away the nausea. Indeed, tomorrow when Midder was not too busy or too tired she would ask her.

Young Emilie Klaasen begged Maunsie for a repeat performance. He said he might, just for her. With Duncan wed, Adelika looked a little happier. Perhaps there was hope for her and Sven Klaasen. Pattie Volker took it upon herself to pamper and pity Malcolm for not being able to dance, while Malcolm would rather be pampered by Siegund. Three mummers came to the door, straw-clad figures with colourful ribbons on their straw hats which covered their faces. No one ever turned a mummer away, for beneath the strawy disguise may well be hidden a god, perhaps the mighty Odin, or Balder, the most beautiful of all gods who had been condemned to the underworld. Woe to the mortal who treated a god with unkindness. Siegund prayed that one of them might be her god Garwulf. The mummers mingled with the guests and, apart from their silence, they behaved in quite human manner, eating, drinking and dancing. Midnight came and revealed no god - just three local lads upholding an ancient custom.

It was the time for Hegan to be escorted to the Harehill cottage by six maidens. She would spend her first night with Duncan in her parents' box bed while the rest of the family would go on celebrating in the barn. Hegan was not at all pleased with the choice of escort in which she had no hand. Adelika and Ingeborg were alright, they were her best friends, but the others she would rather do without, for Hedda Volker could not see, Pottie Pattie could not think, and Sefina Hendricks from the White Owl Crag, with duck-egg eyes, forever talked of her unfortunate grandfather Swaalie. Most of all, Hegan objected to Siegund.

This was one more ritual to be performed, important only to the six maidens. They blindfolded the bride with one of her stockings. Hegan thought it a foolish game, Ingeborg thought it hilarious and Pattie significant. Sefina compared Hegan with old Swaalie because she too could not see now, and Hedda, constantly living in the dark, said nothing at all. The girls stood around Hegan in a circle. More than a little annoyed at such childish pranks the young bride flung her other stocking over her head. It snaked into the air - and missed them all. She took off her blindfold to learn who the recipient, and thus the next bride, might be. Five disappointed faces looked at her accusingly for not playing a fair game. If Ingeborg had felt sure of Rory, and Adelika had hoped that the marriage between Duncan and Hegan had paved the way for Sven and her, now the future looked bleak. Hedda had never held much hope of marrying; Pattie had not been sure but hoped anyway. Only Siegund grinned like a Halloween lantern, deeming herself wed already.

'It's nonsense anyway,' Hegan advised them. 'Wedlock does not depend on an air-borne stocking. Perhaps now you'll let me go to bed; I need time to compose myself.' She talked as if she were preparing to go into battle. Hegan always preached of a right and a wrong way of doing things. They hoped, for Duncan's sake, that he knew what he was on with.

# Chapter 8

Since Hegan had joined the Macalay household Krista, silent as always but a fraction more mobile than before, tried her best to fill Hegan's place. And Siegund - well she just kept feeling sick. Each time she thought of holding conference with her mother, Krista was there, always listening and never getting involved. Indeed, she would ask tomorrow - tomorrow - but tomorrow never came. Had Josefa been a little less busy, had not everything in her life been either black or white, she would have known that her wayward daughter needed her now more than ever before. But she did not see, did not know. She was preoccupied with other matters.

Old Claire was to live with the Nielsens. Siegund and Maunsie were on their way to the Girse croft to carry her things to the Harehill - and carry her as well if necessary. As it happened, Claire, with her possessions wrapped in two small bundles, had no need to be carried; she was quite sober and looked as tidy now as poverty would allow.

'Ha-yee, ha-yee,' was all she said as she walked through the empty byre for the last time. Out in the yard she shook her head at the scanty remainder of the gate as if she had never noticed its deficiency before. With one last glance she said her silent good-bye to the cottage and to the good and bad times it had shared with her. Her advanced age hampered her from walking entirely erect, but she held her head high, smiled and turned away.

'Nay, it's sad, it's wrong that you should have to leave your home,' Maunsie piped and took Claire's arm.

'Always pretend there's no pain and you'll not feel the hurt, Maunsie.' There was no bitterness in her voice. 'The devil take it, young blood is what the croft needs. I hear that Duncan and Hegan are hoping to take it on. It's all the same to me. I begrudge them nothing.' The further they left the Girse behind the more talkative Claire became. Sometimes she stopped to point at a new shoot poking its head through the stony ground by the wayside. 'Ha-yee, your Midder will have told you all about herbs; no one knows them better,' she said.

'Midder doesn't talk much to us of anything and then she calls us stupid for knowing so little,' Siegund complained.

Josefa was waiting for them by the gate and, under massive back-to-front sighs, welcomed Claire into her home and admitted freely that the other woman's help was greatly appreciated; and Claire rolled her sleeves up to show that she was here to work for her keep, though her fleshless arms suggested that to eat and be idle would be more beneficial to her.

Claire went about her work as if the Harehill had always been her home. She lavished motherly affection on the entire family, the kind of affection that none of them had ever known. If age had made her toothless it had also made her sexless, which exempted her from the need to keep proper distance. The cool, formal atmosphere changed within the Nielsen household to a surprisingly happy one; even Rory took to her and seemed more cheerful. In the evenings her tales excited the young ones and delighted the adults. Being the oldest of the islanders her memory went back to the days when Jan's father had been a babe in arms. She spoke of her childhood, of her man and her children, but she never again spoke of Marnie despite Siegund's regular prompting. Claire was content in her new role. She did not mind sharing the box bed with the girls and hoped they would not mind her snoring - and Claire certainly snored.

The rains came back - prolonged and furious; they kept the crofters off the fields and their hand-made ploughs in the sheds so that precious time was lost in a naturally short growing season. It was far too warm for the month of May. A stale smell lay over the island and began to seep into the homes, the wind lacked breath, had no power to drive the foul, earthy air out into the ocean.

Jan groaned and rubbed his aching joints. Something else was troubling him more than the pain, though he would not speak of it. In his eyes glimmered a restlessness that was hard to define, but it was there. The sturdy man's uneasiness made everyone else feel uneasy too. He opened his mouth as if to speak. A flash of lighting shot through the gap in the roof and lit up briefly the white-washed walls; it was immediately followed by a mighty clap of thunder. Josefa, now in her final month of pregnancy, stood up and propped one hand into her aching back. The candle in the cow skull flickered. She crossed herself.

'Bad times are ahead of us, mark my word!' she said. 'Twice within a moon Thor has bellowed at us. What can be the reason for his displeasure?'

'Ha-yee, who can say,' Claire answered, folding her long arms tightly around her thin body so that her hands reached almost her shoulder-blades. 'The devil take it, there's one thing you can be sure of: in every cottage at this very moment, causes and cures will be urgently discussed. They don't forget.'

'It would be wiser not to summon the devil, he may take you by your word,' Josefa told her, withholding from them her own consideration of causes. She tried not to think of it any more, though Hegan caused her concern; she had not looked well at all of late.

They sat in brooding attitude around the fire; in the raging storm there was nothing else to do. Rory, quite needlessly, poked the turf in the grate with a peace of wood that was becoming visibly smaller in the process. In the *ben* Maunsie was playing one and the same tune with maddening persistence. At the next clap of thunder the byre door flung open. To their relief it was not the devil standing in the doorway but Bruno Bideberg from the Beach croft. The sheepskin around his shoulders, complete with a whole year's fleece, dripped like a blanket fresh out of the wash-tub. He probably had never thought of wearing the woolly side closest to his skin; but then, Bruno was not a thinking man. His back was slightly rounded. On a dark night he might easily have been mistaken for a sheep, but there was nothing sheepishly benign in his eyes.

'Holy Midder, what's so urgent that you must brave this hellish storm?' Josefa asked. The Bidebergs were the Nielsens' closest neighbours, though not exactly their closest friends; come to that, the Bidebergs had few really close friends.

'It's our Kate; she's ill. We are at a loss what to do. I beg of you, good woman, cure her.' He brushed his hand over his face, where a massive scar ran from his upper lip to his left temple.

'No one ever needs to beg for my help, Bruno. As for curing her - I must first know what's ailing her. Even then, I can't cure every ailment. Would I could! Kate is a frail child and my knowledge has limits,' she warned him lest he expected miracles. 'Be that as it may, I'll do my best, so much I will promise. How long has she been ailing?'

'Two days she's lain in delirium, two whole days.'

'Two days? Then why didn't you call me sooner, Bruno?'

'I...we..,' he stuttered and shot a shifty glance from Claire to Siegund before casting his eyes to the floor. 'We thought that the tea Martha brewed might make her better.'

'Tea of the right sort is very well; the wrong sort is useless, even harmful, mark my word.'

'You'll catch your death out there, Sefa,' Jan objected. 'Wait till the rain eases. You have yourself and your unborn bairn to consider.'

'Be that as it may, my skills are not given to me to keep to myself but to share them with my fellow neighbours. Come, Bruno, let's not waste precious time in talking nonsense.' Josefa overruled Jan's objection like a mighty judge and the matter was settled. All that was left to do for those left behind was to chant, pray, sigh, sob, curse - whatever each one's inclination might be.

'Blow me, why did Bideberg look at me so?' Siegund asked her father.

'He's a worried man, that's all.' Jan's efforts to show composure went miserably wrong and he looked at her almost as shifty as Bideberg had done. Beneath the pretence of having all matters under control Jan, too, harboured weaknesses and fears, and now they lay exposed for all to see as he paced up and down the *but.*

'The devil take it! The man had no liking for either of us.' Claire folded her bony arm around Siegund. 'For your sake I pray that your Midder will cure Kate. As for myself - I care little.'

Rory looked up at them briefly as if to tell them that they need not fear Bideberg but could not find the words. The sound of the fiddle came to his aid and masked his own doubts.

'Why Kate?' Siegund asked. 'She's the best of the Bideberg bunch. She hasn't yet caught the slyness of her kinfolk.'

'Ha-yee child, we have no right to judge others. Remember it now and forever.' Claire looked forlorn into the fire. Her watery eyes, their colour no longer recognizable through the hazy film peculiar to old age, glistened.

The storm seemed to stop in the midst of its raging fury. The fiddle in the *ben* became silent. A moment of stifling hush filled the air, clogging their lungs and forbade them to exhale. An intense feeling that something awesome was about to happen drained the blood from their faces. Eyes burned in rigid immobility, muscles locked in painful spasms. They strained their ears and heard nothing but their own racing heartbeats. The hard-trodden mud floor under their feet began to vibrate and the clutter on the shelves rattled. From somewhere outside came a deep rumbling and rolling as if the thunder were coming out of the ground - a long, long roll of thunder until at last it stopped and all was silent again.

'The hills are moving again,' Jan whispered, pulling himself out of his stupor. 'Sefa,' he called out as panic took over. He ran out of the cottage, not heeding Claire's advice that the Beach croft would not be in danger. He neither listened nor looked about him, nor stopped running until he reached Bideberg's home. Josefa was already leaving the cottage.

'Jan,' she said, surprised to see him. 'It's no use, Jan, the bairn is dead.'

'The bairn? Dead? No, no, it must not be. You should not have come out here in this storm.' He pulled his hair in vexation and gave a massive curse. 'The green pebble...we should never have left it on the altar. I must go to the church and ...'

'Not our bairn, Jan, not our bairn; Kate is dead,' she called to Jan, but he had already gone. She had no way of stopping him; her sober man had lost his reasoning.

People rushed from all direction to the Kirk croft at the bottom of the knoll. They gazed up at the hill where Jan was already entering the House of God and vanished from their view. Halfway up the hill was Rory, calling to his father. The other men looked on in horror at the foolishness of father and son. The ground began to shudder again, the earth seemed to groan. The hill behind the church moved, slowly at first as if unwilling; it was forced forward by the weight pushing from behind. There was no power on earth to stop its descent. The old church moaned under the onslaught and without struggle submitted itself to its grave, embracing one of the worshippers with its cold, clammy arms. Rocks and debris pelted the lower slower slope, came crashing down into the valley and embedded themselves in the soft meadow. Rory had fallen to the ground and had stayed there until all was still again. Dazed he lifted his head and looked about him.

'Is no one man enough to come up here and help my Fadder?' he called down to the mesmerized Kuans who, for a moment, seemed to have lost all sense of urgency. 'Where is your courage, your sense of responsibility now?'

'Why risk other lives for the one that is no more? The hill might slide yet again,' Fulmar Kon grumbled and spit on the ground.

'Hold your tongue, you miserable coward, aye. You are no brother of mine,' Roland fumed, and immediately headed for the church. He beckoned to the others to follow.

For Siegund it was like a nightmare from which she could not wake up. Nothing made sense to her. Fadder losing his mind? How could that be? And what was the woman, who looked like her mother, doing there at the foot of the hill? And how could it be that Roland the rogue was already catching up with Rory while the other men were lagging way behind? Why the fiddler? Why not Malcolm, or Duncan, or Godfrey? Roland the rogue - a hero? Malcolm, hopping along on his crutches, had only just arrived and was not even aware of the gravity of the situation.

'They are fools if they think they can save a church that is ne mere, ye ken,' he said, standing by Siegund's side.

'Is ne mere, is ne mere!' echoed the words in her head; they echoed and shrieked and shrieked. Someone put a hand over her mouth. The shrieking stopped, and she knew that the awful sound had come from her own throat. She fled from the crowd to run to her father's aid. Her boots sank into the waterlogged meadow. The hill was no easier to negotiate, getting steeper and more slippery all the while. She caught up with her mother, who was crawling on hands and knees, pulling herself up on the scanty grasses; and where there were no grasses she dug her fingers into the even scantier soil for a handhold. One slip might send her all the way down again.

'Midder, you shouldn't be here,' Siegund told her.

'Should I not be with my man when he needs me?'

'Indeed, Midder. And we'll get him out. Give me your hand, I'll help you.'

Men were clambering over the rubble, moving stones or digging with bare hands. Roland gave the two women scarcely a glance as if he did not know them or thought they had no business to be there. He bid the men to stop a moment, knelt down on the ground, and hammered three times against a rock. Placing his ear against the rubble he listened, but he could hear nothing. Robert Macalay found a gap that seemed to lead to the floor of the church.

'Jan, can ye hear us,' he called down with a voice so powerful that the men feared he might make the hill slide again. They held their breath and waited. Nothing happened, no landslide and no reply. Progress was slow and tedious, and once more, time seemed to lose its meaning. They may have dug for an hour, two hours, half a day - who could say.

The clouds hung low over the hills; Siegund fancied she could touch them if she were to stand on her toes and reach up. At last, the long awaited call came. It may have come from Duncan, or Robert, or Roland, she could not say. They freed Jan from his stony prison, praying all the while that the massive altar might have protected him. Alas, it had not. They laid him before Josefa's feet. A sea-green pebble fell from his half-open fist. No one moved, no one spoke. A dozen pair of eyes were fixed on the unholy object that had cost a man's life and yet still sparkled unashamedly in the diminishing light. Siegund picked up the token of her promise and cast it amongst the debris.

'This is where it belongs and where it must stay,' she said with racing heart. She was frightened, but her voice remained steady. 'Let no man take it from here; the Christian God has demanded it so.' Her words were answered by mute stares, by whispers of fear, by murmurs of anger, by rekindled resentment against the evil-doer amongst them. Few pondered over who it may be - others had made up their minds already.

Josefa knelt by Jan's side. Respect demanded silence so that the woman might grieve for her man. Jan's open eyes stared into nothingness; death had not softened the mask of terror. She brushed her hand gently over his waxen face, closing the eyes that could no longer see. For a brief moment she remained there, motionless, only her lips moved, then she got to her feet. She swayed a little, tried to find support in dignity, her arms stretched towards heaven. Over her lips came her cry of sorrow, a long-drawn howl like the cry of a wounded animal. Rory stood by his mother's side, mourning her loss rather than his own as if no connection between the two men existed. He pitied the woman who had lost her man and pitied the bairn that would never know its father. Josefa's hands sank slowly by her side. She shook herself like a dog after a dip in the sea, and with it the moment of immense grief seemed to have passed.

'Take him home men,' she ordered in her matter-of-fact voice. 'Darkness is coming down on us fast.' And with that, she started her descent down the slippery slope, helped along by Rory and Siegund. Her composure was deemed neither particularly brave nor peculiar; it was the Kuans' way.

Women and children were waiting by the Kirk croft. At a corner of the cottage, in the dusk of the evening, huddled Krista and Maunsie. They had heard their mother's cry of sorrow and knew the truth long before the six men with their morbid burden passed them. Head bowed in condolence they went on their way to the Harehill. The Nielsens followed them, walking tall and erect with their heads held high. If shame could dampen pride and dignity - grief could not; and if weakness on Krista's behalf occasionally manifested itself in two or three clucks - Maunsie, who was greatly in need of comfort himself, was at hand to instil courage in her.

Claire, expressionless, motionless, in ill-fitting dress that hung limply in the airless dusk, stood by the gate like a scarecrow that had mistakenly wandered in from the field. She asked no questions nor did she show any distress. She knew, somehow, that disaster had struck and knew there would be more. Mishaps were like the ocean, they came in waves; fate held good and bad - no one but the gods could choose.

The door creaked its macabre welcome as the men entered the barn and laid Jan's body down. Duncan, Godfrey, Johannes and Sven bowed their heads deeply to Josefa and departed, leaving Robert and Roland to do whatever needed to be done. Rory intended to stay by his mother's side, ready to offer comfort and support, but Josefa sent him away to fetch the things she needed.

Claire had taken the young Nielsens under her wings. She spoke quite uninhibited of their father's forthcoming journey and of the beautiful place in the sky where he would be happy. She spoke as if she had already been there and could not wait to get back to it; it made death seem less severe, less final. From the barn came frantic hammering as if Noah had just begun to build his ark and then realized that the waters were already lapping around his ankles. A driftwood coffin on a driftwood bier with driftwood legs, humble as the man who must rest in it, received the washed and freshly dressed body.

'One must start the last journey clean and tidy,' Josefa said, quite matter-of-fact.

Just as Roland and Robert were leaving, Hegan rushed into the barn. Her face that had been lacking the ruddiness of late was now as white as someone with her complexion could be.

'I had no idea, Midder,' she said, quite out of breath. 'Duncan has come home this very minute...Midder; he looks a beaten man. He says...oh, Midder, say it isn't true...it can't be because of the redness! I'm with child, Midder, oh, Midder, say that the redness is not cursed.'

'No one is to blame. Be that as it may...' Josefa bit her lip and refrained from speaking her thoughts.

'But Midder, how could this happen?'

'It has! Let that be the end of it,' Josefa replied and busied herself with the tasks ahead. She lit a candle and placed it by Jan's head. It flickered momentarily before it took hold. She picked up the blue dye Rory had prepared for her. 'Blue for sadness, blue for faith,' she said and began to neatly paint the coffin with Nordic signs and symbols. She stopped briefly, propping one hand into her back and one hand on her stomach. 'The bairn is restless tonight,' she said, then nodded her head towards the cottage from where Maunsie's fiddle sang a tune of Valhalla and of snow-white sails.

'Why does no one stop that boy?' Hegan grumbled and Rory agreed.

'Let him play if it comforts him,' Josefa shrugged them off. 'Fadder won't mind. He was so proud of the lad. Go home, Hegan, your man needs you, and I wish to be alone with mine for a while. And you, Rory, see to the livestock; they have their needs too; there's nothing else you can do here now.'

Reluctantly Hegan and Rory left the barn, knowing well enough that alone in the stillness with her man, Josefa's grief would be mightier than dignity.

'Jan, Jan, why did you do such foolish thing, you who were strong and wise? Now you have gone from us, left us to fend for ourselves.' She leaned her head against the painted box, unwittingly transferring some of the sadness-and-faith paint to her brow. She vowed to pray each night for guidance from him so that her courage and strength might be nurtured to help her through this life without him until the day they should meet again. A prayer for young Kate ended her moment of grief. Perhaps Jan was guiding her already as she remembered her duty to her children. A massive shake of her whole body restored dignity at once.

Straight and proud she entered the *but*. All eyes were on her, searching her face for advice as to in what manner to behave, searching for security despite their loss, searching for permission for life to continue. And Josefa, in all her sorrow, showed them how to accept what could not be altered. That night, when the wind whined its mournful song, Krista and Siegund huddled close to Claire who, for once, managed to go through the night without snoring - and probably without sleep.

In the morning the islanders went about their work as if it were just another day despite the pain and anger in their hearts. The humid air forced an early burial, especially since Jan's and Kate's coffins had too many gaps; and thus, at noon, friends and neighbours gathered, some at the Harehill, some at the Beach croft. The temporary division of the community was unavoidable; perhaps it was not even significant that the families themselves had split up. At any rate, soon the two assemblies would meet at the Beach croft to take the sad journey to the cemetery together - the Nielsens and the Bidebergs, united in their grief despite their differences in the past.

Six men had carried Jan down from the hills; now six men carried him back to them. Robert Macalay led the bearers, carrying a cross made of two flat pieces of driftwood. It bore no name, but on it was painted a blue sea eagle, its wings spread wide as if about to soar into the sky. Two by two the mourners walked behind the coffin, most of them still wearing the clothes they had worn in the morning while tending sheep, cattle or pigs.

At the Beach croft young Emilie Klaasen stumbled forward to take her place beside Robert. Her slate eyes were cast down. The black shawl that covered a mass of dark blond hair made her pale cheeks look almost transparent. She carried a cross for Kate on which was painted a white dove. In her apprehension to walk ahead of death her timid face with its upturned little nose seemed to grin a little, but had she not grinned she would have cried. She was fifteen, the age when one was treated as a child, but was no longer allowed to behave as one. Unlike the rest of the Klaasens she was small and fragile; Robert's sturdiness made her appear even smaller. A blue sea eagle and a white dove moved side by side and the white dove trembled in the air.

Josefa walked upright behind the bearers, proud almost as if she had just achieved some megalithic feat instead of having suffered a loss; at least the equally proud Rory by her side had gained in status, now being the head of the family. Behind them trudged Hegan with Maunsie whose hand she held in tight grip; and behind them walked Siegund - alone. There was no malice in that; it was just that the path was too narrow to accommodate three people side by side and that they happened to be of an uneven number. She was glad to walk alone yet also felt slighted. From behind her came Krista's occasional 'Cluck-cluck', followed by Claire's 'Hush, bairn, hush.'

They had walked this path on Candlemas night full of hope, now there was only gloom. Jan and Kate were no more - the dilapidated church was no more; its ruins were painful reminders. Grim-faced the people passed this once holy place while some minds were filled with unholy contemplations despite sorrow.

Siegund cast a sideward glance to the heap of rubble, anxious that no one should detect her distraction from grief. Her eyes searched for the pebble. There was no sign of it; perhaps it had dropped between the rubble, perhaps it had stopped shining forever. She thought of Garwulf, thought of the fiddler who was walking far ahead of the cortege so that his fiddling, mournful though it was, should not be too intrusive. The fiddler, always the fiddler! It annoyed her that she could not think of one without thinking of the other. Yesterday, on the hill she had almost admired Roland - almost; now she loathed him again.

All sorts of things went through her mind. She felt guilty for her lapse of grief. She wondered why Duncan's usually ruddy face looked so pale. Did he feel guilty too? She remembered Claire telling her to beware because folk do not forget. She shuddered, tried to think of pleasant things, but it was too difficult a task when they were about to bury her father and poor young Kate. How strangely connected they seemed - Fadder, Kate and the green pebble. All three of them belonged to the earth now.

The cemetery lay only a short walk from the church where the hills eased out into boggy marshland - hostile land where even the sheep where denied access because of the large areas of unsafe ground. The sun behind a hazy sky seemed to mock rather than smile. It sent a chill through many a spine despite the humidity. The cortege passed though the gate in the hilldyke to the place reserved for the dead. A sheet of mist hung over the ground of the lower marsh with its rotting earth and vegetation from where the stale smell had come to their homes and had called for a sacrifice. It had taken its due.

Two open graves, one large, one small, lay waiting to receive the spent flesh. There was no priest to sprinkle the ground with holy water, no churchman to preach a sermon, only the pig man with the thunderous voice and the fierce Macalay redness who tried his best to fulfil his temporary role of spiritual shepherd, conducting his haphazard service and offering his prayers as best he could. The earth closed over Jan and Kate. Two mounts of peaty soil was all that was left of them. No flowers graced their resting-place, no names to tell who might be sleeping the eternal sleep beneath the marshy turf; just two mounts and two crosses. The sea eagle and the dove rested side by side, and the dove no longer trembled.

# Chapter 9

Josefa crouched by the fire, her mind uneasy with her recent loss. The pain of labour cramped her body at ever- shortening intervals. A strand of hair hung over her white face. She did not notice it; not that she was normally disinterested in her appearance nor in her work. Now and then she closed her eyes and gave a faint groan.

'Are you ill, Midder?' Siegund asked concerned.

'Not ill child, mark my word, not ill.' Again she groaned. Awkwardly, as if giving some long-kept secret away she said: 'The bairn is coming.'

'What, now? Blow me down, can't it wait until Rory and Claire are back?'

'Bairns come when they are ready, not when someone comes back. Don't stand there gaping, Maunsie, make yourself useful, go to the beach and look for driftwood.' It was not that wood was needed just now; she simply wanted him out of the way. 'And Krista, fetch Hegan and then see if you can find Rory and Claire in the hills above the Northstane.'

'I'll go, Midder,' Siegund offered. I'm faster than Krista; I can run with the wind, indeed.'

'Be that as it may, you may forget your errand if something else takes your fancy. Go, Krista, don't dally.'

'But Midder, I know nothing of such matters as bairns.' Siegund covered her mouth in horror, and through spliced fingers she mumbled: 'I'm afraid, Midder, blow me, I'm afraid.'

'There's nothing to be afraid of; nature will take its course.' Josefa licked her dry lips. 'Help me to my bed.' Her voice momentarily rose with sudden urgency. 'Holy Midder, the bairn is in a hurry.'

'Midder, why do you have another bairn when you have us already?' Siegund asked for want of something more appropriate to say.

'What talk is that? Children are given to us by the grace of the gods. We don't choose and we don't question our purpose in life. Mark my word, unfortunate is the barren woman who has no reason for existing.'

Everything happened very quickly and yet seemed an eternity to Siegund. A miracle, a messy, gory miracle happened before her very eyes. Miracles should gladden - she was not glad at all. If miracles cost so much pain and distress, then why, oh why did folks pray for them? She did not want to be a woman and certainly wanted no children, now less than ever. Her chest felt tight, her stomach churned. She closed her eyes. Bed and walls seem to rotate in antagonistic directions. She wanted to tell her mother of her own indisposition that still troubled her from time to time and ask for a remedy.

'I shall see to them now,' came Hegan's cold, sharp voice. 'Go and clean yourself up, girl.'

Siegund flung the doors open without bothering to shut them behind her. She ran as fast as her shaking legs would carry her. Down the common path she fled, heading for the beach since the hills would be swarming with men folks tending their ewes and lambs at this time of year. Unfairly perhaps, at this moment she hated them all for being spared the pain of childbirth. If pain was the women's purpose in life - what was theirs?

A lively surf met her and stopped short by her feet. She looked at her blood-stained hands and wondered if some of it was the babe's blood. Perhaps she had wrenched his head too much - he had yelled so the moment he had been born. She clambered over the stony terraces to get to deeper water. The surf washed the stains off her hands, but it could not wash away her anxiety. She stepped back over the smooth rocks, wishing that the sea would also smooth the rough edges of her young life. Back on the sea-sprayed shore she sat down, leaned her head against a rock and cried.

'I'm ailing something, blow me, and I dare not speak of it to any one. Fadder, why have you left us? Not that you would have listened. And Garwulf, why have you abandoned me? Perhaps, the fiddler is right about you, or perhaps, you were only a dream.'

'Nay Siegund, what are you doing here? Should you not be with Midder?' Maunsie stood beside her, carrying a fair few pieces of driftwood.

'Blow me down!' She jumped to her feet. 'Why do folks sneak up on people?'

'Nay, I didn't sneak, I called to you from yonder.'

'Indeed? Anyway, we have a baby brother and I helped him into the world,' she announced proudly, her moment of self-pity already forgotten. But that is how it was with her ever-changing moods.

'Nay, Siegund, what yarns you spin! You have no such skills.'

'Believe what you will.' She picked up a handful of pebbles, skimmed them one by one across the surf. 'He looks a bit like you, Maunsie,' she added cheerfully.

'The gods forbid that he should be like me, Siegund.' With a clatter the macabre harvest of someone else's death and destruction dropped onto the pebbles. Maunsie jerked one shoulder up as if to readjust the hump on his back. He could not follow his sister's rapidly changing emotions and instead emulated Roddy the rooster by stretching and retracting his neck in vexation.

'If he is like you, I shall love him. Let's climb onto the ledge over there,' she suggested, pointing to the lower part of the cliff. For a short while Siegund the child returned; Siegund the child was happy - Siegund the woman was not. Siegund the child felt the sun in her face and the joy of springtime in her heart - Siegund the woman had mostly known anguish and nausea. And now the child climbed the cliff, leaving her brother way down on the ground. Higher and higher she climbed, sure-footed like a mountain goat, her laughter echoing from the cliff. She stood on the narrow ledge, her face turned to the sea. The sun sent its amber rays down on her so that, against the slate-grey background, her face and bare arms seemed to turn to gold and her hair fluttered like strands of brocade. The saline breeze was far more cleansing than the sea had been - it cleansed her soul and set her free once more. She felt like a bird, fancied that she could fly; if she were to spread her arms she would fly with the terns across the ocean or fly to the sun.

'I am the goddess of Skerra Kua!' she cried, her arms raised high. 'Can you hear me, you Kuan miseries? No one can harm a queen of the heavens. And you, Garwulf, god of the night, I command you to return and keep your promise.' Her arms dropped suddenly when she added on sudden reflection: 'Blow me, else I must wait for ever and a day.'

Maunsie was shouting and waving his arms, looking small enough to fit into Fulmar Kon's pocket; his words did not reach her.

'Nay, Siegund, why do you take such risks,' he reproached her when pity for him had brought her to his side again.

'The gods take good care of us unless we anger them; and then, blow me, you're not safe in your bed.'

'How you alter your moods by the minute! And how carefree you are, Siegund! Sometimes I wish I could be like that.'

'Carefree? Is that what you think? Midder calls it waywardness. It's never that. I worry about many things and care for many more. I care about the hills, the rocks and the fresh air, I care about you and Midder; I care about Malkie - a little. I care about Garwulf.' She shrugged her shoulders in apology for speaking his name. She listed all sorts of things she cared about, but she avoided to mention the things that worried her.

'You should have climbed to the ledge with me; close to the sky you can make peace with yourself and the world.'

'Nay, I'm not at war with any one, nor with myself.'

'Indeed? All the same, the nearness to the sky makes you feel good and powerful...and humble, Maunsie.'

'Humble? Nay, it's not your way to be humble, nor would it suit you. A crown would suit you better, but a crown you shall never have.'

'I have the next best thing.' From her pocket she drew the string of shiny red beads with three tear-drop pendants at the centre. Quickly she cast a sly glance towards the mainland as if to reassure herself that it was quite safe to show off her shady acquisition. 'Have you ever seen anything as beautiful, Maunsie?' She placed the necklace on her head so that the pendants rested on her forehead.

'Nay, it looks like blood on your brow. Robert Macalay says that Jesus had a crown of thorns and that blood oozed from it.' He shuddered at the idea and became thoughtful.

'Blow me, it's not blood and I'm not Jesus and not at all divine, not yet anyway. But one day Garwulf will make me his goddess. One day it will come true.'

'Yay, and you talk like a duck's rear end again. Let's go home; I'm starving,' Maunsie piped in his highest pitch. He had no liking for the weird stuff and showed his agitation by severely reproaching her, but he spoke in such jumbled fashion, it was not clear whether his uneasiness was on account of the beads, of Garwulf or of the possibility of having a goddess for a sister. Preferring to put his trust in reality he stooped to pick up the carelessly dropped wood. His legs buckled a little under the weight, but Maunsie had pride too, or dignity, or whatever else they wanted to call it, and would not ask for assistance.

'If you had got your legs going instead of your mouth we would be halfway home by now, Maunsie,' she advised him as they idled along. When he did not reply she tried to humour him by talking of Erik - whether he would come home soon or whether he had drowned. Maunsie did not like that sort of talk either and for a while they walked without speaking, but such moments of silence never lasted very long with them.

'Where did you find those beads, Siegund?'

'I bought them on the mainland when you were all at church praying with - and for - Hegan.'

'Nay, you have no money.'

'Indeed not. One bawbee and a plack! Oh, Maunsie, my sins are great.'

Maunsie was at a loss. What could he say - what could anyone say? They fell into silence again.

'Blow me, I can see Martha Millipede and Slim Tim!' Siegund suddenly giggled. Martha Bideberg had earned herself the name on grounds that she was never seen except running at high speed, knitting some garment or other on the way as if she had more arms and legs than everyone else.

'I wonder where they are heading for.'

'The Mulvoens, most likely,' Maunsie replied. After a short pause he gave a jerky sigh. 'I think he's a decent fellow though, when it comes down to it.'

'Who is?'

'Roland! He was braver than the other men when Fadder...'

'Shut up about the fiddler,' she cut him short. 'He has two faces and I've seen them both, and the one you don't see is worse than the one you see.'

'Yay?' Maunsie grinned.

Martha was bawling at Slim Tim who had the roundness of a suckling pig and little pink eyes to match. Martha, wearing her husband's sheep-skin coat despite the warm weather, was as piggy as Tim. All the Bidebergs were piggy - all except Bruno. He was something different altogether; he was quite weedy, round-backed and bow-legged. His management of Martha was often the subject of jocose conjecture amongst the men, who argued over who was easier to handle - his wife or the bull he kept in a stone-walled enclosure near the cottage. To be fair, the scar on Bruno's face was not Martha's doing; it stemmed from an encounter with the four-legged brute, which she had fended off him with a broomstick. With two such fierce creatures at hand it was little surprise that most folks only ventured near the croft when the bull's services was required or when a supply of the brownish candles were needed; their top-secret ingredients were equally subject to conjecture. Bruno claimed to be a descendant of King Guthrun the Viking, though there was nothing royal, or even vaguely noble, about any of them. As mother and son came closer, their progress became precariously retarded as if in two minds whether to pass the Nielsen kids or turn back.

'Greetings, Midder Bideberg; greetings, Tim,' Maunsie called to them and smiled perhaps a little more than might seem proper for someone so lately bereaved. 'We have a brand-new baby brother.'

Martha seemed asleep despite the fact that her knitting needles clicked furiously in her hands. She neither replied nor acknowledged her young neighbours, instead boxed Tim's ears for trying to return the greeting. Martha looked the other way and, as she passed, her pursed lips ejected a sizable volume of foamy saliva. The rude demonstration of her feelings seemed to have given her fresh energy, for she hastened away at full speed, her bulky hips and buttocks bouncing up and down with every step.

'Blow me down, what's got into her? She spits more viciously than Fulmar Kon. I bet that's why they have a liking for each other; they ought to have a contests,' Siegund suggested in anger.

'Nay, it was thoughtless of me to speak of our new bairn when she has just lost one of her own. She is bound to be grieving still.'

'Indeed, she may well be grieving - we are grieving, too. But she hates me - me and Claire, and so does her man. Blow me, you think I'm making it up! My mind isn't addled, Maunsie.'

'Nay, not addled, just over-ripe. Come Siegund, I want to see my new brother.'

'They'll not let you see him. Men folks are not allowed in the ben for two weeks.'

'I'm not a man yet. And where do I sleep if not in the ben?'

'In the barn with Rory.'

'Why?'

'Because! Blow me, I don't know why; something to do with purity, I think.'

Claire, old as the hills and gentle as a breeze, met them by the door and took them both into her arms.

'Hush now,' she said, your Midder and the bairn are asleep. And what a sprite little bundle he is. He'll make a fine fellow one day.'

'He's alright?' Maunsie asked timidly. 'I mean, he's not like...like me?'

'Ha-yee, no, not like you.' Claire stroked the boy's head. She always comforted even when comfort was not asked for. 'You are a fine fellow, too, in your own way, Maunsie.'

Krista stood over the fire, stirring with monotonous frequency a stew that was bubbling in the blackened cast iron pan. She threw a hasty glance at Siegund - quite shiftily for someone of meek disposition - then quickly stared back into the pan. She wanted to say something, but could not find either breath or the courage for it; instead she just clucked and was still clucking now and then when Rory came home for his meal. His desire to talk, if not his word power, had markedly improved since Claire had joined them and had further improved since his father's death.

'All is well with the ewes,' he volunteered, 'though Bideberg complained that he had lost two lambs. I have no idea what he wanted me to do about it, nor what he was trying to say.

Weird folks! Can't make them out.' Rory did not ask about his mother's progress, in his opinion, ewes and women were made for that sort of thing and usually coped well enough. He was told the good news anyway to which he nodded his acknowledgement and asked to be fed.

# Chapter 10

Summer came early with a bracing air that might have inspired wary souls and healed weary bodies. Even Claire, old as she was, could not recall such glorious weather - and there was no flaw in her memory. Folks were willing to shrug aside the mishaps of the past months. The women and children toiled in the fields and tended the livestock; the men harvested the sea, their slender boats, criss-crossing the tranquil panorama of gentle seas. It was delightful to watch the boats glide with ease before vanishing from sight to return two or even three days later with a tidy catch.

'One or two we've caught,' the men would say when asked the measure of their success, believing it offensive to Aegir, god of the ocean, to brag of good fortune or even to be precise.

But all was not well. Whenever the young Klaasens were safely out of the way to be spared the unpleasant sight and smell, Tobias would take the rags from his festering hands and feet to seek his cure from the scorching sun, but the sun's healing powers were limited after all; it did not heal his sores, which had now spread to his face, much to Josefa's dismay.

Martha Bideberg thought she could do better; it ended in an exchange of harsh words between the two women and placed the Klaasens in an awkward position. Out of desperation they gave Martha a chance, but after a few days of Martha's unclean, incompetent handling of the malady Tobias begged Josefa to come back. And while Josefa agreed - under a fair deal of matter-of-fact complaints - Martha came away with a huff and with sore hands of her own.

Folks waited with increasing uneasiness for the rain that would not fall. Week after week the sun beat down relentlessly and became a burden; the constant heat sapped their energy, the glare became painful to the eyes. Parched lay the shallow, stony earth, stunted and wilted lay barley and oats. The subdued wind spread minute particles of saline spray over the prematurely autumn-hued land, crusting over the fields and destroying the little that was left of the crops; the grass in the meadows and foothills succumbed to the draught.

'Ha-yee, our land is truly cursed,' Claire sighed and folded her mottled hands. 'The devil take it, my knees are sore with praying to the Christian God and my voice is hoarse with calling to Odin. I've done my best.'

'We all have, mark my word,' Josefa answered. 'But why are we punished so? It has been a bad year, and it isn't done with yet. Holy Midder, it's a bad business all around!' She turned to the cow skull for help and reassurance, hoping that the already much repeated exercise might be fruitful this time. Young Jan was growing steadily plumper while Josefa seemed to loose flesh at the same rate. He began to wail in his mother's arms. She was preoccupied with other matters and did not seem to notice it.

'Hegan is not at all taking well to expectant motherhood,' she told Claire. 'Not that she's unwilling, but something is amiss, mark my word.'

'Ha-yee, she'll make out alright,' Claire offered with a half-confidence that reflected the present general attitudes of all the Kuans.

'Only if it is the will of the gods, mark my word. Tobias, too, is in the hands of the gods now; I can contain his sores no longer; they are eating flesh and bone away. The Klaasens have brought a medical man from the mainland. Not that I blame them, but what humscum the learned man speaks by summoning all men, women and children to the Heather croft for examination. I shall not go, nor my kin; over you, Claire, I have no say.'

Before Claire could reply, a pale, lanky figure, which looked like a malady himself rather than a medical man, stood in the doorway and introduced himself as Doctor Lundquist.

'I shall not waste time on lengthy preliminaries; you are not the kind of folks who need pampering,' he said and bowed his head slightly. 'I think you should know that Tobias Klaasen is a very sick man.'

'Have you come to tell me what I know already? Then you're after all wasting time,' Josefa replied sharply.

'That is not all I have come to say.' His evaluating eyes glanced briefly at Josefa's hands before he continued. 'The malady is highly contagious and the outlook is bleak unless you heed my advice. The leprosy is already rife in parts of the mainland. You, good woman, are more at risk than any other, having tended the old man's sores.'

'I tend all the Kuans' ills. Holy Midder, I do my best. Don't trouble yourself with my family; we're all well; nor do we want charity, for times are bad and we could never pay your fee.'

'No one could have done more than you, god woman. A cure for the malady is beyond medical knowledge, but hear me out - it is a desperate thing. Let me help stem it before the whole community succumbs. I'm quite willing to take my pay when times are better for you.'

Josefa considered the proposition carefully, laying dislike for her rival aside. It made sense what he was saying; she allowed the examination to go ahead.

'Hm, you are indeed in good health,' Lundquist stated with a hint of admiration for Josefa after he had checked hands and feet through a magnifying glass, carefully avoiding all physical contact. 'Yes, yes, all...except...hm...I can't be sure,' he said, looking past Claire instead of meeting her eyes. 'The signs are there...hm...I cannot be sure. It is the same with young Emilie.'

'Emilie?' Josefa expelled in horror. 'But she's a mere bairn. How can it be?' The sharpness in her voice subsided. 'Any one else?'

'Martha Bideberg. There's little doubt about her.'

'That will teach her to meddle with affairs of which she knows nothing,' came Josefa's voice sharp and matter-of-fact again. 'Holy Midder, what am I saying? Our pride and dignity has turned to mistrust and hatred; the gods have mercy on us all!' She quickly crossed herself. 'What will you have us do, Doctor?'

'Build two huts in the hills, one for Martha and Tobias, one for Claire and Emilie lest I am mistaken. There they must live. Build an enclosure around the huts. No one must venture either in or out. Leave food and other requirements by the gate.'

'What will happen to them?' Josefa asked, for once shaken to the core.

'Nothing can be done. There is no cure as yet.'

'Holy Midder, are we to leave them to die?'

'They have each other. As for the rest of you - it will pass. Now I shall beg the ferry-men to row me home, my work here is done. I bid you good day.'

The new calamity had transported the islanders into a temporary state of mental impotence. They all knew the pain of loss; it was part of life, but to abandon their fellow men, through no fault of their own, was unthinkable; to sit in judgement over - and condemn - the sick was more than they could comprehend and cope with. Too much had happened - they could take no more. Morose contemplations took over. Someone amongst them must take the blame. But who? Not Claire, for she was a victim of the leprosy; not the stranger, for he had long left the island. Perhaps it was the Macalay blood, perhaps the fiddle or the bairn born on Yule day. But Siegund's Yule-day disgrace and the Malcolm Macalay affair at the Kilcairn ledge overshadowed all other possibilities. The fragile bubble of slowly regained trust over the past two months finally burst. Despair rather than reasoning brought the Kuans to the Harehill. Every step on the parched ground hammered into their heads the need to resolve the matter of the evil-doer once and for all, some more aggressive and determined than others. Their commotion brought Josefa and Rory to the gate. The fierce expression of the islanders told Josefa at once that some of them had come for a more sinister reason than building huts, but under her firm and open address the tempers mellowed a little.

'One hut will suffice,' Claire told them from a safe distance - safe for the folk's sake rather than her own. She had no intention of leaving Tobias to Martha's slap-happy ways, though her own had not always been up to much either. 'The devil take it, my best days are gone and I have no fear of what's to come, nor is loneliness a new experience for me. I'll take good care of them until my breath leaves me.'

That seemed to calm the situation a little. Still muttering they made for the hills; amongst them were Josefa and Rory. Claire too left the Harehill and idled towards the beach, alone with her thoughts, alone with her troubles. Her eyes, with lids bereft of lashes, were empty, her mouth merely a blue slit held together by masses of radial lines. She, who was older than any islander, she, who had outwitted death while her contemporaries had long gone, seemed suddenly aged by another hundred years, her back a little more bent; but still, she tried to hold her head high.

Siegund had hidden behind the half-open byre door and had peered at the angry mob. Frightened she ran back into the *but.* Maunsie and Krista were holding one of their wordless dialogues in which twitching faces, jerking necks, rolling eyes and shrugging shoulders did all the talking.

'Sometimes I think that Midder was right about the fiddle, and then I don't want to play any more,' Maunsie said, turning to Siegund. 'But it demands me to play, it will not let me rest, and. when I play again I feel at ease, I feel it is good and a sacred gift; and then I think Midder was wrong.'

'The fiddle is not to blame for our misfortunes, indeed not.' Siegund cast a sideward glance at Krista. 'Blow me, Krista, you give me the mortal jitters with your silence and your eavesdropping.'

Young Jan knew nothing of misfortune except his own, and noisily he let his kin know. Shrewdly Siegund considered which end of him might have the greater need. While she tended the babe she mentioned, so by the way, that Claire might have drowned herself by now, which in turn sent Maunsie in see-sawing motion down to the beach. He returned with Claire who clearly had not even got her feet wet.

When darkness fell, Josefa and Rory returned. The hut was finished, they said. Furnishings and provisions would have to wait till tomorrow. Claire nodded her ancient, white head.

'I'll be ready when the time comes. As for tonight, I'll sleep in the barn if it is all the same to you, Josefa.'

'Holy Midder, what nonsense is that? All these months you have shared our home with us; what's so different now? You shouldn't have to leave at all, Claire. As I see it, there's nothing wrong with you.'

'If they can send a bairn like Emilie away, then why not an old woman? Ha-yee, I shall have a home of my own again and no one will want to make me leave it.'

'I'll get your blankets and prepare your bed,' Rory offered all too quickly, and instantly guilt and shame for his selfishness coloured his face scarlet. Embarrassed he looked down to his feet and began to stutter an apology, but Claire cut him short.

'Ha-yee, you do that, lad, I'll be snug enough there; it's for the best.' Claire's eyes became vacant just for a moment. She smiled a little as to herself. Her toothless mouth sank a fraction deeper into her face. 'Today on the shore, when the sun began to sink into the ocean, when the evening sky glowed crimson, I prayed to Odin to preserve young Emilie. Wind and waves answered me. All will be well with the poor mite in the end; for the rest of us lepers I did not plead; we've had our lives, and my share was greater than I deserved. I, for one, shall not fret.' The door gave a click; Claire had left the but.

By noon on the next day the awesome task was completed. Building and preparing the hut had been the easier part, toilsome and depressing though it had been; abandoning the sick was too gruesome a business to deal with. Neither Claire nor Martha had enjoyed much esteem amongst the Kuans; their abandonment might have been accepted as a relatively simple matter of punishment, severe though it was even for the likes of them. Tobias had never wronged anyone, but he was coming to the end of his days anyway, which might have scaled down the horror of his plight. But Emilie - kind, timid Emilie - what could anyone say against this child to justify such gruesome deed, except that Jesus wanted her to walk by his side? The idea did not ease their horror.

The sun beat down on misery and despair, mocking mankind's pitiful endeavours, yet insisting that life should go on. And life did go on, but nothing persuaded the folks that their selfishness and cowardice could ever be forgiven; neither could anything hold them back from doing what must be done. In the face of such calamity their most powerful weapons were the ritual procedures that brought things into perspective, and where no ritual was known, their natural inventiveness soon created one. Thus, they gathered together as if attending a funeral, and in a way, it might have been regarded as one, but a funeral far more tragic than any other could have been; their dead were still alive - feeling, fearing. Ahead of the cortege walked four people, one for each of the lepers. Hanno and Katrine Klaasen, their loss being the greatest, lead the way. Then followed Josefa and Bruno Bideberg. This arrangement cleverly hid an important factor - no neighbour should ever be accused of being more responsible for the abandonment than the nearest kin. The Kuans would take the responsibility together and would have to live with it for the rest of their days; those who were children now would have to live with it longest.

From time to time Katrine stopped. Hanno, his face and body rigid, took her arm to steady her and led her forward. Both walked bravely on, their farewell tears left behind the walls of the Heather croft. Now and then a cry of sorrow rose from Bruno's chest and lodged in his throat; Josefa's hand reached out and touched his arm. Some ten strides behind the leading foursome walked Martha and Tobias. The old man could barely set one foot before the other. They were followed by Claire and Emilie. Ten strides behind them followed the rest of the Kuans. Already the isolation had begun; already the outcasts felt the creeping, lone death come ever closer. They were faceless, shapeless figures, loosely draped in blankets, their identity lost, their pain and fear hidden beneath the woollen covers as they were herded along. No force was applied, no resistance offered; their unsteady gait alone betrayed their distress. Far ahead of them all walked Roland in Puritan coat, carrying his fiddle. He knew of no tune to fit such sadness and refused to play.

A Nordic rhyme was being chanted somewhere, a Christian prayer said, a doleful tune hummed. The sob of a child was hushed away. The parched hills echoed in faint, mournful undertone the unstoppable tragedy. It might have been rehearsed, so orderly and purposeful was this death march. It was the death of a father, a mother, a wife a daughter, a sister, a friend - and the death of trust. Who could say how far the malady had spread? Who might be next to take this path for the last time? And who was to blame?

In this compassionate mercilessness they came to the end of their walk. Practicality being the essence of the Kuans' existence the hut had been build next to the cemetery wall - not as an infallible exploit to induce insanity and early death of the occupants but to allow them to bury their dead if and when death occurred. What should happen to the last of them to die was too awful to contemplate.

The leaders stepped to either side of the gate and bowed to the four wrapped figures as they, one behind the other, passed through. They neither flinched nor looked back; no wave of the hand, no nod of the head hinted a goodbye. The door closed behind them. They belonged to another world now, lost forever to the people outside. Katrine reached for the gate to follow her daughter; Hanno held her back. Her single cry of grief pierced the air. Children wept - at least children were allowed to do so. They wept for Emilie and Tobias, for Claire, for Martha and for themselves.

From the peaty roof of the hovel came a thin twist of smoke; life had not ended after all with the closing of the door. Smoke meant warmth, and warmth was soothing. It seemed to whisper of hope. Hope for whom? There was no power on earth to change the inevitable; it had to be done. Now it was done.

The heat and gloom weighed heavily on the islanders' minds while their hearts turned as cold as graves. Philosophy and ritual had done little to ease pain and anger. The stale smell had come back from the marshland. People whispered of sorcery, crossing themselves and chanting something ridiculous when a more sensible rhyme would not spring to mind.

'What is it with folks that they go out of my way, Midder? I've done no wrong. Even Hegan prefers to see me gone when I visit her at the Girse.' Siegund complained.

'Hegan is not well; she is working too hard to get the croft into a decent state again. Mark my word, if you are innocent you have nothing to fear,' Josefa told her, but even she showed signs of doubt, turned her back on Siegund and went outside. She joined Rory, who was standing by the gate. Rory was looking idly at the bluish grey haze that obliterated the late afternoon sky and almost blotted out the sun.

'More omens – more bad times to come,' he said.

When Siegund joined them she found Rory and Josefa nervously looking up and down the common path. Rory stubbed the parched soil with the tip of his boot.

'Dust, nothing but dust,' he mumbled through clenched teeth. His face was sullen, his skin tightened over his high cheek bones, his jaws locked with tension. The heat and humidity had finally wilted the last shred of rationality.

'I have a good mind to join my brother at sea; there's nothing in this tedious place for me.' He seemed to have forgotten Ingeborg. 'I'll earn good money for all of us. There surely must be a better life somewhere.'

'Would you leave us to fend for ourselves, son? Once you leave, you'll be lost to us forever. This is our home, our land. Would you forsake it for a whimsical dream? Mark my word, the day will come when our island will be abandoned by all, when our fields turn into wilderness because folks are forgetting their loyalty. William Macalay, Pete Klaasen, Bjorn Volker, Erik - they have all gone. If you are searching for a paradise, son - it does not exist on earth.'

Someone was running along the edge of the fields, crouching low and using the hilldyke for cover. The near-black hair gave away the man's identity. He headed straight for the Harehill, edging his way around one of the outhouses and crept behind an open door.

'Fiddler, what is the meaning of this? Has the whole island gone mad?' Josefa asked.

'You must run, Siegund, run to the hills and hide. The Kuans have lost their reasoning; they are blaming you for all that has happened and are intent on driving you over the cliff.' He spoke fast while peering from behind the door. His piercing eyes flashed arrows of intense fury in the direction from where he had come. 'Make haste, they are on their way; men and women with peat axes, sickles and stones - aye, shame on my name, for my brother Kon is leading them.'

Siegund looked to her mother for help, begging her to call him a liar and send him on his way.

'There should be a trial if they have cause to suspect someone,' Josefa objected. 'Folks must be given a chance to clear their name; that is the rule.'

'That's what the Macalays and the Klaasens and some of the others told them, aye that they did, and they want no truck with it. But the rest - senseless with hatred they are, not at all human. No one can stop them now.'

Roland left his hiding place and carried on along the other side of the hilldyke in the direction he hoped Siegund would flee. Josefa and Rory stepped out onto the path to see for themselves where the truth might lie - and the truth was terrifying, for over the brow of the hill, where the path climbed steeply out of a deep trough, came the rowdy rabble of men and women. Their angry shouts, the flailing arms, the glistening weapons, though still some distance away, persuaded Rory that this was no time for reasoning.

'Run, Siegund, run like hell,' he yelled at his sister.

'But I have done no wrong,' she yelled back at him.

Rory's heavy hand against her shoulder-blade sent her stumbling forward. She saw the plea in her mother's frightened eyes. Siegund fled and could not think why - apart from having been told to - nor did she know where she was running to. In her confusion she thought of it as some absurd exercise for which she was out of practice, not having been outdoors much since Claire had left them. She wondered why her body had become a little larger and clumsier of late and vowed to eat a little less from now on. Her mind was filled with trivialities because she could not think of anything useful. She stopped to look back only to see the unruly crowd reaching the Harehill, saw her mother and Rory step into their path, trying to halt the senseless pursuit.

'Out of the way, woman,' big Fulmar Kon bellowed, brushing both Rory and Josefa aside. 'We have no quarrel with you. It's the witch we want; we'll take no more of her sinister work.' Konrad would not listen to reason, nor would the mob allow him to linger.

A stone hit the ground. Siegund turned her head and saw Roland climb over the wall onto the path. How ordinary he looked in his workday garb. She thought that she would have preferred him in his red and purple pantaloons and immediate cursed her frivolous notions; the Kuans were after her hide and the fiddler was hurling stones at her. He was a bad shot though; the stones fell way off target. She laughed hysterically at his incompetence.

The shouts of the rabble behind her grew louder. She tried to run faster. The blood hammered in her temples; her heart seemed to have climbed into her throat and threatened to choke her. The wind that had slept for all too long had at last woken and momentarily took her struggling breath away so that she began to in and exhale several times in bi-tonal wheezes that sounded much like the brays of a donkey. The moisture that should have been in her throat, had instead collected in her eyes and blurred her vision. Through the mist of tears shimmered the Northstane. Malcolm stood by the door, looking her way.

'Malkie, help me,' she cried. 'Blow me, Malkie, friends should...' Her voice broke. Malcolm had turned his back, had limped into the cottage and closed the door behind him as if he had neither heard nor seen her. So, Malcolm too had deserted her, had denied her his friendship. She slowed her pace and almost came to a halt. She deemed a life without friends worthless and was ready to surrender to fate.

The fiddler, keeping the same distance, stirred the fear in her anew, drove her on mercilessly with pungent accusations and relentless bombardment of badly aimed missiles. Too tired to go on and too frightened to stop she stumbled uphill through the straggly heather, and each time she looked back, the fiddler was there and the rabble was gaining on them both. The wind was gaining too. It brought billowing clouds from the east and spread them across the sky as if a change of theatrical props where required to enhance the next scene.

She lamented, cursed and hated the Kuans. She despised herself for belonging to the kind of unfortunate people who always tried hard, always meant well and yet never succeeded in finding the delicate balance between right and wrong. What seemed right to one person seemed wrong to another, it had little to do with facts but with interpretation and degrees; the mob laid down the rules, their strength being in number rather than individuality.

'Bear right, Siegund. You'll be out of their sight, aye. Then drop your shawl, go to the cave and hide within. I'll lead them astray; I'll take them to the Wizards Bench. Go!' Roland grabbed her shawl and hid it under his tunic while continuing the ridiculous game of chasing and throwing stones at nothing and no one. Now and then he waved to the men to follow him. The women were still on the lower slope, unable to match the pace of the men, though they were not handicapped in matching their shouts and their fury.

The mouth of the cave seemed to have grown smaller and resisted Siegund's entrance; it did not entirely refuse to let her in. She poked her head out just far enough to survey the situation. Dark-haired and red-faced, Konrad Mulvoen's head bobbed up and down like a red and black ball being bounced on hard ground. He looked straight ahead, avoiding even the slightest glance toward the cave.

'Blow me, big Fulmar Kon is afraid of the little people, yet he thinks nothing of sending me to my death,' she gasped, still out of breath.

The storm clouds were turning daylight into an ominous yellow. She withdrew into the rocky sanctuary where the shouting no longer reached her ears and where she might rest and think - if she could. The musty smell of decay in the cave reminded her of the fiddler to whom she now ought to be grateful; he had helped her when no one else had the courage or even the presence of mind to do so. But still she mistrusted him, doubted his motif - gratitude had no chance.

'Blow me, you've brought me to the very place where we rose together through the flames of sin that have scarred me forever. And on Hegan's wedding day I rode with you to hell and back. Indeed, we ought to have gone to the bottom of the ocean.' A flash of lighting threw its spiky beam against the wall. Under the rolling thunder that made the air tremble she quickly retracted her words. The heavens opened all at once, pouring down the long-awaited bringer of life and growth. It had come at last. But it had come too late; too late for the crops and too late for Siegund.

She curled up on the musty straw and pulled the damp blankets over her. Her heart was heavy and her limbs were aching. In the rapidly cooling air she thought she was turning to stone, to become part of the cave just as Garwulf had seemed. She tried to smile at the idea, but stone cannot smile; it can only sleep a deep, long, dreamless sleep, which came mercifully quickly to her. Eventually the cold woke her up again. In the shadowless darkness she raised her hands close to her eyes. For a frightful moment she thought that she must be lying in her cold, damp grave.

'Stone doesn't smile and hills don't laugh and corpses don't move,' she told herself. 'Unless… unless I am a ghost?' Her mind became troubled with pictures of shattered legs and shattered souls, but her growling stomach told her that she was still very much alive, which induced just a little gratitude and a great deal of self-pity. The lepers had food to eat, a fire burning in the grate, and above all, they had each other's company. The thought came to her to join them, if they were willing to have her, and in turn she was willing to like Martha - if Martha would try to like her. She stood up. With arms stretched forward she fumbled her way to the exit of the cave to escape the musty air within. It was dark outside, though the rain had stopped falling. Somewhere a twig snapped. She drew back into her shelter.

'Don't be afraid, Siegund. I've brought you food and a dry blanket, aye, that I have, and wood for a fire,' Roland called to her softly.

'Fiddler,' she exclaimed, gratitude forgotten. She was surprised and angry at the same time at his sudden appearance. 'Blow me down, what right have you to steal to me in the middle of the night? It's not decent! I don't need your help and I'm not hungry,' she said spitefully.

'Is that so? But you'll be hungry and lonesome ere long, aye, that you will,' he replied, inviting himself into the cave. 'I've brought you oil for your lamp to brighten up your dark existence.'

'Why do you say that? Do you, too, think me guilty of sinister deeds?'

'Would I be here if I did, Siegund?'

'The devil is not afraid of evil; he likes its company. Why have you come, Fiddler?'

'Why? To help you, aye, to take good care of you,' he said casually, giving his attention to lighting a fire.

The glow reflected on Roland's face, which seemed to hold all the calm and dignity other folks had lost; it swayed Siegund's esteem of him in an almost favourable way until he spoiled it by saying all the wrong things. A little less self-assuredness, fewer references to her and him as a single unit – those things might have served him better. He ruined his chances altogether when he flippantly remarked on the clutter left behind by the former occupant, calling it a marvellous foresight on Garwulf's behalf.

'Why do you speak of *us* when you have a home to go to? And why mock the man who is a hundred times better than you?'

'Is he? Then where is he now?'

'On his way back to me,' she replied with a hint of doubt and huddled a little closer to the fire.

'Aye, and perhaps not,' he said, displaying the sort of self-confidence that comes with maturity and personal freedom. Being only a worker and lodger on his brother's croft he could leave whenever he cared to - he had often considered doing exactly that. He had not meant to distress Siegund with his words; he now did the sensible thing and became silent. But silence was tedious to her as much as to him, and since she had nothing pleasant to say to him she attacked him with crude verbal ammunition, the kind that was meant to wound and scar.

'Blow me, you're a legless coward. You chased me, but you never caught me. And...and you're a swivel-eyed toad; you threw stones at me, but none hit me.'

'I chased you, fair Siegund, to let folks think I was with them; I missed you because I never aimed at you.' He smiled at her accusations of cowardice and incompetence. 'Even I, who am not fit to kiss this Garwulf-fellow's boots, can aim better than that. There are things I have done in my life of which I think with anything but pride, aye, but a coward I am not, nor am I a fool. Tell me, Siegund, what would be the good in both of us lying at the bottom of the cliff, waiting for the fish to eat our flesh or for the birds to pick our bones? There is life ahead of us, aye, that it is - a good life if you wish it so.'

His words, so gently spoken, did not prevent her mind from straying to Garwulf. Perhaps he really was on his way back - perhaps this, perhaps that. Her predicament being what it was, she weighed up the fiddler's offer against loneliness and decided that loneliness was the more beastly thing of the two. 'Perhaps...,' she thought aloud, dreaming once more of Garwulf's return. Roland took it as an answer to him. A definite yes would have been preferred, but the 'perhaps' was a start. By the glowing fire he began to talk of the afternoon's events.

'Aye,' he said, '...way above the Kilcairn ledge up to the Wizards Bench I led them. And when they got there, blowing and puffing and with all the rainbow colours in their faces, they dared not come close to me at the edge of the cliff to look for your body in the broiling pot below. And your shawl flapped merrily from the overhanging rock, aye, that it did.

Kon came as close as he dared, he never came close enough to get a glimpse. Bruno Bideberg tried it on his knees, aye, but he got scared and got Slim Tim to crawl on his belly while Bruno held onto the lad's legs. Tim did not get far for yelling. Then a flash of lighting turned all the faces a uniform blue for a second, aye. After that, no one was interested in looking down any more.'

'I suppose they blamed me for the lightning, too!'

'Aye, I suppose they did. When the rain began to fall they went on their knees, deeming themselves right in what they thought they had done.'

Having heard his tale Siegund thought Roland worthy of a smile after all. How strange the fiddler was! He was not like the other Kuans or the half-highland Macalays; he had more moods than wind and ocean - stormy and calm, robust and gentle, wicked and kind, with a certain dignity in all his moods.

'I'll bring clean straw for comfort, aye,' he said. 'Not tomorrow, mind. If the weather is favourable I have to go fishing with the men.'

'Go fishing then!' she told him with renewed hostility. 'As for comfort - what comfort are you talking about and for whom? What is in your mind, Fiddler?'

'Nothing you don't agree with. It's one of the things I have done first and regretted later - aye, and perhaps not. Let me take you away from here, to some place where we can live in peace. If you insist on waiting for the other, then I must wait, too, aye, until you realize how futile your loyalty to him is.'

'We shall see. Roland, tell my Midder and Maunsie I'm well.'

'That, I cannot do. For your safety's sake, no one must know. Your Midder is a strong woman, she will cope well enough, aye, and Maunsie has his fiddle to comfort him.'

'So, that's your game, to keep me away from my family and friends! Blow me, you've made all this happen by saying bad things about me. I hate you, Fiddler, I hate you.' In a fit of anger and frustration she rattled her fists against his chest.

'Not so, Siegund, I would never wish degradation on you, but you must understand, your family cannot help you now, and you have no other friend beside me. Did you not see Malcolm turn away from you? Even he, who admired you in earnest, abandoned you. Do you really think I am to blame? Then let me tell you: people have whispered about you since Yule day; with every mishap they whispered a little louder, aye that they did. Folk have forsaken their way of keeping their thoughts hidden. I heard them talk; I listened well. There were disagreements for a while as to who might be the culprit, aye. Then Krista let it slip to one of the Volker's girls that you had seen the stranger long after his disappearance.'

Krista? Blow me, I don't believe you.'

'Aye! Krista - not me.'

'So, that is why she looked at me so shifty and clucked so. Leave me, Fiddler,' she yelled at him, pulling her hair in vexation. 'I need to think, and I'm not at all sure my head shall not burst in the attempt.'

'I'll go then if that is what you want, though there will be more hours for thought than you care for, aye that it will.

It need not be so. Think it over, Siegund,' he said calmly and turned to go, leaving her to consider her position. He was convinced that loneliness and fear would do the rest. He had no hand in her predicament, but now that it had come to this, he did not wish it away.

Roland had gone so swiftly it took her quite by surprise. Now that she was alone again, all attempted sensible thought was smothered by paradoxical resentment. Quite irrationally she felt slighted by his sudden sense of propriety. Had he pawed her, at least the continuation of severe hatred for him would have been justified. In her jumbled emotions she yearned for affection when all she was left with were promises - promises from Garwulf and Roland, and neither of them was there now and promises were easily broken. Her thought went from one consideration to another. One moment she was sure to be called home, then she was sure that no one would come, for no one knew that she was alive; besides, her mother was powerless, Rory spineless, Malcolm gutless, Hegan heartless and Krista brainless, in short - they had all a part of their anatomy missing.

She wished she had not sent the fiddler away; after all, his friendship was better than no friendship at all. Garwulf had once told her that in solitude there were no enemies except the ones within oneself, which could be mastered. His theory gave her no comfort; there were too many of the hostile blighters within her and without. She flung herself onto her bed. At least, in solitude no one would see her weep, which stopped the heart from bursting and numbed the senses; it brought sleep, soothing, glorious sleep.

The new day sent its narrow beam of light into the cave - a new day with old troubles. She bathed her soul in that light while listening to the sea birds, to the rolling waves and to the ever-wakeful wind. She marvelled that there could exist so much sound and yet such silence at the same time. It seemed to call for prayers. Promptly she knelt down, but as always, her prayers were too hurried to be respectful. The air smelled clean, the earth fresh after the downpour. She stretched herself, feeling refreshed like the earth and happy to be alive even in solitude. A young rabbit raised its head out of the heather, sat erect for a moment and regarded her with twitching nose before withdrawing into its hiding place. It reminded her of Emilie Klaasen, somehow, which made her sad again. She wondered if Emilie too had cried herself to sleep. The sound of laboured breathing came from the slope.

'Maunsie,' she whispered. Instinctively she crouched low beside a rock lest he was not alone. He was leaning forward, digging his outward-pointing toes into the soil-starved ground. Fiddle in one hand, bow in the other he looked smaller and more hunched than ever; he might have been a trowie come late off nightshift. He walked past the cave, not even giving it a glance. Siegund wanted to call to him, to run to him; her voice and legs disobey. His wheezing was still audible long after he had disappeared from sight. When the numbness left her she crawled on hands and knees after her brother, and each time he stopped for breath, she stopped too.

At the Wizards Bench, where the cliff fell off in perpendicular descent, Maunsie stood still, his breath rasping in his throat while his head gyrated with every desperate gasp of air he took. He laid down fiddle and bow, then stepped a little closer to the massive rock that hung precariously over the cliff's edge in defiance of gravity; by everyone's reckoning it should long have crashed down into sea below. From the rock fluttered the shawl in the wind, much like the memory of his sister who he feared lost to him forever. As he stood there, mourning her plight, he began to sway to and fro until on one of his backward sways he fell to the ground. There he remained for a considerable time, grasping his coat as if for a handhold, and all the time he mumbled to himself. Then he crawled on his stomach onto the rock and reached for the shawl.

'You'll need it to keep you warm,' he said all of a quiver and dropped the shawl over the edge.

'Farewell, Siegund, my loneliness is complete. It should have been me, not you. Nay, not you.' He lay still and wept.

For a while he lay shivering in unwholesome contemplations, then thought better of it, crawled back and began to play a tune. The wind seemed to halt its breath, the seabirds to stop their calling as if not to taint the sweet, melancholy sound. In his sadness lay peace, a peace that in time might heal all wounds, though the scars would mar Skerra Kua forever. He began his walk down the slope from whence he had come, his breath reasonably controlled, his face composed as if he had been relieved from a cumbersome burden.

Siegund had watched him while cowering behind a rock; she had watched her own funeral and had cried with the only mourner, and again she wanted to call to him - again she had no voice. She reasoned that perhaps the assumption of her death was less painful to him than the knowledge of her miserable existence. How hard it was to let him go, to let go of all she had ever known, never to belong again but to live as a memory or as an evil best forgotten.

'Maunsie,' she suddenly cried with a voice too throaty to be her own.

He stopped and slowly turned round. When he saw nothing he shook his head and went on his way, unknowingly closing the door between her and her family and leaving her to face pain and sorrow alone. She thought of the young Macalay women who had been forced to leave their folks – of Bridie who had preferred death, of Marnie whose memory was forbidden. Midder too had left her folks on Papa Kira when she had wed, and had never seen them again; perhaps that was why she was so cold. Siegund vowed neither to die nor to allow herself to be heartless, and out of her wealth of emotions, out of moderate sense and profound sensibility she drew new strength.

Survival was the game now, and what better start was there than to make the cave homely as ever a cave had been. The scanty light that fell through the funnel-shaped entrance gave everything a morbid hue; layered patches of creamy fungus, laced with darker edges, clung to one side of the wall. In a more cheerful place they might have looked quite pretty; here, in the gloomy twilight they indicated decay. Her own special world of oh so long ago was rotting away. With fierce determination she swept fungus and all useless debris into the fire; the chores of which she had wanted to be free at home now gave her a purpose. The collection of iron and wooden necessities, the intrinsic factors of her common fate with Garwulf, clattered into neat stacks. She stood back to examine her domestic achievement - how lamentable that in the murkiness of the cave clean and dirty looked alike. She began to ponder again, but since she had done that already she decided to sit by the cliff's edge. How majestic the ocean ebbed and flowed! The sea was a goddess in her own right; she suffered insignificant men to trespass when her mood was a generous one.

Too much freedom can easily become as tedious as too much restraint. In a moment of inexplicable giddiness, tired of watching the waves, tired even of counting the seals that popped up their whiskered heads here and there, Siegund thought it a good idea to go to the Wizards Bench and say a prayer or two, and perhaps lay a cross of stones for herself to complete her funeral ceremony. She foolishly discarded all caution and ventured away from the cave while humming a cheerful tune. Higher up on the slope walked clumsily an enormous basket on legs, and from this basket came a whistled tune that resembled nothing on this earth; it immediately gave away the identity of the missing head and torso. Udo Patersen made a half-turn, shielded his aging eyes against the sun, shook his head and walked on again.

'Blow me,' Siegund huffed as she slithered like a snake on hands and knees across the stony ground. She thought it wiser to abandon her foolish idea of cross and funeral service.

The day seemed endless, the freedom became a burden, the boredom was torture. When evening drew in and darkness fell once more, she felt a strange sense of relief and of safety.

She could not say why night should gladden her, for she would be as lonely as she had been all day. She poked the dying embers and piled wood and peat onto them. At daytime the fire had to be kept low so that no escaping smoke should give her presence away. The straw, partly dried by the sun and partly by the fire, felt more comfortable and smelled a little more of fresh air and smoke rather than mildew. She stared into the fire that was much like her own spirits - alive, fluctuating, demanding to be nurtured lest the flames extinguish. She wished that Garwulf would send his silent message. Perhaps the fault lay with her for not concentrating hard enough. But even now, the fiddler's words came to her mind, and from the fiddler her thought went to Malcolm and Krista, which brought the misery back to her.

'I need none of you, do you hear? None!' she cried out.

The silence of the night gnawed at rationality and implanted in her mind thoughts of revenge against the people who had betrayed her. She pulled the blankets over her head to blot out the wicked thoughts. When sleep eventually came to her, shattered bones and shattered faces tormented her anew, she saw the fiddler in gaudy costume sitting in a field of ruined barley, smiling his knowing smile. Kicking and yelling she was jerked out of her sleep in mindless panic.

The new day had been no easier to face than the last one had been; so many hours to fill - with what? She sat by the cliff's edge, perhaps had sat there all day in worshipful passivity. She did not know. She was hardly aware of the sporadic drizzle of rain that obscured the view and made sky and sea appear as singular vapour. Seven boats hovered somewhere in the greyness, either riding the waves or the clouds, their progress slow and laborious. The sun was trying to break through the low clouds in one final effort, but not even the mighty sun was all-powerful; soon the approaching darkness would proclaim itself ruler once more. The sea that had kept the fiddler away on the previous night teased out of her a peculiar longing to see him - to see any one - and in anticipation she found herself wandering nervously in and out of the cave, talking to herself and wishing the hours away. She sat down by the fire, stared into its glow while asking herself questions to which she knew no answers, and the more she thought the less was she sure of anything. How frightening and frustrating uncertainty was! By the time the fiddler arrived late that night she had reached the deepest deep of a demoralising abyss so that under tears and with much ado she flung her arms around his neck.

'I'm so glad you've come, Roland, indeed I am,' she told him. She really meant it. 'It's so lonely here, it drives me mad.'

'I am pleased to hear that you have missed me, aye, that I am, but tell me, am I still second best? Or worse?' Roland dropped the armful of straw he had brought, but refrained from returning her eagerness.

I'm glad you've come, blow me, isn't that enough?' She let go of his neck, regretting her moment of liberality.

'Aye, for now it will do, that it will.' He sat down by the fire, rubbed his hands over the glow. He lowered himself onto the straw and patted the blanket as invitation for her to sit beside him.

'The nights are getting chilly.'

'How is my Midder?' she asked. 'And do folks still say bad things of me?'

'They will not speak of you, Siegund, they want to forget. You know their ways as well as I do. You shall live on in folks' minds forever, aye, but they will not speak.'

'Shall I never be able to go home, never see Maunsie again?' Her eyes searched his face.

'It need not be like this, Siegund; you know the alternative, aye, that you do, but I cannot carry you off against your will.'

His calmness and the talk of a future with him raised her anger anew, and in a fit of wild lamentations she blamed him for all the bad things that had happened to her, which included the apparently shrinking dress and the daily shrinkage of the cave entrance. Roland shook his head but let her have her say anyway. He reckoning that, when her feelings were thoroughly vented, she might be persuaded to listen without throwing another tantrum. He had guessed the reason for her fuller figure for some time, had made it his business to notice it. To find the right questions at the right time was not easy and too often before had he said all the wrong things.

'Your mind is becoming twisted, Siegund, aye, that it is. I have done none of the things you accuse me of, except one single matter which I cannot deny, and for that, I suppose, I deserve your mistrust. But it is no worse than the other has done. I tell you, had you been pure, I would not have touched you. You must understand, I had wedlock in mind, aye, and I am standing by you now. Tell me - where is the other? Ere long, your need of me will be greater than you realise. Siegund, is all well with you? I mean your health? Have you been sick at all - apart from the day on the swell?'

'What makes you talk of sickness?' His questions turned her rage into curiosity. 'I used to feel sick,' she admitted. 'That was when I was growing up. The sickness has left me now, but sometimes my inners are doing a mad hop and a skip, and I feel all jittery with worry, yet, I don't know why. It is doing it know; feel for yourself.'

'Siegund, don't you know you are with child?' he blurted out quickly for fear that the moment to make her face the truth might pass.

'Blow me, it can't be so; I'm not wed - not properly.'

'Bairns do not concern themselves with wedlock. They come along when...' He could not go on explaining. 'The gods help you if you will not listen to me.' He began to count the months from February to September on his fingers. 'Only two moons to go, by my reckoning. Siegund, you and the bairn cannot stay here, with winter not too far away. Let me take you to a safe place.'

'But Garwulf...'

'Garwulf! Garwulf! I am tired hearing of him,' he cut her short. 'He has left you to face the consequences of his actions alone, though...' his voice took on the gentle sing-song tone again when he added, 'though the bairn might just as easily be mine.'

'What makes you think you know of such things,' she asked, preferring to believe in her growing-up theory.

'I know because I have lived a little longer than you, aye, that I have,' he said with a degree of modesty and regret. He spread out the things he had brought her - one of his mother's warm dresses, food, soap, and a comb with which he began to tidy her tangled hair while his gentle voice sounded like a lullaby, calming, protective, soothing. For the first time she thought a life with the fiddler a fair possibility, but when she wanted to tell him so, Garwulf came to her mind and would not let her speak. That is how it was with her; the more she pondered the more she got confused, which might have explained her general habit of doing first and pondering later. Roland left without an answer while Siegund blamed her plight on having parted with the green pebble, which caused yet more conflicts with her own interpretation of right, wrong, necessity and unavoidability.

The following day her loyalty belonged entirely to Garwulf, Roland once more faring second best despite the fact that he had been a thoughtful companion of late who had made no demands on her. That evening, when darkness fell, she decided to search for the pebble, hoping in all sincerity that the Christian God would not mind too much; after all, He had only asked for a token - any token. Roland would not be calling; he had said so - to give her time to think.

Wrapped in a blanket she set out on her mission - a fallen woman on her way to the fallen church. On a midsummer night daylight only faded rather than died, but now, already being autumn, she became just another shadow of the night. She stumbled through the darkness along a sheep track that might as easily lead her astray as to the ruin. The flickering lamp did little to preserve a sense of direction, though she figured that if she stayed on the same level, if she neither climbed nor descended, she would get to her destination. The quiet of the night was yet filled with subdued noises; her own rustling footsteps seemed to come from all around her and for a moment she thought she was being followed. She spun around in horror. An obscure creature with plump body and countless spidery arms stared at her in silence. She stared back at it. It came neither closer, nor did it retreat. Stupefied with fear she assumed a similar rigid stance.

'I mean you no harm,' she whispered at length.

A silvery moon crept from behind the clouds and shone its light onto the ghostly monster, revealing nothing but a rock and a straggly gorse bush. Siegund giggled nervously and went on her way. Her eyes wandered longingly towards the valley. Far below, the Harehill cottage seemed no larger than a shed. She yearned for its comfort, yearned to be with her people. Folks were afraid of her - her, whose heart was filled with thrice their fear.

Whenever the moon illuminated her way she walked briskly, her heart filled with hope, and whenever the moon disappeared she stumbled along, her heart filled with self-pity. In a small hollow she saw a sheep cast on its flat, broad back, its legs pointing to heaven like four symmetrical sticks. The rescue of the ewe was surely a good omen; she was meant to be here at this time to safe the animal from certain death. Sheep always reminded her of stupid Krista, but stupid or not, her sister was at home in her bed while she, Siegund, was in a great deal of trouble. Self-pity, reflection, hope - one followed the other in rapid succession. The sleeping landscape with its strange, sinister kind of beauty frightened her as much as it pleased. She began to hum a tune as she went on her way, quietly as not to offend the creatures of the night; it seemed they did not mind.

The ruins of the church lay before her like a grave that in its gloom forbade all song or even humming. Her eyes searched across the mournful heap of misconceived permanence, her hands groped and dug, turned a stone over here and there, and when the moon once more disappeared behind the clouds and the night turned black, Siegund fancied that God had blown the candles out and gone to bed. Disappointed and tired, with sore back, sore head and sore fingertips, she hurriedly knelt down to pray before God should fall asleep.

'Blow me down, I mean to keep my promise to you, indeed I do,' she told the Almighty while closing her eyes in respect. 'I can't build you a church just yet; you see, I have no friends to help me. And I've not come to steal the token, only to exchange it for my beads. Without the stone I must wed the fiddler - or die.' She opened her eyes to learn the effect of her plea. In the returning moonlight sparkled the decider over her fate. She slipped the stone quickly into her pocket and drew out the string of red beads. She pressed them against her face to feel them for the last time.

'I suppose you wouldn't like to share them with me?' she asked the Almighty. 'If you let me keep the three tear-drops you can have the rest,' she suggested. When God said neither yes nor no to her proposal, nor gave a sign either way, she deemed the deal acceptable to Him, and instantly she broke the string so that the beads rolled over the ground. 'There, they are all yours! I'm content with what I have left. I must leave you now, but I'll be back. And if you see Fadder, tell him not to fret.'

Her mission was completed. Had her mind been focused on her retreat, had the moon not denied her its light more often now, had her eyes not wandered too often to the relentlessly moving clouds which had no home to go to either, she might have found her way back easily enough, but darkness and dreaming took over, clouded her judgement of direction and led her to the dark abode of the living dead. Despite its sullenness the acute longing to speak with Claire and kiss her wrinkly cheeks, to ask Martha for permission to stay with them, prevented her from bolting into the night there and then. Instead she hid amongst rocks in the fluctuating darkness. Stone and darkness - darkness and stone! The hut itself seemed like a huge cairn where the living dead were buried. No glimmer of light, not a single sound came from the hut; only the faint twist of smoke testified that within the walls hearts still beat.

At length the door opened inch by inch as if some great effort were required. A dark figure, draped from head to toe in a blanket, stood in the doorway, then limped a few steps forwards the gate. Tobias pushed the blanket back a little and raised his eyes to heaven, then seemed to look straight at her, yet showed no curiosity; he must have thought her part of the landscape. The moon momentarily poured its silver light over his face and revealed deep-sunken eyes and a lipless mouth. Where once his nose had been was an empty hollow. He stood in prayer to the gods who had forsaken him, nodded his head as if he had received an answer, then covered his face and limped back indoors again.

Siegund fled in panic, stumbling, falling, picking herself up and stumbling again in rapid succession. She still managed to wonder why Tobias was punished so. And Emilie - did poor Emilie look like that now? Her senses began to swim in a whirlpool of imaginings that conjured up swarms of hideous creatures hard on her heels. She felt too heavy to run at great speed and cursed her clumsiness, but still she ran, she could not stop herself, not until she was in sight of the cave. Ah, Claire was waiting for her - good old, rugged, loving Claire with wispy hair and out-stretched, spiky arms. Siegund fled into her embrace - and felt the thorns tear at her face. Her senses returned. Under groans of realisation, and more than a little surprised, she untangled herself from the straggly hawthorn that was trying to grow into a tree and would never make it. Exhausted she staggered to the cave, leaned her face against the cool rock and looked back in the direction from where she had come. There were no ogres, no demons, no grotesque faces in sight, only rocks, brooding moors and the cave.

The fire was waiting to be fed so that it might repay the tenant with its warmth; the bed invited her to rest. She curled up on the straw and fell asleep. Sleep was kind when it kept the bad dreams away; it allowed her to forget her troubles for a while. If only she could sleep forever, she thought each time she woke up; then she would creep deeper under the blankets and pray for peace. But only the dead sleep forever.

When she awoke, another day was already fading into dusky obscurity, turning the island once more into grey uniformity. She wondered if Roland would be calling tonight. Her need for companionship was great indeed, but so was the need for intense concentration so that she might send her silent message to Garwulf. She was confused, found it too hard to give either the one or the other a decisive vote of preference. The fiddler's caring usefulness had gained him a little affection in her heart while Garwulf's prolonged absence had lost a little. Indecision was best left to fate; besides, her body's need of food and fresh water had to take priority over the needs of the soul. With that in mind she cautiously made her way to the brook above the Northstane and filled her pail with the clear water. She lingered a while, set the pail down and playfully dropped a twig into the tumbling brook. She watched it swiftly race downhill towards the cottage.

'Tell Malkie I'm hungry and in need of friends, 'she whispered and followed the brook slowly downhill. 'But, blow me, friendship was inconvenient to you, Malkie, when I asked for it. I wish I had no need of anyone, but you see, body and soul are interlinked; where there is companionship there is food.' She wished she were blessed with her mother's kind of self-discipline that quenches all useless emotions, though it might not ease hunger. She longed to stroll down to the valley, to walk along the common path, to stand outside the Harehill just to gaze, just to feel the nearness of her kin. What if she were to walk into the cottage? Would Midder wring her hands? Would Krista betray her again? Would Rory send her away? The thought came to her that she knew them even less than she knew herself, but she set off to risk it anyway.

A mist rose from the calm sea and came rapidly inland. It blanketed the landscape and concealed Siegund under its opaque, dewy mantle; the obscurity of murky evenings, the anonymity of the nights kept her secrets. Siegund got no further than the Northstane. The mist, in its over-protectiveness, was turning to dense fog. Malcolm was hanging a lamp up on a wall facing the sea. She strained her eyes to see if his eyes held even the minutest trace of regret, but all she saw was a faceless figure disappearing indoors. She gave a little cry of sorrow. No one seemed to pity her; no one knew she was there. She was truly a wandering soul with broken heart, tattered shoes and growling stomach, empty of food - yet not empty. She got annoyed with the fiddler again. What did he know of bairns?

'I want no bairn,' she cried in defiance.

The fog muffled her words, muffled all other sounds as if life had suddenly ceased to exist on earth. She scrambled back up the slope. The pail still stood by the brook. She found her way to the cave more by instinct and good fortune than by landmarks. The fire in the cave was a welcoming sight. She knelt down and poked it vigorously, then took the pebble out of her pocket and held it between her folded hands. In a moment of reminiscence, fantasy and ardent wishing her heart began to beat faster.

'Is this concentration?' she asked herself. 'Blow me, how am I to know, when my mind is as volatile as barley pudding and my stomach is yearning for food? Come back to me, Garwulf,' she pleaded. 'I need you dreadfully. The fiddler says...' she stopped and bit her lips. 'I suppose I shouldn't tell you of him. Have you got someone else, too? Have you? Perhaps you could let Roland take her....' She covered her face in horror at her willingness to swap partners. 'Still, a fair exchange is not wrong,' she reasoned. 'The fiddler says..., blow me down, to hell with you, Fiddler.' Furious at Roland's intrusion into her haphazard concentration she cast the stone with one mighty swing from her; with instant remorse she hastily retrieved it again under the most compelling explanations and pleas for forgiveness. 'Blow me, Garwulf, the loneliness bends my mind. It makes me angry, it makes me sad, it makes me yearn, it makes me hate. Can't you see that? I even long to see the fiddler. I don't know how many days and nights I've already been here alone - nor do I know any more what I feel.'

She gave up on meditation and concentration, crawled to her bed, chewed on a remnant of dried-up cheese to still her hunger. She began to surround herself with imaginary friends, which served no other purpose than to pass on time and preserve sanity. Fantasy took her to flowering meadows, took her deep into the hills where wild ponies performed their midnight dance; fantasy took her on a white dolphin out onto the ocean where seals sang their doleful songs in chorus. Sometimes Maunsie was by her side, sometimes Garwulf, sometimes the fiddler, sometimes Malcolm, sometimes her father. She saw young Kate waving, and Bridie, and Emilie, and Claire, and Martha, and Adelika, and Marnie, and Tobias - all of them happy, cheerful people. But always, reality came back, which had nothing to offer but a smoke-filled cave, meagre rations, and loneliness.

Roland did not come that night, or even the night after. Three nights of emptiness, of waiting and pondering, of uncertainty and hunger had brought her near breaking point. On the fourth evening the fiddler appeared quite suddenly and silently before her. She flew into his arms, hugged him and kissed his face; had he been the devil himself she would have welcomed him with no less enthusiasm.

'Blow me, I thought you had forgotten me or that something untoward had befallen you, indeed, I did,' she told him, relieved that such was not the case.

'I'm honoured that you feared for me, aye, whatever the reason for your affection may be. As for forgetting you - you are not one to be forgotten easily. And what, in heaven's name has happened to your face if Freyja's cat-drawn chariot has not run over it?'

'Hawthorn,' was all she said on the matter, intent on questioning him over his absence.

'Two days and two nights fishing, aye, and one night of Kon and Arlene's busy-bodying have kept me away from you. Folks are talking again, some say your soul is wandering the hills at night, some folks claim to have seen you in broad daylight; others say it cannot be so, and then they argue.'

'Blow me down, does Konrad suspect the truth?' Her eyes grew large with fear as much as with hope of the Kuans' forgiveness.

'Kon? The truth? No, not that! The truth is too simple for his tangled mind, but he watches me with bloodshot eyes, aye, that he does; and Arlene rations daily all food and keeps painstaking account of every movable item on the croft. I cannot blame her entirely; the winter is going to be long and our supplies are scanty this year.' Roland stretched out on the straw bed and grunted his present contentment. 'I have taken to sleeping in the barn, aye. It makes it easier for me to slip away unnoticed.'

'You are risking your neck for me?' Siegund asked and planted herself beside him on the straw.

'Aye, I risk that and more, and do it gladly. I have no fear of my brother, nor any great liking for him, and he has none for me.'

'I'm glad you are my friend, Roland. I've been thinking of what you said, of going away with you and getting wed. Indeed, I have thought of it a lot. If you still want me - I am willing.'

'I want no one else, Siegund. I once loved another girl, and since you have agreed to be my woman you have a right to know, though even now it is hard to speak of it - aye, even now.' He sat very upright as if his confession required at least that much courtesy. One arm folded loosely around her shoulder. 'Her name was Marnie!'

'Marnie of whom no one will speak?'

'Aye, I loved Marnie Macalay.' He seemed relieved to have spoken her name. 'She was Robert's youngest sister,' he went on. 'Aye, and she was beautiful, full of life - and headstrong, just like you. The day I saw her bathe in the pond beyond the Bracken Hill my boyish heart was lost. I should have discreetly made my retreat, aye, that I should, but the spell of her pure white nakedness against the setting sun was more powerful than all the sense of decency in the world. That is how it all began. I was fifteen then - she was almost twenty. No one knew of our meetings; folks rarely ventured as far as the pond.

She taught me the secrets of love and passion, made out of the boy a man and I intended to wed her as soon as I was a little older. I made one dire mistake - I told Kon of my liking for her.' Roland rested his head against Siegund's shoulder like a child seeking comfort.

'Was that such a terrible sin?'

'It was! It was! Aye, because Kon put it into people's heads that Marnie was breaking the hearts of boy children. Robert swiftly dispatched her to the Highlands. But Marnie ran away from her Scottish kinsfolk and mixed with bad folks. She should have known better than to come back to Skerra Kua a year later, unwed and large with child; they would not suffer her to stay, said she was undesirable company for men, women and children; not even Robert would have her under his roof, and Ethel, not then having the esteem she enjoys now, was powerless. It was Claire who offered Marnie a home and protected her the best way she could; it was Claire who was with her when the child was born. Folks never forgave the old woman for going against their rules. I would have wed Marnie even then, but folks would not stand for it, and I was young. They took the bairn by force out of Marnie's arms. Robert and Ethel, who raised her as their own named her...Adelika.'

'Adelika? Blow me down. I think I've always known somehow. I once saw Marnie's image in Adelika's face and body.'

'Aye, the night they took her bairn from her, Marnie disappeared never to be seen again. No one knows what has become of her, though all sorts of rumours were spread. Some folks say she is lying at the bottom of the Bracken Hill pond.'

Roland spoke very quietly and slowly as if he felt the pain even now. 'Aye, many a night I lay awake and wept for her, that I did. I blamed myself, though as a mere boy I could have changed nothing. But time heals many things, aye, though I never loved another woman again until..., ah, but you know of that. No one shall ever harm you - not while there is breath in my body.'

Roland's confession, her own predicament, the days of loneliness and despair - it was just all too much for Siegund, she wept in his arms, wept for Marnie and Adelika, for herself and for Roland, for Claire and for all who had suffered injustice in the name of pride and dignity. Garwulf came briefly to her mind and then faded into the background. Roland the rogue, who had cried for Marnie, who was capable of compassion, needed her as much as she needed him. His gentle kisses sealed their destiny. That night he stayed with her, his arms wrapped around her until dawn greeted them with a timid light. Against all odds fate had united them, fate, loneliness and Marnie.

'I have stayed a little longer than is wise, aye, that I have,' Roland said...'not that it should be my brother's concern where I spent the night. All the same, we shall leave as soon as we can, all we need is a calm night to cross the swell.'

'Fiddler...if you've lied - I mean, about Garwulf - I'll curse you to hell,' she told Roland, who was taken aback by the sharpness of her voice. He gazed at her surprised.

'You have cursed me in the past, aye, that you have; I am prepared to take the risk.'

'Why do you say risk, Fiddler? Does that mean...?'

'It means nothing,' he cut her short and smiled. 'Is your heart wavering already? No matter; one day you will learn to trust and respect me, even if I cannot expect your undivided love.' He shrugged his shoulders in mute resignation and left the cave.

Siegund grew quite used to the idea of a life with Roland. Each day she waited, studied the flight direction of the birds, noticed the shape and drift of clouds and looked into the fire for clues of what the weather might do the following day. Each night she stood near the majestic cliffs in their nocturnal silence, listening to the thundering waves that warned her to keep away. Not even the fishermen dared to take to their boats, which meant that Roland was able to visit her often. He carefully chose different routes to avoid being followed, and brought news from the Kuans, to which she listened with more interest than might be assumed reasonable for someone who claimed to have done with them all. He told her of Potty Patty losing her sister Hedda on their way to the Blue Bane and how folks had found the blind girl wandering around in a meadow. His peculiar, asymmetric smile faded a little when he spoke of Hegan.

'Her bairn is due around Yule time. I hear she's having a bad time of it even now. If you ask me, your Midder is fretting more than she will admit.'

'And what of Maunsie? Is he well?' Siegund asked a little distracted. 'And how is it that Hegan with her right and wrong ways can't get things done properly after all?'

'Don't slight your sister; it doesn't become you. As for Maunsie, aye, he is well. He shall help me play at the harvest celebrations, though heaven knows why they want to celebrate when there is no harvest. As for myself, I hope the pleasure of playing will be all his.'

'Blow me down, how can they think of celebrations? Will you really play for them, Roland, while I am here alone with my sorrow?'

'It's not callousness on my behalf, Siegund, nor forgetfulness on theirs, come to that. It would never do for me to neglect my duties while I live amongst them; your survival depends on it. Life must go on, aye, and it does. A little less food on the tables, a few people missing from their midst - they have known it all before; it does not break them, though Krista is taking it very badly. They say she has not spoken a single word since the day the mob came for you. Aye, it is hard to live with guilt, that it is.'

'Would you have me pity her, Roland?' Siegund threw back her head in defiance.

'Don't be too harsh on her, a. little compassion never goes amiss. She is not entirely to blame for your misfortune - perhaps, no one is, or perhaps, we all are. It seems to have got to Malcolm, too. He mixes seldom with the young folks now and rarely speaks to anyone.'

'Blow me, the two should get together, I mean Krista and Malcolm. Both are traitors, both are yellow as hell.' She was in no mood to grieve for those who did not deserve her pity. 'When can we leave, Roland? I no longer have a family, nor do I care, indeed not.'

'We might try tomorrow night, aye, tomorrow; the signs are good. Be ready.'

'Blow me, I've been ready and waiting many a night,' she complained.

'Can I control the weather? It would be madness to risk our lives; we might just as easily jump over the cliff here and now and have done with it. But dead heroes are of no greater use than dead cowards or idiots.'

She looked at him long and hard, as if she had really seen him for the first time. His features were strong and rugged, not even the long eyelashes that spread out like tiny black fans could soften his roguish appearance. His full crop of dark hair showed a hint of greyness at his temples while his beard was at last in the process of growing into a permanent feature.

'All will be right in the end, aye, that it will,' he smiled and playfully ruffled her hair. 'I am content; I pray that you will be content, too, and that our bairn will be born healthy, aye.' It was the first time that he said *our bairn*; it sounded natural as if he really believed the child to be his; or at least that, by believing it, it would become his own even if it were not, just as he might have become Adelika's father all those years ago.

Time passes slowest when impatience is at its worst. In late autumn, calm waters were as rare as a glimpse of the sun. But the calm day had come at last, and as evening drew in Siegund waited for Roland and thought of Garwulf - where one was, the other one was too, much like the cliffs that flaunted beauty and recklessness as if one could not exist without the other. In the fading daylight Siegund vowed to be a good wife to the fiddler, at least she would try to be. She began to wrap her chattels into two blankets - all of it stolen and none her own.

She huddled by the fire and waited, prayed, doubted, hoped. Somewhere in the distance an owl hooted its warning to vole and dormouse. From time to time she stepped outside, her eyes searching the darkness, her ears anticipating eagerly the sound of snapping twigs. Sometimes she thought she heard him approach, then all was quiet again, and each time her heart sank and she would go back into the cave and scorn Roland for playing a wicked game with her.

Morning came. Warily she trudged up to the Wizards Bench, careless of the risk of detection. She edged close to the brink of the cliff, secured a handhold on the massive rock and peered down into the broiling sea below where folks had wanted her to be, where perhaps fate wanted her to be. The sea roared; it beckoned and repelled. She imagined that Marnie was waving to her from the foamy depth, a wayward, jealous Marnie who wanted Roland for herself. Siegund shrank back.

'Blow me, I'll not die willingly, indeed not. I'll fight with all my might.'

A pale sun broke through the clouds; she took it for a promise of life. Six boats rose and fell on the mildly choppy sea and headed for the sandbank - six boats rowed by eighteen men, their faces obscured by a silky haze of light. She fancied she could see Roland amongst the men - she might have been mistaken. One of the men pointed her way, which was enough reason for her to slide to the ground. The boats moved away, the men turned their backs to her. She retreated to the safety of the cave, knelt by the rock where she and Maunsie had wept together. She flung her arms around the stone and pressed her face hard against it.

'Blow me, Maunsie, what fools we were. It seems a whole lifetime ago now, yet nothing has changed. You're still what you are and I'm still a fool greatly in need of wisdom and clarity. My need to know, to understand, and to endure is as great as your need was to be cured.' With Garwulf's token she began to scratch the Nordic rune of Wunjo into the grey stone - Wunjo, the symbol of light and joy and restoration. 'This is for both of us, Maunsie,' she said. 'One day the light will shine into our hearts as it has never shone before.'

She crawled into her shelter. With unhurried fingers she untied the bundles and spread the contents around her. How pathetically inadequate the clutter was, and how pathetically inadequate she was herself! She stretched out on her bed and tried to sleep, but sleep would not come. The wakefulness chewed and tore at her sanity and in this inner turmoil even the imaginary friends seemed too frightened to come near her.

Roland did not return to the cave - not that night, nor the next, nor any time later. Siegund remembered her curse and his apparent hesitation. Perhaps he had really lied about Garwulf and had, in consequence, sailed to hell. She regretted her curse now. A liar and cheat for a companion would have been better than no companion at all. If Roland had lied, should that not mean that Garwulf would be back? But how could she still hope when she had lost faith in them both?

'Rats, all rats,' she lamented. 'Indeed, that's what they are - Roland, Garwulf, Malcolm, the drunken sailor - rats all of them.'

# Chapter 11

Self-pity is a wasteful pastime when the stomach growls for food. By fair or foul means, Siegund was forced to find a way to still her hunger if she wanted to live - and she did want to live despite loneliness. In the midst of night she set out to raid a Kuan larder, hurrying over the muddy ground along the hilldyke, her head bowed low, her shoulders hunched under her blanket. Icy rain stung her cheeks as if to punish her for her dishonest activity. But hunger hurts, too, so that the foul means may seem fair. Any larder would do. The fear of the trolls would keep the Kuans in their beds; she nevertheless, headed for the Harehill, wondering whether it was a greater sin to steal from one's own mother than from a neighbour, but apprehension either way was counteracted by an excitement of seeing the valley again.

Her thoughts went to the cows in the byre, they too suffered hunger every winter, and to make matters worse, folks drained some of the cattle's blood when the milk yield ceased; mixed with barley meal it provided a kind of black pudding for the family. In spring, when the animals were little more than skin and bones, when their lethargic brains seemed to have forgotten the rare commodity called fodder, they were half coaxed and half heaved onto their unsteady feet and slowly nurtured along with obnoxious-smelling concoctions of shellfish, eggs, fish oil, seaweed, barley meal and warm water. All this Siegund remembered with a shudder, remembered their weak lows that had sounded like short groans as they accepted the food without a hint of accusation in their doleful eyes. Krista had said that they must be used to it. Did that make everything right?

The Harehill lay in brooding silence as if it neither knew the night-visitor nor cared. Her heart hammered to the rhythm of the rainwater that dripped from the roof with needless urgency. She listened for a moment with one ear placed against the byre door, then stepped inside. The warm, distinct smell of cows, of deep litter and home comforts poured into her nostrils. She probed her way through the byre where old Daisy greeted her with what seemed a minute sigh.

In the *but* the inevitable peat fire smouldered. Again she listened. From the *ben* came Rory's heavy snoring. Apart from his variegated vibrating grunts all was quiet. She reached up to the shelf and helped herself to a piece of mutton, a chunk of pork and a couple of smoke-dried herrings. Maunsie coughed. It stopped Rory's artless music instantly and sent Siegund seeking refuge under the table. She did not emerge until Rory resumed his irritating sound effects, now in a different key entirely. Hunger being greater than fear and shame put together she helped herself to eggs, cheese and barley meal.

'I'll pay you back, Midder,' she whispered. 'Indeed, one day I'll make up for all the pain I've caused you, but for now I have only my three red tear-drops to leave you, though what you should want with them I cannot think, and I would rather like to keep them.'

She wrapped the loot into one of her mother's aprons, then placed the three pendants into a small wooden dish and left her token of thanks on the table. For a moment she allowed her eyes to scan the *but.* It looked as it had always done - plain, tidy, everything in its proper place. And as always, the bowl of clean water for the trolls stood by the fire. Nothing had changed - nothing could change. Young Jan began to cry. Siegund fled from the cottage, fled from her home, from her mother when she would rather have stayed and spoken with her. On her way back to the cave she cursed her own cowardice. How absurd it now seemed to have run away from her mother instead of having faced her matter-of-fact reproof; she had so longed for a single word from her, no matter how unkind it might have been.

The pilfered pork sizzled and crackled over the fire so that the delicious aroma made her mouth water like that of a rabid pup. If patience was a commendable virtue - for a hungry girl it was downright agony. She could wait no longer, grabbed the spit, wafted the hot meat in the air one moment and vigorously blew at it the next to speed up the cooling process. In her frantic activity the meat slid off the spit. She stabbed at it with ferocious determination, picked it off the floor and, without a thought for cleanliness, tore with her teeth large chunks off the half cooked pork and filled her mouth with meat and grains of dirt. Under greasy, pork-flavoured sighs she reminded herself to go easy on her rations while her long, dirt-lined fingernails dug into the meat as if never to let go again. For a brief moment she held it at arm's length and surveyed it in a torment of indecision, then took another bite on the grounds that there was no sense in saving food for tomorrow if she were to die of hunger today. And who could argue with that?

Now that her immediate needs were satisfied the successful excursion to the valley gave her a feeling of power. Power tends to encourage wickedness. She, who nurtured a promise to rise as goddess one day - and was meanwhile branded a sorceress - would make the islanders pay for the wrong they had done her. She would frighten them out of their shrivelled minds; indeed, a toad, a handful of grubs, a dead rat - they would make perfect tokens of appreciation on her nocturnal visits to the Mulvoens, the Bidebergs, or the Volkers. The idea filled her with impish delight; at the same time she was aware that to create more havoc in the valley might jeopardise any chance of forgiveness. Yet, she thought them beneath her station; she knew far more than her folks, knew that there were no trolls and no ogres in the hills, who despite their non-existence kept the crofters in their beds at night. Their fear had helped Garwulf to survive; now it was helping her. Considering every fact, her feeling of superiority waned fast. She had been cheated by the two men she had trusted and the third had turned coward. The thought brought the wretchedness back again. At such times, when her spirit was at its lowest, she contemplated death as an easier option, to which the gloomy cave echoed its agreement while the lusty fire crackled its ridicule.

She passed her days in ever changing moods, talking to the cave, the fire, and to the brute of a spider that had made its home in the cave. It lived close to the floor to avoid being smoke-dried like Macalays' bacon. Siegund tolerated its presence as a companion - not one she would have chosen, but still, a companion. She called it Rollo because it reminded her of Roland. Her nocturnal visits to the crofts were kept to an absolute minimum lest she were found out, and yet she wished for it to happen; but as always, folks stayed in their beds.

She was entering the Harehill for the third time, a little less excited, a little more desperate to speak with her mother and beg for a remedy to stop her body from growing ever larger. She refused to accept Roland's explanation of her condition and much preferred her own interpretation – the growing-up theory; or perhaps it was something more sinister. In the wooden dish on the table still lay the three pendants and beside the bowl lay a neat little pile of food, a tub of sandy soap, a candle and a shawl. Quite obviously, the provisions were laid out for the night visitor, whoever they thought it to be. How readily she would have exchanged them for a kind word, how gladly she would have gone hungry in exchange for a little affection!

'Midder,' she whispered, '...if you know of me, why don't you come and speak with me? Blow me, I'm your daughter, not a witch - indeed, not a witch. I'm bloated with dropsy, Midder. It's killing me. I can feel it twist and turn inside me. Why won't you tell me what to do?'

Rory's nasal concert petered out into a faint mumbling, then into silence as if the cottage were deserted. Were her folks listening? Were they holding their breath? How could they live with their cowardice? Why did they not come and welcome her - or chase her away? To be ignored was worse than to be chased away. She tried to convince herself that they did not know of her presence. Their rejection overwhelmed all hopes and fears and turned them into dull indifference. She shrugged her shoulders and collected the gifts; had hunger not been greater than rejection she would have left them on the table.

'I came because I'm hungry and sick. I'll never come back again, not ever as thief or beggar,' she said neither particularly loud nor subdued.

Outside the rain pelted her face without mercy. The notion of ending it all had never been stronger, but she preferred to leave the unpleasant details of it to chance. The cold rain began to soak through the blanket, through her clothes down to her kin. Death's icy breath was quivering down her spine. She might die of the wheezing sickness like one of the Johansen boys, but she would rather not; it had been a slow and tedious business with him and the memory of his suffering turned her rapidly against seeking an early demise. Oh, how she longed for the simplicity of her earlier monotonous existence when she had knitted socks, worked the fields and walked with Maunsie. She might go to the mainland and seek work or seek Garwulf if she knew where to look. The thought directed her feet, as if by mechanical action, towards the beach.

The sea was neither calm nor in its most turbulent of moods, but still, the white crests of on the swell did their eternal dance around the impressive stacks that discouraged strangers from intruding and natives from leaving. How was she to row past those stony guardians? Perhaps she would just drift like Garwulf had done; hopefully, someone would find her, too.

The boats lay wedged keel-up between the rocks far out of the water's reach. She heaved, pulled, prayed and cursed, biting her lips sore in the process. Through her own wild vociferations thundered the roar of the ocean. It took numerous attempts before she managed to free one of the long, slender vessels. Step by step she dragged it across a stretch of sand and pebbles while frequently stopping to rest for short moments. A sudden pain cut through her back and ended somewhere in her right leg. The sickness from months ago came back and poured the bitterness of her pain out of her, rendering her momentarily quite incapable of any sensible thought. She hardly noticed the rain now that was still pouring down on her. The pain eased away. The briefness and severity of the sudden malady confused her yet more. She made another attempt at dragging the boat to the lapping water that seemed to play a game with her, for it seemed to draw back a little more each time she came close. Her strength gave out. Skerra Kua was holding her prisoner; she should have heeded its demand for loyalty. She thought she heard the hills call, or perhaps it was only the wind; either way, she followed the call.

The walk back to the shelter seemed like the endless walk of a lost soul wandering aimlessly in limbo until eternity. The pain that forced her to her knees returned spasmodically, followed by emotional numbness and semi-awareness which alternated like ebb and flood tide. She plodded on through the rain, stopping now and then to allow the pain to pass. The sodden blanket weighed her down; each step she took was a little harder than the last one had been. At last, at long last, the fire welcomed her home. With tediously slow, mechanical movements she took care of the fire so that the fire, in turn, might take care of her.  She lay on her bed, hardly noticing her wet clothes; the straw was always damp anyway since the autumn rains had come. Once more she became distant; whatever was happening to her seemed not to concern her; she wanted to sleep, but the pain came back, stronger, fiercer and more frequently.

'Midder, why have you rejected me? I stayed with you when Jan was born.' She gave a cry of fear, admitting to herself for the first time that the fiddler's diagnosis had been right, though according to him it should not happen just yet. 'But I want no child, blow me, I have never prayed for one.  Was it the same with you, Midder?  Did you feel the same about your children - something you never asked for, yet, was burdened with? Is that why you have always been so cold, so remote? But you were not frightened, you did not yell as I am doing. You said nature would take its course. Cruel nature! I used to think nature gentle and beautiful.' She cried out for Garwulf, then for Roland, then cursed them both, then herself, and in the end she scarcely knew who to blame.

One last pain, one last piercing yell. She lifted her head, laughing, crying and shaking with cold and exertion. What to be done now? She regretted her squeamishness when she had fled from her mother's bedside. But if the wild ponies in the hills had no help, nor the rabbits in their warren, should she not although be able to cope? Necessity showed her the way. Before long, too weak to stand up, she crawled to and fro across the fungus-speckled floor, fetching the things she thought she might need. She felt humbled by the gift from the gods - asked-for or otherwise - humbled also by her shame; indeed, mostly by her shame. It seemed fitting for her to crawl on her belly like a snake, for she had lain in sin with Roland the serpent.

The tiny girl, wrapped in a blanket, lay snug and warm in Siegund's arm. Its warmth spread into her own heart. She was no longer alone. She vowed there and then to banish for ever all uncharitable thoughts. Exhaustion was getting the better of her, and as she lay on her bed, eyes open but only half awake, the glow of the fire became a light of redemption, a light that brought her a kind of peace.

'Farewell, loneliness,' she whispered. 'The rune of Wunjo has worked its magic for me; one day it will work for Maunsie too.'

She drifted into a world of gentle dreams in which her mother was reaching out to her with open arms – a loving, caring mother. She slept until a flock of rowdy kittiwakes boldly proclaimed the new day. And where the dreams ended a new reality began. How was she to take care of the babe when she had nothing but a shawl and a damp blanket to wrap it in? She asked the gods to bless this child born in the darkness of a cave, an unholy child, fruit of her sins. No sunray as sign acceptance fell into the cave; the best the gods could do was to temporarily stop the rain from falling.

'No matter, babe of darkness, you'll have the sun in your heart. I'll name you Sonwill, will of the sun!' she pronounced with solemn expression, hoping that the name might not be regarded by the deities as presumptuous, but as far as she was concerned, no was name too grant for the tiny bundle of rather loose skin over minute bones. The babe was much smaller than young Jan had been, with a mouth unproportionally large when it opened to cry. 'You'll be my companion, my comfort and my salvation. You'll grow up in the hills and never fear the night as other folks do, indeed not.'

Siegund would have been content - happy almost but for the realisation that something was amiss with the child who was not feeding well. For two days and a night Siegund fretted, tending and nursing the babe almost continuously and getting little sleep and nourishment herself.

'Blow me...there, there now,' she cooed, being quite near tears while rocking the whimpering babe in her arms. 'Midder Josefa will make you better, indeed she will; she'll know what to do.' Siegund was whimpering too, whimpering because she too felt desperately ill, whimpering even more at the loss of her so recently gained companion, her precious gift, wrapped in a blanket that smelled of rotting vegetation, as did everything in the cave.

Ocean and north wind roared their rowdy symphony, drowning the pitiful whimpers of mother and child. Siegund picked her way through the darkness, feeling so weak, so wretched that at times she thought she could not go a step further, but each time anxiety drove her mercilessly beyond the limits of her strength, allowing her no rest. The menacing ague turned her thoughts into a jumble of unclear fragments; she made no attempt to bring them into order and fit them together, even the shadowy cottage and the cosy *but* failed to revive her. The child was quiet now as if it knew of its mother's plight.

'Make her well, Midder, even if you loathe me,' Siegund whispered her plea for compassion, which was smothered by Rory's snoring. On the table lay a neat little pile of food and a root of some kind. She took the gifts without much thought and laid the baby in its place. She retreated into the byre and listened behind the closed door. 'I'll come back for you when you are well again,' she whispered. Sonwill began to cry.

'Holy Midder! Holy Midder Mary,' Josefa was lamenting in the *but.*

Siegund stood in the byre and waited. Her heart was pounding; her head whirled with hope and fear. Would her mother come out to call after her? She heard pans clatter, rhymes being chanted. Her mother was too busy to trouble herself with a fugitive who was supposed to be dead anyway. The babe needed help; it was barely alive.

With a heavy heart Siegund acknowledged that Sonwill's need was greater than her own, though her own was great indeed. A moment later the rain beat into her face, cooling with over-zealous activity her feverish body. Reluctantly she headed back to the cave - slowly, wearily, often stopping to rest. Sometimes she knelt on the sodden ground, pressing her burning face against the cold earth while her mind functioned only in patchy comings and goings in this seemingly endless, pointless struggle for her young life. It had begun in the Harehill cottage and would surely end in the cave - if she ever got there. The relentless wind urged her to return to the fire.

Bereft of the last ounce of strength she reached the cave. It seemed the end of her world – a decaying world to which she belonged. She crawled onto her bed and felt herself sink into deep emptiness in which all emotions, all hopes and dreams, all sorrow and shame left her. If eternal sleep was like this she would not mind dying, for the emptiness was not empty at all; there was solitude instead of loneliness, awareness of existence but not of life itself. She tried to speak out Garwulf's name but had no strength to do so and remained mute.

# Chapter 12

It might have been a hundred years, a hundred days or just a hundred blinks of the eye since her emergence into this peaceful dimension. Sometimes she drifted close to the world she had known and then she could hear a deep voice call from afar, though no words could pass into the tranquil void, this space between spaces that had no concept of pain. She resented the intrusion and tried to distance herself, but the voice came louder and occasional words came to her ears. A menacing light shone into her face so that she had to shield her eyes. She saw the fiddler bending over her, wondered why he looked so much like Garwulf, and when her vision became clearer she knew it was not the fiddler. She blinked and swallowed, then blinked again.

'Blow me, Garwulf, is it really you or have I lost my senses? How long have you been here with me?' she asked with a voice that sounded like rusty hinges moving in a breeze.

'A few nights and as many days,' he replied, brushing his hand gently over her hair. 'You were asleep most of the time except when you were rambling about things that made no sense. What has happened? Why are you not with your family?'

'Fear and ignorance, remember? Those things brought me here.' Siegund hesitated, wondering what to tell him first and what not to tell at all. 'I...I...you...we have a child.'

'I know,' he said, as if the news were no news at all. Then he shook his head. 'It lives?'

'She's ailing and is with Midder. But how did you know?'

'I took care of you these past days; I could not help but notice the state of affairs.' He took her in his arms and rocked her to and fro. 'Get well, Siegund, get strong enough to cope with the journey; I have a home waiting for us, a good and safe home.'

'You have no wife? Blow me...you're not wed already?'

'Would I be here if I were? If only I had known - God in heaven, I should have known.'

'I tried to call you. You said it could be done. I'm not clever enough. Forgive me for that and for…'

She stopped short of confessing her infidelity, stopped short of freeing herself from the weighty burden of her dark secret. If she did not speak of it now, while his own feeling of guilt was at its strongest, her courage might wane, and perhaps one day the fiddler would tell the tale. On the other hand - so she reasoned with herself - leaving the island may well avert such disaster, in which case it may be better to say nothing at all.

'We shall leave Skerra Kua soon and never part again.'

'But I can't leave without Sonwill. I've vowed never to abandon her. Don't ask it of me.'

'She is my child too, but, Siegund, think on it; a journey across the swell is too hazardous for a frail child. I promise you, we shall come back for her when winter has passed.'

Once more she was prepared to believe in the strength of his promises. Under his resolute care and guidance, substantiated by nourishing meals of meat, fish and barley concoctions, her health improved with each passing day. Before long she was able to stand with him near the cliffs at day break. They looked across the swell while talking of their plans in much detail. Garwulf, now dressed in well-fitting clothes, looked truly handsome, a god indeed, and on their lofty outpost she too felt elated - not like a goddess but like a butterfly freshly emerged from its chrysalis.

It was on one such early mornings when they stood close together under the cloudy sky, his arms drawn around her shoulders, that they had a feeling of being watched. They turned their heads, slowly, both at the same time. They saw Maunsie peering from behind a rock some twenty paces away.

'Maunsie,' Siegund called out. She tried to hasten to her brother. While her heart had suddenly grown wings, her feet must have grown corns; perhaps she had forgotten how to run. 'I'm alive, Maunsie, look, I'm alive and I'm quite well.'

He stared at his sister, uncertain of her existence even now. His whole body twitched and jerked convulsively and was still twitching when brother and sister fell into each others arms.

Siegund laughed and Maunsie cried, then Maunsie laughed and Siegund cried.

'I knew I would see you again, yay, I knew it all along,' he stammered feebly, 'Midder has sent me to find you. Come home, Siegund, no one will harm you now.'

'You mean that folks will have me walk amongst them? I don't understand.'

'They have seen you. Nay, it's sad, it's wicked. Some say you have the skills of the most powerful witch that ever lived; they dare not offend you any longer, others deem you innocent; they say you have the protection of the gods, for no one has ever survived a fall from the Wizards Bench, nay, no one.' He stared at Garwulf as if he had just seen him coming out of thin air, which immediately turned Maunsie's face that pale shade of orange again. 'Nay what do you want to come back for, stranger?' he asked. 'I doubt folk's hearts have altered enough to accept your presence, too.'

'Blow me, Maunsie, don't ask me to return to the valley without my man-to-be. Don't make me choose.'

'Maunsie is right,' Garwulf intervened. 'You must go without me. Would you have them think we lived together in sin all the while and have yourself slighted for it? It cannot help matters.' He stopped to consider the sense in what he had just said, for the child would certainly more than call her purity into question. He thought it far safer if she did not go at all, but he had neither the heart nor the wish to tell her so. 'Go with your brother. As for you and me - nothing will change if you do not wish it so.'

'What do I care for folks? They have made me suffer the insufferable; they can do me no greater harm.'

'Come, Midder is waiting. Yay, the grief is breaking her heart,' Maunsie told her, tugging at her sleeve.

'Is it indeed! How can her heart break when she has none?' She stretched her hand out to Garwulf, partly wishing that he would persuade her to stay instead of nodding his silent encouragement. Her heart cried out to him, it cried just as loudly for her child and even for her heartless mother. If she could not have them all, she hardly knew which one of them she needed most just now, but since options always proved as bewildering as the lack of them, indecision left room for outside influence; she allowed Maunsie to lead her home.

They walked hand in hand as they had done so many times in the past. How strange it seemed to walk in daylight again after her night activities! The thought of meeting her folks frightened her. When they came to the Northstane they saw Malcolm in the yard, tending the pigs as he had always done. He looked different; the Northstane looked different, though nothing had changed - the same muddy yard, the numerous sties and the same number of squealing pigs. Yet, everything *was* different and could never be the same again. Malcolm stopped his work and stood motionless with an awesome stare of incredulity, then bowed his head as if he had seen Freyja, the beautiful lady of the skies, the patroness of sorcery who was led by her brother Frey, the god of sunshine and rain.

Brother and sister, positively mortal, walked on without acknowledging Malcolm whose show of respect and reverence had instilled in them a temporary feeling of uniqueness that filled them with unwholesome pride. Their spirits rose high above the clouds while the air, heavy with the awe of the unknown, forced spasmodic sighs out of their heaving chests. A woman with thin body, thin face, grey hair and seemingly dead eyes, was walking towards them. She opened her mouth either to speak or to cry out, but she stood aside without making a sound until they had passed.

'Who was she?' Siegund asked, still dazed by her emotional trip.

'Don't you know her? It was Katrine Klaasen. The grief for Emilie has broken her.'

Siegund clutched her brother's hand tightly. Instead of feeling stronger for having endured the unendurable she felt exposed now, vulnerable, and when at last she stood outside the Harehill cottage she trembled even at the sight of the stepping stones, trembled when she saw her mother in the *but*, trembled when she looked at Krista, her cherub face now dull and drawn.

'Midder, I've come home,' she mumbled and could say no more than that.

Siegund had stopped in the doorway as if waiting for permission to enter. Her mother came with unsteady gait towards her. Her hand brushed carefully over Siegund's face to feel for herself whether the figure before her was flesh and blood or merely an apparition called forth by her own grieving. Josefa took her daughter into her arms. Her matter-of-fact attitude had given way to an unprecedented softness; her silent tears said all that was to be said.

At this brief moment of wordless gratitude came Krista's pitiful sobs. 'I never meant to hurt you, Siegund, no never though. I forgot myself and gave your secret away. I have punished myself ever since, I never spoke another word, no, never though. Now my punishment is over if you can forgive me.'

Josefa's temporarily damaged discipline was immediately restored with a violent jerk of her body. 'Mark my word, blessed is this hour.' She let go of Siegund, praising with raised hands the gods for their mercy. 'The one who was lost has been returned; the one who was mute speaks again.'

'Midder, where's the babe?' Siegund asked eagerly.

'Jan is asleep in the *ben*.' Josefa cast an uneasy glance at Krista and sent her on an errand.

'Not Jan, Midder; I mean Sonwill.'

'Child, your grief is my grief,' she said at length and lowered her head to avoid Siegund's searching eyes. 'The bairn was sick and weak. She could not live.'

'Nay, Midder, it's wicked, it's sad,' Maunsie intervened, making his presence known for the first time since the reunion. 'I can't let you do that, Midder. Why do you lie when all our lives you've urged us to honesty? Nay, if you can't admit to your wrong-doing then I must tell her. Can you really live and die with a secret so dark? Nay, but it's no secret - I know what you have done.'

'Leave it son, it can do no good, mark my word!' She tried her old matter of fact attitude; the tremor in voice and hands indicated that she was not entirely in control of herself, but her lips remained tightly closed about the matter.

'Tell her, Midder,' he urged. 'Tell her how you took Hegan's dead bairn, born long before it's time, and buried it in the midst of the night. Yay, and tell her that you took the other bairn to Hegan, and how Hegan, near death herself, never knew any of it, and still knows no better now that she has recovered. Yay, it had to be said.'

Siegund's eyes had moved from Maunsie to Josefa and back to Maunsie again, her mouth ajar, her body fixed in perpendicular suspension.

'Blow me, Midder, you have given my child away? I entrusted her to your care and you gave her away like a kitten? Indeed, you have no heart. I'll fetch her home directly.'

'Holy Midder! Hannah is Hegan's bairn now - Hegan and all the other folks think it is. It can't be altered.'

"Hannah? Her name is Sonwill – not Hannah!' Siegund flung herself at her mother, clawed and scratched at the tormented face that yet remained cold.

'Nay, nay,' Maunsie yelled at them while trying to pull them apart. 'It's wrong, it's wicked that you should lay hands on your Midder.' And for want of anything more decisive to say he added in the same yelling tone: 'Rory lost faith in our land and has left us for a life at sea.'

'Has he indeed? Siegund yelled back, but despite the bitterness she halted her vicious attack instantly. 'A family of traitors!' she hissed, feeling suddenly disarmed and broken. After a moment of silent contemplation her voice came soft and pleading when she asked: 'Will you come with me to see my bairn, Maunsie - just see her?'

Maunsie declined. He wanted no truck with the business as it stood. He deemed the laws of nature supreme; the rules of the land should bow to them. A bairn belonged to its rightful mother. Maunsie had grown somewhat in stature, that is, his legs had grown longer while his torso was still lacking height. His voice had at last passed through the phase of breaking from low to high and high to low tones and, being the eldest son at home now, he might have thought himself as head of the family, but it was Josefa who held the reins; in truth, she had always done so.

Siegund's emotions began to run riot again. How was she to endure her loss? Had Sonwill died she might have accepted her loss. But this, a gift to Hegan - to Hegan the miracle worker - it was monstrous. The fury rose in her like a raging wild beast. She screamed again, lashed out, tore her own hair and banged her head against the wall so that the blood ran from her forehead.

'Let it be, child, let it be, I beseech you,' Josefa pleaded, trying to restrain her daughter who seemed to have lost her senses. 'There was no other way, believe me. No one else knows - no one ever must know.'

They heard Krista enter the byre, which prompted her to go along with her mother's shameful deed, at least for the time being, though she would not be prevented from seeing her child. That seemed reasonable enough even to Josefa who, to avoid the risk of irreparable blunder, offered to accompany her daughter to the Girse croft there and then.

They walked along in silence. Siegund felt like a visitor to the island who was seeing Skerra Kua, if not exactly for the first time, perhaps for the second time only. The passing neighbours seemed like strangers who did not seem to know her either. Tilo Volker crossed their path, bowed his head slightly and went on his way without as much as a word. She looked at her mother for an explanation.

'It will pass; they'll get used to you again,' Josefa said, shrugging her shoulders.

'Midder...if you knew I was alive, if you knew I was coming to the cottage...why didn't you wait up for me? Why did you forsake me so? How could your heart be so cold?'

'Cold? No, not cold, mark my word, child, not cold. My tears could have easily filled the ocean. Rory forbade me to speak with you, he being the head of the family then. He said he would leave if I spoke with you. Be that as it may, he's left us all the same to cope with our lot. The Macalays have promised to help us in the fields. Already, young Malcolm does what he can. Mark my word, Malcolm is a good lad, but he has changed - Holy Midder, we have all changed.' Josefa was troubled by Siegund's presently adopted aloofness; she was beginning to fear Siegund for what she might say or do.

'Why did you give my bairn away, Midder?' she said louder than was necessary. 'Hannah, you call her - Hannah. Her name is Sonwill,' she told her mother once more.

'I wish I could undo what is done, all of it, mind. There are times when the things we do are wrong, yet they are also right. What would folks have said about Hegan's still-born baby? The affairs on the island being what there were, Holy Midder, who would they blame? The men were out fishing that night; who was to know if I exchanged one babe for another?'

'And you want me to pretend I have no child? How can you ask it of me?'

'It's the best course to take - with you unwed and the bairn's Fadder dead.'

'Who is dead? Blow me down, you have told me many times that I talk nonsense, but now you are talking more nonsense than I have ever done.' Siegund felt her cheeks begin to burn at the mentioning of the bairn's father. 'Who is dead?'

'The fiddler, child - the fiddler, of course.'

Siegund gave a little cry and instantly her hand flew to her mouth to cover the sound.

'There was much talk of the fiddler's excursions into the hills at night,' Josefa continued. 'One night he did not return. They found him washed up on the shore. He must have fallen from the cliff, though some of the Kuans suggested far more sinister reasons for his death. His body was strangely twisted and he had no longer a face. All in all, he was scarcely recognizable; he might have been anyone, lying there in shreds and tatters and half decayed. Some folks said that it was not him at all; Konrad said it was.'

'Stop it, Midder, blow me down, stop it,' Siegund cried out once more, feeling her stomach turn and the blood drain from her face. Her guilt in the matter was weighty indeed; she had wished him to hell, and that was where he had gone and had taken their dark secret with him. For that she was grateful, but she had never really wished him dead.

'You have much to thank him for,' Josefa said. 'While he lost his face yours was gradually restored. Rumours began that it had been the fiddler all along who had brought down the curse on Skerra Kua and had cleverly steered the blame towards you.'

'But that isn't so, Midder. He was not an evil man. He helped me when no one else had either power or courage to do so.'

'I know, child, I know. But, Holy Midder,' Josefa said, frowning and shaking her head, '...what made him come back and tell me that he had failed to save you? I'll never understand it. After that day he avoided me, though I gave him no blame. It was only after his death that I guessed what his business in the hills might have been. It stands to reason.'

'He had nothing to do with the bairn. I'm betrothed to Garwulf, he is the Fadder, no one else. And you have given his child away; you shouldn't have done it.'

'Holy Midder, for the sake of sanity and peace, let it be.' This new revelation of the stranger's role in all this shook Josefa anew and made her voice unsteady again. Her hands fidgeted when, on nearing the Girse cottage, she said: 'Your sister is still ailing. If the truth be known to her, mark my word, the grief will drive her into an early grave.'

'And my grief, Midder - does it matter so little? How can you measure grief against grief? It's my right to be with my bairn.'

'You had no right to her in the first place, nor have you the right to give the bairn a bad name - you not being wed and all that; she would carry the shame of your sins through life. Giving her up is the noblest of all sacrifices you'll ever be asked to make. Do it bravely and without malice, do it for the child, for you, for Hegan, and for Skerra Kua.'

For all the sense Josefa spoke, the truth was too hard to bear; truth had a habit of being painful; pretence was often kinder, and in the name of pretence Siegund was not allowed to grieve over her loss, was even to deny any cause for grief. The day the Kirk Knoll moved, Josefa had howled her complaint out into the hills, and later, Katrine had done the same for Emilie. Siegund's hand went to her throat as she tried to swallow the emerging cry that seemed to turn to mature leather in her gullet. She felt her mother's hand on her shoulder, begging a promise without allowing a refusal.

'You are blessed with immense strength, child, more than some of the men folk around here,' Josefa told her. 'Use it wisely and you'll find it an advantageous gift; use it carelessly and it will bring more pain. I'll help you, counsel you if you seek it. You think me hard, child. Be that as it may, am I not also a Midder? Seven children alive and just as many dead; Holy Midder, I too have lost bairns and know the pain. I shall never see mine again in this world while you will see yours grow up - the gods willing.' She squeezed her daughter's hand as last reminder of her duty when they entered the Girse cottage which, under the new tenancy, had lost its air of abandonment.

Hegan, startled into useless haste, jumped to her feet. She stared at Siegund and shook her head in disbelief. Swiftly she picked the babe from its cradle, drew her close to her ample bosom and folded both arms around the small bundle.

She seemed unsure whether to retreat altogether or stand her ground at a safe distance from the intruder.

'Where, pray, where have you been, girl - if the dead don't come back?' Hegan stammered.

Siegund stepped forward to reach out for young Hannah. Hegan took the same number of steps back, her cold eyes filled with a strange fear, a madness almost. But what was she afraid of? Did her unreasonable behaviour, the absurd over-protectiveness, suggest that perhaps she knew more than she would admit? The thought crossed Josefa's and Siegund's minds.

'The bairn is fragile,' Hegan explained quickly. 'It's only for the goodness of the gods that she still lives.' She allowed Siegund to take a peep from this safe distance. Hegan's mouth formed something like a smile - a wary, fearful smile. 'She's beautiful, to be sure. And see, her hair is beginning to grow; there's no sign of the Macalay redness in her.' Her own statement seemed to reassure her, which seemed to take a little of the fear from her. The combination of her pallid face, her bleached-straw hair, the matronly figure, the black shawl draped over her shoulders, and the dark, wide sleeves of her gown gave her the appearance of a white-headed eagle clinging with powerful talons to a new-born lamb.

Siegund craned her neck as far as it would go while her feet remained fixed on the spot. Her chin quivered a little. Tears began to blur her vision. With erratic movements of her hands she brushed over her face and over her dress for want of what else to do with them. Hannah puckered her wrinkly, still slightly jaundiced face that looked not too unlike a partly inflated pig-bladder ball that suddenly began to wail. It was all too much for Siegund.

'Midder, she doesn't know me,' she lamented.

'Holy Midder, could you expect her to?' Josefa's hand dug into her daughter's back to warn her against foolish errors. It was just as well that Duncan and Malcolm arrived at that moment, carrying between them the carcass of a pig for the celebration, which was planned for the following day when Hannah was to be introduced to all the Kuans.

The two men were not sure how to react to Siegund's presence and only managed rather dumb, awkward stares, which made the whole thing an embarrassing affair. Josefa attempted to get at least a bitty conversation going - clearly there would be no sensible one. She reaped only pathetic replies until in the end Siegund yelled at them all.

'What is it with you? Blow me down, is my homecoming disturbing you so? I'd best leave you then, so that you may talk freely instead of stuttering.' Anger and frustration sent her scampering headlong outdoors. She leaned against the restored gate at the end of the yard and propped her head into both hands. Someone called to her. She knew the voice, knew it was Malcolm's. She flung round in anger, ready to send a shower of poisonous verbal arrows at him, but when she noticed his heavy limp, which had become a permanent encumbrance to him, pity overpowered anger; the once so dashing youth looked old and tired somehow; it was not the tiredness that age brings along - it was a weariness induced by prolonged sadness. He smiled, or tried to smile, and for a moment his handsome face seemed rejuvenated.

'I'm glad ye're heme and safe, ye ken. Can ye ever fergive me, Siegund?'

'It matters little now - nothing much does, come to that; so, why speak of it? All is well, they say. I say that some wrongs can never be put right.'

'Perhaps it can, if ye let me try. Perhaps in time; och, perhaps not.' He was still at a loss what to say or how to say what he had in mind and looked into the distance for inspiration. 'I saw in yer face how fond ye are of Hegan's bairn, ye ken.'

'I like her well enough,' Siegund replied casually.

'Why give yer affection te someone else's bairn when ye should have yer own. Siegund, will ye marry me?' The words tumbled over his lips with sudden clumsy desperation, knowing well that this was neither the time nor the place for a proposal, but he persevered stubbornly. 'Could ye still like me, Siegund? Ye did once.'

'Indeed, Malkie, I did once. I was a child then. I still like you, but I can't wed you. I'm promised to another, you must look elsewhere. Midder says you are fond of Krista. Why not ask her?'

'I looked to her and pretended it was ye, not because of similarities - there are none - but because she is yer twin. Can ye understand that?' Malcolm closed his eyes as if he were in great pain.

'Maybe I can, maybe I can't. It's not important now, nor are the dreams of childhood. Wed Krista and be content. I wish you both well. We were never meant for each other, Malkie, indeed not.'

Josefa joined them to take Siegund home. Malcolm was left by the gate, looking lost and wretched with his hopes gone from him. Siegund looked back just once. It seemed that his auburn hair was all that was left of the dashing harvest sun. Her mind wandered back to Garwulf who was waiting for her in the hills, and the hills reminded her of the lepers whom she had not given a single thought since her homecoming.

'How is it with Claire?' she asked her mother, ashamed of her own neglect of them. 'Blow me, my selfish prattle made me forget all else, yet I pondered much about them in my solitude. Indeed, solitude makes one think, but its taste is bitter as bile and its embrace is cold and stifling.'

'Be that as it may, it's all a matter of discipline,' Josefa replied, having no liking for that kind of talk because she did not understand it. 'Claire and Emilie are still alive,' she said. 'As to their exact state of health - no one knows. Tobias and Martha - Holy Midder, bless their souls - are no more.'

'So soon? But the medical man said...'

'No one knows what happened. Claire will not speak and even refuses to show herself when food is brought, though folks say they sometimes see Emilie's shadow by the half-open door. Claire signalled Martha's and Tobias' end by displaying their clothes on the wall facing the cemetery as they had been instructed to do. It's strange, mark my word, that Tobias and Martha should both have perished on the same day.'

'Blow me, I shall go and see Claire this very day. I shall make her speak with me.'

'Child, you're in need of rest. I see the weariness in your face. You can't help them - no one can. Don't dabble in things you know nothing about; Martha did, and see what has become of her. Mark my word, no good will come from it. Forget them; no, Holy Midder, that's not what I meant to say - I meant, leave things as they are.'

But Siegund's mind was made up. After a short rest at home she prepared to climb up to the lepers' hovel. 'You must not mind me, Midder, but I shall never pretend they don't exist; don't ask it of me.'

'Would it make any difference if I minded?'

'Indeed not! I'm old enough to think for myself. Not long ago I was a child, now I'm grown up. Where my youth has gone I cannot say; I guess it has passed me by. I'll make good use of the lessons I've learned, but I'll no longer be forced under the yoke of obedience. Indeed, things are different now. From now on I'll do as I see fit, not out of malice, Midder, but you owe me a debt. I am ready to exchange my silence for freedom.'

'Mark my word, obedience never weighed heavily on your shoulders,' Josefa told her. 'You may be grown up, but you're still dreaming. What good can your fanciful charity do the lepers when there's no cure, no hope?

'I can talk with them, comfort them. It's far better than denying their existence. Their flesh and bones may be rotting away, but what of their souls?'

'Then I pray that your meddling will not revive the madness that took our pride and dignity away from us; without it we are nothing. It's only now that folks are beginning to come to their senses again. Don't destroy the slowly healing spirits a second time.'

'The madness was not my doing, Midder; it came from within the folks themselves. Why should compassion offend them? Don't they understand such feelings? Don't you, Midder? Then I pity you all.'

Josefa shuddered ever so slightly. This was not her daughter who had come back but some stranger, someone she did not know - someone she feared.

'Go then,' she said. 'You have my blessing, though I give it with a heavy heart. Promise me not to go beyond the walls of the enclosure, lest you bring the leprosy back.'

'I'll take no unnecessary risks, Midder, indeed not; I promise that much and no more.'

When a little later she climbed the hillside a lively breeze lifted her spirits and filled her lungs with invigorating breath. For the first time in weeks the sky was trying to clear and the late autumn sun was making its appearance as if in a grand finale before retiring to the land of everlasting ice once more. She might have been happy had not the ghosts of the recent past forbidden even contentment. Before her lay the ruins of the old church - derelict, a site of chaos and destruction. Yet, it was a permanent memorial to her father. Already time was changing sorrow into remembrance. Sleepy lay hills and moorland - it was their nature. In the progressing day the scene became that of morbid stagnation, which seemed to intensify as she came closer to the hovel.

The light of a fire fell through the half-open door of the hut, its smoky aroma mingling with the stale smell of the marshland. Siegund stood by the gate and waited. Her skin crawled a little at the memory of Tobias' grotesque death mask. Would Claire look like that now? And Emilie - had the sickness devoured the turned-up, happy little nose and the sweet young face? Siegund quickly called for Claire lest her courage should leave. She yelled with such desperation, it sounded like a cry for help. Two figures, draped from head to toes in blankets came to the door. And there they remained as if afraid of the visitors.

'Come to the gate, Claire. What dialogue can there be in shouting? I've brought you some of Midder's herbal remedies.'

Through the fold of a blanket peered one watery eye. Slowly Claire advanced to the gate, with Emilie close behind her.

'How is it with you, Siegund?' she asked with tired voice. Contrary to Josefa's report she seemed glad to talk. In fact, she had much to say and the talking seemed to bring a little life back into her. She spoke of the fiddler who had often come to the gate of the hut, of how one night he had called on her, fearing that his life was in danger. 'Ha-yee, he begged me to help you, should anything untoward happen to him. I never saw him again. The devil take it, I broke the rules and went out looking for you in the night, but how could I find you when he never had the chance to tell me your hiding place?'

'Roland is dead,' Siegund told her with low voice that conveyed a certain degree of sadness; she knew she had lost a genuine friend and was willing to forgive him for all that had happened.

'I guessed as much.' Claire nodded her head. 'For all his faults, he was a better man than most of the Kuans. But what of the child? He said...'

'There is no child,' Siegund cut her short. 'He was mistaken. Do try the herbs Midder sent you.'

'Bless my old bones; we have no need of remedies. We are as free of leprosy as any of you.' Claire exposed her hands and face, which seemed a little thinner, a little mottlier, a little wrinklier, but there were no sores. I'm biding my time, Siegund. I must prepare Emilie for her return home. You see, she's not well in mind.'

'But why don't you both come home?'

'We can't leave until she's better and the Kuans have come to their senses. Ha-yee, it's far too soon - the way she is. She's not ready yet to endure more stress; nor are, no doubt, folk ready to accept her back in this state.'

'Why not let Emilie decide for herself, Claire? Will you both walk with me for a while? Folk will be near their homes, now that darkness is not all too far away.'

'Is it wise to risk unsettling them? Their madness, when it comes to them, is worse than any malady,' Claire said with a great deal of hesitation, but then stepped through the gate.

Emilie clung tightly to the old woman's hand, repeatedly stumbling even over the most insignificant obstacles. Siegund offered her hand for support. Emilie ignored it with blank expression. They settled at a spot from where they could see the peaceful valley that looked sleepy but not yet asleep. A hint of red sky painted landscape and cottages in a pale rosy hue while up here, so near the marshland, the air was moist and chilly. Claire pulled her blanket a little tighter.

'Can you see the smoke rise from your Fadder's cottage, Emilie?' Siegund asked softly. 'Your Midder will be preparing the evening meal and your brothers and sisters will soon be gathering by the fire. Do you remember the tales they told? Emilie, would you like to be with them again?'

'The poor mite's mind is damaged and her eyes can no longer see,' Claire explained, and with a sudden urge to ease her burden she poured out all that had happened in the hut, living through every moment of misery as if it were happening now; a story filled with tragedy and desperate heroism, a story that marred the serenity of the dying day. The island's rugged beauty was intertwined with tragedies - to know the one meant also to know the other.

Emilie had sat quietly at first. Now she began to rock forward and backward, fast, rhythmically, continuously, in the only way she knew how to express her emotions these days. Her dull eyes stared into nothingness. Siegund reasoned that, if Emilie could still get upset, if she remembered, then surely, she might be coaxed out of the darkness. Gently she folded her arm around the girl.

'Speak, Emilie. Blow me, I know you can speak. No, no, rocking is not the answer. Tell us that you want to go home.'

'Leave her be,' Claire intervened. 'It was a bad idea. The memories are too painful to her. The devil take it, she has taken a step backward; she had given up his rocking of late. Let's say no more of it and bide our time.'

'I meant well and have yet again done harm. I'm cursed to bring bad fortune to those I love. Could it be that in loving those who have suffered as I have, I only truly love myself? I'll go then and trouble you no more. Goodbye, Claire - goodbye, Emilie, and if you don't want to be my friend, I understand, though I'll still be yours.'

When no answer came, neither from Claire nor her young companion, Siegund prepared to leave, accepting the failure with good grace, yet fretting none the less. As she turned away from them she felt a timid tug on her skirt, no stronger than if twig had caught it. Emilie's hand was holding the seam of her dress. Her pale lips moved, but no sound came. Siegund stood still, waiting, holding her breath so as not to miss the slightest utterance.

'I...want...to...go...home,' came the girl's neglected voice, throaty with a tone or two too low, almost as if someone else was speaking through her.

'You shall, Emilie, you shall,' Siegund promised, hugging and even kissing under a flood of tears the bewildered girl. 'Tomorrow you'll be in your Midder's arms.'

'Ha-yee, the time is not yet right.' Claire's eyes too had become a little more watery.

'There shall never be a better time, indeed not,' Siegund stated while drying her eyes on her dress. Folks dare not oppose me just now, they are in awe of me, think me to have weird powers and bow to me, some in reverence, some in cowardly submission. Blow me, they are mad indeed, but let me tell you what you must do.'

A moment later Siegund descended the slope, her spirits high. The last of the sun sank into the ocean and a white paper moon began its night watch, looking on with morbid impassivity at the rapid transition from day to night. Flickering stars between almost transparent clouds offered guidance and promised hope. Siegund fancied that the setting sun symbolized Sonwill while the moon represented Hannah and that one day her sun would rise again - one day. Until that day came she would watch over her, love her as her moonbeam; she would make Hannah love her too, teach her compassion and not allow Hegan's iciness to take root in her heart. With that, Siegund would have to be content.

'Well? What news is there?' Josefa asked, waiting impatiently by the gate. Her ever vigilant eyes rested on her daughter, her once impersonal dogmatism pared down to impersonal ambivalence.

'I spoke with them,' Siegund informed her in a way that meant to safeguard her present power. 'They are as well as you might expect,' she added, which might have meant anything from being quite well to not being quite dead. She spoke no more of them.

Krista was busy with the chores Hegan used to do, be it a little slower and a little less efficient. For all her release from self-punishment she seemed no happier, nor had she any more to say now than in the past. Maunsie, his fiddle propped under his chin, looked up at them with blissful vacancy of mind as true musicians are apt to do, then lowered his eyes again and slid back into his own, private world.

When later Siegund lay in her warm, dry bed with its soft, dry blankets she felt for the first that she had truly come home, but the longing for Garwulf and her promise to Emilie would not let her rest, and when everyone was asleep she stole out into the night, carrying with her a small bundle of food.

'Has it come to this that my woman should walk alone in the night and provide for me?' Garwulf greeted her. He was glad to see her all the same despite the mild reproof. 'Have you been treated in a civil manner?'

'Indeed.' She crouched by the fire and huddled close to him.

'Then I rejoice with you, yet, my selfish heart weeps, for you shall be tempted to stay with your people - and by right, that is how it should be.'

'Blow me, I used to dream of leaving Skerra Kua and I have been punished for my disloyalty with an everlasting burden. I can't leave the island, not now - not ever. I am part of it and it is part of me. Stay with me, Garwulf, be part of us, too - of me, of my land, of my people. I shall make them see reason, indeed I shall.'

'Can you work miracles, Siegund? Nothing less will do. You know the ways of simple island folk.' He cradled her in his arms. 'Alas, I cannot leave without you. I am prepared to give fate a chance. Now, what of our bairn? Is she well?'

'We have no bairn. She's lost forever.' Siegund stared into the fire. Her lacy eyelashes fluttered nervously and the tears began to roll down her cheeks.

'Then let me grieve with you, for I too have suffered a loss. I know not what else to say; words cannot express the sorrow I feel. If only I could turn back the tide!'

They held each other in tight embrace, united in their grief, drawing comfort and strength from each other. In the wake of the tumultuous storm of life, and the devastation left behind, they would build a future, its stability fortified by the traumatic events of the past.

'Tomorrow shall begin a new day - for us and for the other outcasts. Tomorrow...'

'Never speak of tomorrow, Siegund. Today were are together; tomorrow - who knows?'

But she did speak, had to speak. She told him of her plans, which she thought quite ingenious. Garwulf thought them foolhardy, but could think of nothing better.

The cold air discouraged any lengthy farewells and good-lucks by the cave entrance; thus, in the first glimmer of daylight, she hastened down to the valley. She reminded herself that she had no need to give explanations, should her mother ask any questions. She was free of all that now. In this present sentiment of being in control of her life she made her way to the Girse to say goodbye to Sonwill and get to know Hannah.

Hegan lifted her eyes at the early visitor, yet, seemed to look through her in sombre passivity, in languor almost, but somehow, the strange fear she had displayed yesterday was still there or had come back. It was like a kind of calm revolt, a madness smouldering beneath temperance.

'A magnificent bairn, don't ye think, Siegund?' Duncan said with obvious pride. 'She has battled fer life like a true Kuan. She reminds me of ye, though why I should think so...' Hegan's disapproving glance stopped him in mid-sentence. He began to busy himself with the fire and then went into the byre to ponder over what it was that he had said wrong.

'She's special indeed,' Siegund said, still standing by the door where her sister had wanted her to stay. 'And today is a special day that will be remembered as long as people shall dwell on Skerra Kua.'

'What is the meaning of your illogical ramblings, girl? She's a bairn like any other, not some miracle. Nor would I wish her to be.' As far as Hegan was concerned the matter was closed.

Sonwill was no more, just as the fiddler was no more, but Sonwill might one day live again - the fiddler would not. Siegund stretched her neck like a goose on a rack, searching the babe's face for a likeness to Garwulf - or Roland. A child born out of love or sin - which one was she? How sad for a mother not to know her child's identity. From the babe's dark hair Siegund deducted, rightly or wrongly, that Hannah had to be the fiddler's child and that for her sake she ought to think kindly of him, and after all, he had given his life for them both; through the child he would live on. Poor Garwulf! He had grieved with her for the loss of a child he never had; how much greater his grief would be if he knew the truth.

Hegan, against her better judgement, preoccupied herself with the miracle of Hannah's dark hair. She preferred not to believe in miracles. She sank into morose silence. But if a babe had the blessings of the gods, she pursued the line of thought, then why should its mother feel so uneasy? She shook herself as if to shake off her uneasiness and slanted a suspicious glance at her sister.

'Are you coming down with a fever, girl,' she suddenly shrieked at Siegund, emerging from her momentary apathy. 'You're all of a tremble, to be sure.' Her concern was not for Siegund but for what the bairn may catch. The madness in her eyes intensified and it was just as well that Krista walked in at that moment, lisping that Midder was fretting and had sent her to look for Siegund.

'Midder - fretting? Ah yes, indeed, she would be,' Siegund replied with a great deal of cynicism.

'Take your sister home this very minute, Krista. She has no business coming here if she's ailing.' Hegan's dismissal cut as sharp as a blade.

They met Malcolm on the way home. He nodded his acknowledgement in a by-the-way manner, showing preference to neither the one he loved nor to the one he was fond of, but for all his pretended indifference his face could not hide the hurt. Krista blushed and cast her eyes to the ground without noticing his distress, which was no real surprise; to her, simplicity and uninvolvement were far less painful than sensitivity. Siegund saw his struggle to come to terms with life as it was. The bond between them since that day in the hills had never been quite broken; it had seemed like a promise then, but that was a long time ago - time and events had made the promise null and void.

That evening the whole township gathered at the Girse and filled the barn with marginally apprehensive chatter and cautious goodwill. Krista had braved the darkness and now sat forlorn in the shadowy background, quite overwhelmed by so much festive activity while Malcolm kept his distance from her as from Siegund. Maunsie played his fiddle and the young folks danced, just as they had done to Roland's tunes. Siegund sat beside Maunsie, watching the mottled crowd and trying to estimate each man's and each woman's reaction when they would be faced with the result of her carefully designed plan. And as on all occasions, they had all come, the Klaasens, the Volkers, the Hendricks, the Johansens, even Bideberg and big Fulmar Kon with Arlene, all hoping to put the unhappy past behind them.

Under her breath Siegund prayed to Odin to guide her with his wisdom, doubting her own more and more as time went by. She pleaded to the gods to prevent the destruction of this delicate peace. Folk's mingled with pretended ease. At length Siegund left Maunsie's side and slipped out into the moist autumn night. With the flickering lamp she drew three circles above her head, which signalled to the uninvited guests who were hiding by the hilldyke to make their appearance. She returned to her brother's side. Maunsie played as if he were truly the fiddle's soul and his soul belonged to the fiddle, his happiness as complete as he deemed it could ever be, and his music transferred his contentment to the listeners.

Three knocks at the door silenced all talking. Three figures stepped over the threshold, one clad in straw, the other two draped in blankets. Gasps of displeasure, unwholesome murmurs and whispers passed through the barn; the lepers had come amongst them. The crowd shrank back in fearful dismay. Duncan looked around helplessly. They may have sent the lepers away, but no one dared to offend the mummer, lest he be a god. It took Duncan a fair while to think of what to say.

'I de ne ken who ye are Skekler, but ye are welcome. Our rule demands it so. But why have ye brought the lepers here?'

A god was not expected to answer a mortal's questions, but his silence, his disinterest in food and drink, and the way he stood his ground close to his two companions disturbed the Kuans. Slowly Siegund walked towards the visitors, then turned to face the crowd.

Good people of Skerra Kua,' she said with a minute quiver in her voice. 'We have cause for much gratitude instead of fear and anger. Claire and Emilie have been returned to us.'

'...And brought the sickness back with them?' Tilo Volker called out red-faced.

'Indeed not. The leprosy has passed. See for yourself.' With that, Siegund removed the blankets. 'Come closer, good people, look at them and see for yourselves. There are no marks on their hands and no blemishes on their faces.' And to display her own absolute confidence in her diagnosis she kissed Emilie's face. 'You see? I have no fear of them, why then should you?'

Some craned their necks a little, but none came forward. Claire looked the same as she had always done in folks memory, just older, more wrinkly, like the bark of a tree, but

Emilie, empty-eyed, was no longer the girl they had known; she seemed like a ghost - a shadow.

'How can this be when the medical man told us there was no cure?' Fulmar Kon asked and spit on the floor. 'I tell you, folks, it's sheer sorcery that has brought it about. She has made us blind to the malady, but it's there alright.'

'I have no such power, and if I had, I should not abuse it. Remember the medical man's doubt? He was right to doubt. Claire and Emilie were never sick, they should never have been sent away. But blame has no place here. For pity's and for decency's sake, take them back.'

'Then why did they stay silent? And why did Tobias and Martha perish so soon, and on the same day? Seems more than chance to me,' Bruno Bideberg hinted full of scorn, pointing a finger at Claire. 'Well? How do you explain that?'

'You are asking why they stayed silent, Bruno? Would you have taken them back at a time when the madness ruled your heads? Indeed not. Even now you're wishing them away. And how could they be sure to be free of the sickness when they lived with the lepers all those moons? As to your hinting of foul play, you'd do better to go on your knees and beg Claire's forgiveness. Claire took care of the lepers and of Emilie.'

Siegund was no longer afraid of them now; the power of truth, folk's fear of her, the skekler - they were all on her side. Undaunted she continued her unrehearsed speech. There was no option now anyway other than to complete what she had started.

'Let me tell you their story, let me tell you of their misery. Tobias' pain was immense and all hope had had gone from him. He chose to die so that young Emilie might live. And poor Martha - her mind had become mercifully twisted under the stress so that she no longer knew what she was on with. One night Tobias left the enclosure; Martha followed him. Claire and Emilie watched them go, not then realizing what was to follow. The two lepers walked away, together - yet alone in their suffering. Across the graveyard they walked and far beyond, down to the swamp where the ground will not carry even the weight of a child. There they stood, in a hazy moonlight, hand in hand, their faces turned towards heaven until the wet, cold earth closed over them.'

Siegund paused and searched the listeners' faces for signs of compassion, or at least for signs of regret, or acceptance. Bideberg looked ashamed to the floor. Here and there some sternly denied tears glistened under downcast eyes. Katrine was reaching with both arms out to her daughter; Hanno and Sven held her back, because folk told them to.

'Let Katrine go to her daughter, I tell you. What right have any of you to deprive a Midder of her child?' Siegund looked straight at her own mother when she said those words. 'Most of you still have homes and families intact. You carried on as if nothing had happened, though I see the unhappiness in all of you.' She addressed them as 'good and wise people' while thinking them bad and stupid. 'Imagine just for a moment to be Emilie on that night,' she continued. 'After all that had already happened to her - what would you feel? The pain addled her mind so that she had the sense of a babe. Had Claire brought her back in such pitiful state - who would you have blamed then, since you always seem to need a scapegoat?

Would it have been me - the fiddler - the stranger? Who? Who would have been next to suffer humiliation and even death? Claire, mistrusted by all, cared for Emilie as if she had been her own bairn, spoon-fed her when she would not eat, talked to her when she would not speak, and sat with her when wild dreams tore her out of her slumber. Emilie is getting better now, but her eyes that have seen too many bad things now refuse to see anything at all.'

Siegund licked her dry lips. She wondered whether her words had stirred sufficiently the consciences or whether she had carried things too far; no one had ever spoken to them that way. Until midnight she and her two friends had the protection of the skekler whose strawy hand rested on her shoulder, after midnight even the skekler would not be safe. The four outsiders stood like accusers who by most unfortunate error were awaiting the judgement of the accused. A great hush ensued. Maunsie limped towards them, took Emilie's hand, looked at it briefly and planted a kiss in to the middle of the thin, white palm, much to the Kuans' surprise and horror at such unprecedented show of affection.

'Nay, it's wicked, it's sad! I'm glad you've come back, Emilie, and you too, Claire.'

The crofters responded to his earnest declaration of loyalty and confidence with whispers, mutterings and uncertainty. Katrine rushed forward, no longer heeding permission or denial to embrace her daughter. 'I'll take you home, child,' she uttered with a dry voice. 'It's over now.' Her voice broke altogether, but even now, for the sake of dignity, she did not cry, though she wanted to; she would rather choke on her tears than let them flow. And Josefa was like the rest of them, full of that awesome dignity, but she invited Claire back into her home and spoke of the work to be done instead of regrets.

Hegan brought young Hannah into the barn and quite unexpectedly presented her to the skekler in the hope that he might truly be a god. He held Hannah in his strawy hands and raised her above his head, then bowed to Hegan and laid the babe safely back into her arms. Siegund had yet one more task to complete; there was yet more to be said - and it was none the easier, especially since the attention was turning to Hannah and Hegan.

'Good people,' she began again, 'the gods have forgiven us our days of weakness and our cowardly ways. We are united again. Should we not give thanks to the higher beings?' Her words prompted most of the men and women to kneel and mumble prayers. 'I don't mean prayers alone,' she continued. 'Let us build a new church in gratitude to the Christian God who demanded my promise on Candlemas night. Will you help me?'

They looked at each other, surprised perhaps that no one had thought of it before. Robert Macalay, the occasional spiritual shepherd was the first to reply.

'It makes sense when we ne longer have a church, ye ken. Ye can bank on us, Siegund.'

'Aye, aye,' called others, and one by one the volunteers made themselves known.

'We shall build it near the lepers' hut in memory of Tobias and Martha,' she said. 'And each year, on this very day, we shall go there and pray for them and remind ourselves of our duties towards each other.' So powerful had been all that she had said, so remarkably serene had been her countenance, folks could not altogether be blamed for believing in her unearthly powers - divine or otherwise.

'What are you - goddess or witch?' Fulmar Kon blurted out, took a few steps towards her and lifted a threatening hand, his face red with rage. The skekler's presence forbade him to come any closer, which infuriated him all the more. 'Who is it you think you are, speaking to us in your presumptuous manner? And - and you have turned my brother into an evil-doer and caused his death.'

'I'm neither goddess nor witch, nor have I any special powers. If you are intent on harming me I should not be able to prevent it; I would not be alive now had it not been for the help of a good man. Indeed, those you accuse of wicked dealings have committed far fewer sins than you, Konrad Mulvoen. Your brother may have sinned, but he was not evil, nor has Garwulf the stranger done you any harm. He came to us for shelter and you have chased him off the island. But you shall see him again, indeed, for I shall be wed to him as soon as it can be arranged.' And with that she removed the skekler's mask. Good people, if you accept me you must also accept him, for we shall never part again.'

'She's a witch, I tell you. She makes things happen, don't you see, friends?' Fulmar Kon yelled. 'My brother's death...'

'What is it with ye, Konrad Mulvoen?' Ethel Macalay asked. 'De ye ken mere aboot yer brother's end than we de? If so, then let's hear it, else hold yer tongue.'

Konrad grimaced. His face turned ashen when some of the men began to question him on the matter. Things threatened to get out of hand.

'Leave him be,' Siegund demanded. 'It can do no good. The fiddler is no more; why not let him rest in peace. Make an end to all the hatred lest the madness returns.'

Konrad looked at Bideberg for support. Bruno turned his back, no longer valuing the other's friendship. Having Martha's memory honoured at the new church meant far more to him. Quite apart from that, he seemed to prefer Josefa's company to whose side he had clung all evening. Whether or not she noticed his modest advances was hard to say, but it might have been quite reasonable to assume that a woman without a husband and a man without a wife had more than just neighbourly interests in common, though for now, their losses were too recent to think on those terms.

'If before God you are to be wed to my daughter,' Josefa addressed Garwulf, 'then I'll accept you as my son. Holy Midder, an extra hand is sorely needed on our croft. Play Maunsie, play!' Let your tunes sweep away the gloom of the past so that we may celebrate joyfully the reason for our gathering tonight, which, it seems, we have all forgotten.

With Josefa's acceptance of the stranger the people, tired of bad feelings, came one by one to introduce themselves to Garwulf, chatting freely and without malice, all except Konrad, who fired thunderbolts of scorching glances at Siegund and then stormed out of the barn. Folks crooned over the Macalay babe whose dark hair was hailed as yet another miracle. They were not aware of the tears in Siegund's eyes, of her private moment of mourning. Malcolm was talking to Krista, Sven was dancing with Adelika; Ingeborg, though looking a little lost without Rory, was responding with radiant smile to Harry Volker's corny jokes while Garwulf was talking with Robert Macalay. And now that all was accomplished Siegund felt quite exhausted. Through the moist film on her eye lashes she saw two dark eyes searching hers, eyes that seemed to say: 'We know of the cave, of our passion, aye, that we do, but we won't tell.'

'Roland Mulvoen,' she cried out. 'You're dead, you have no business to come amongst us.' Her cry had made everyone swing round in confusion. What happened next took no longer than a few blinks of the eye, if indeed their eyes managed to blink during the horror that unfolded itself before them. Fulmar Kon had re-entered the barn; with wild, bulging eyes he headed for his brother Roland, brandishing a knife.

'You murderous dog of a brother,' Roland snarled. 'I have a score to settle with you, aye, that I have.'

Garwulf tried to step between the brothers. The blade glistened in the half-light of the oil lamps. With an expression of shocked surprise the stranger sank to the floor. From somewhere in the barn came a single, hysterical scream. Konrad fled into the night. In the confusion of the moment folks crowded around Garwulf. Josefa was kneeling by his side to see what could be done. She shook her head and got to her feet.

'Come child, 'she said, '...it's over with him.

Siegund felt nothing much at all except that she had died with her man and with Sonwill.

'I am truly sorry, Siegund, aye, sorry for everything, that I am,' she heard the fiddler say. Josefa and Ethel were pulling her away; somewhere, anywhere - she did not care where to.

# Epilogue

It had been a bad year, the worst that any of them could remember - a year of madness when pride and dignity had fallen by the wayside. Battered and shaken they had come through their ordeal, a little wiser now, a little more tolerant so they said, though people rarely change all that much from one year to the next, if indeed they ever do. Now it was behind them and a new year was beginning; pride and dignity had returned and would survive.

As the long dreary nights spread their winter sleepiness across the island Yule day came around once more. They had turned a full circle, had lost much and gained little, but gain was hardly on the Kuan agenda even in good times. Roland, clad in merry shades of green instead of his sombre Puritan dress, performed his duty as he had always done, bringing his Christmas cheer. Beside him walked Maunsie. In his dull grey garb, and half the other one's size, he looked much like Roland's monochrome shadow. Maunsie enjoyed the fiddling - Roland mostly the brandy. His message of love came to the Harehill, not impatient as the previous year but gentle as a reminder. Siegund, though still grieving over her loss, understood the message and gave it serious thought.

The two fiddlers trudged on to the Heather croft, their breath steaming and their hands a tinge of blue. Maunsie had a message too. His fiddle sang entirely for Emilie who came to the door with Hanno and Katrine. Emilie raised her hand in greeting, though her eyes did not see the gallant young musician. Maunsie seemed to grow a little taller in Emilie's presence. Katrine smiled her generous smile again, her face having lost its ashen gauntness of recent days; she was well in the process of regaining her maternal plumpness.

When evening came, folks gathered at the Blue Bane croft. It was the Johansens' turn to lead the festivities this year; Johannes the weaver with his great white beard, and his plump little wife Anna who had the same laughing eyes as Ingeborg, were as jolly as any hosts could be. Folks smiled again, neighbours talked to each other without first looking over their shoulders. And they all had much to talk about, especially the fiddler.

'And Fulmar Con really laid hands on you - your very own brother?' Bideberg asked,' though he had already been told the story. 'Fancy that! Who would have thought it of him?'

'Aye, Bruno, he stalked me, that he did. We had a brawl there and then, way above the Wizards Bench. Aye, and he, being bulkier than myself, got the better of me. Sailing over the cliff I went like a guillemot, aye.'

'It's a miracle you're alive to tell the tale,' Johannes joined in.

'Aye, I fell onto a ledge, just far enough to make my ears ring and my head buzz, and the light flashed before my eyes like ten of Bruno's candles, aye, that they did.' Roland had told his story a dozen times or more and would rather not go through the same old narrative again. The trouble was, folks liked to hear him talk. In his green pantaloons, green cloak and leggings he had more in common with a court jester than a musician, but he was nevertheless hailed a hero. He seemed ageless somehow, or rather, of all ages according to mood and occasion; only his slightly greying temples put his years a little into perspective.

'Ugh, weren't you scared? I would have been,' Potty Pattie asked, her dandelion-clock hair standing on end more than ever.

'Scared? No, not that. I blew out the candles and went to sleep right where I was. I guess the fall had made me sleepy. It was daylight when I woke up again, aye, but some fool had lit the candles again. I thought I must have drunken a whole bottle of brandy and regretfully could not remember the taste of it.

'The devil take it,' that stuff is worse going over the edge for, eh, Roland?' Claire piped and gave an out-sized grin so that her withered face seemed to collapse over her toothless mouth.

'Why didn't you climb up again?' Sefina Hendricks asked, not being particularly bright. Her rolling duck-egg eyes flashed admiration and her lips pouted an undeniable come-hither invitation.

'Why? Let's say, my fingernails were too short - that's why. So I climbed down instead; it seemed to make sense at the time, though where I should have gone from there I can't imagine. Then I fell a little further, aye, and the candles went out again. I remember nothing more; I can only repeat what a handful of fishermen from Papa Kira, who found me clinging to a rock entirely surrounded by sea, later told me. I must have rambled a fair bit, aye. They could not make out what I was saying, even doubted my native origin and thought me a survivor of a shipwreck. A good woman on Papa Kira took care of me. My head soon mended, but it seemed I had left my memory on the cliff; I could not remember who I was for a long while. The rest goes without saying. I'm home now, safe and sound, with my most precious memories restored.' He smiled, closed his eyes and seemed to loose himself in those memories.

The Kuans were content. In Fulmar Kon they had finally found their scapegoat; without it, peace of mind would have been doubtful. Although Konrad could scarcely have been blamed for the drought, the landslide and the leprosy, but what he had done deserved their wrath. So why should he not be burdened with the sins and the guilt of all the Kuans so that their slates might be wiped clean? And the fulmar - he had not waited for his punishment, he had fled the island. Now Roland was master on the Moorholm croft, taking care of his mother, of Arlene and the young fulmars.

Skerra Kua was redeemed, and for that, the island vibrated with joy and gratitude. Folks had not forgotten the church. Whenever the weather allowed it, men, women and children made for the hills, collected suitable stones and humped them to the site by the leper hut. And while carrying out their enormous task with severe solemnity they regarded it as an unselfish service to the Christian God, though secretly they hoped for a divine reward in one way or other. While their hands and backs became sore in the service to one god, their singing and chanting hailed another. Slowly the walls began to rise from the ground. It would be a humble church, not grand and imposing like the one on the mainland, but one that had been built with the islanders' hearts and souls. What better tribute could there be to any god!

After each day of toil Siegund stole to the cemetery where a driftwood cross bore a single symbol - Dagaz, the rune of self-transformation. She was kneeling there now, took the green pebble from her pocket and placed it on Garwulf's grave. She gazed at the cross and folded her hands in prayer. Her face was streaky with the grime of her previous occupation and with the tears that presently ran down her cheeks. Her long, blond hair fluttered in the wind that roared hollow across the bleak winter marshland so that the stunted grasses bowed their heads.

'Now you'll be a proper god again, in your rightful place. Your world I shall never know. Gods aren't meant to wed mortals, and I could never be a goddess; my sins are too great and my heart is fickle, for even though I grieve for you I'm forgetful of you at times. I feel lonely without you, and when I look at the fiddler I don't dislike what I see, and the passion in his eyes awakens desires in me, and then I tremble. Roland and I are two of a kind and... Sonwill is the fiddler's child; I can see the likeness in her. Can you forgive me my sins,

Garwulf? I have lost her and have lost you, but you still have my heart and now I ask you to give it back to me and set me free so that I may wed Roland; I've nothing else left of you except memories.'

She remained on the ground until the cold began to chill her bones. She told him she would come back because she had not heard his answer, then got up and walked away, rubbing her hands vigorously to bring the life back into them. She glanced up towards the new church. Beyond, it in the distance, against the dusky skyline stood Roland, alone, looking across the marshland - a tall, motionless silhouette. He was too far away to have heard her words; he would not have intruded anyway. He allowed her to grieve - pain needed time to heal. She looked back at the cross. On the grave twinkled the green stone like a brilliant star.

'The pebble is yours, Garwulf; I'm giving it back to you. And when the grass has grown over both of you I shall be free, though I shall never forget you.'

To give back the stone had seemed the right thing to do at the moment, but she loathed parting with it, and immediately she changed her mind, deeming it careless to allow the grass to grow over it, lest it grow over the memories too. She begged it back of Garwulf and told him it was to grace the new church, so that at least once a year folk would remember him even if they forgot him for the rest of the time. Her remarkable talent to make up the rules as necessity required proved, as always, a reliable way of coping with the pitfalls of life.

Candlemas came. The holy flames from Maalie Voe threw their flickering lights against the by now man-high church walls. There was ample room for all to worship together, which emphasized and hailed the new-found unity. Prayers and chants rose to the open, starlit sky. A massive rock anchored the incomplete House of God to the ground and represented an altar, which as yet bore no resemblance to a holy table; it would take years of chipping and chiselling before it was deemed worthy of God's approval. For now, relics and candles adhered to it, wedged, perched or imbedded with a handful of mud the best way they might be adhered. It had been quite a tricky manoeuvre for the three maidens to prepare the altar; added to that, Sefina Hendricks was clumsy and had talked all the while of her Grandfadder Swaalie, Emilie Klaasen was unable to tell night from day, and Siegund, who initially had refused the invitation, thinking herself unworthy of such high office, had pondered over her sins.

But folks deemed her, who had the protection of the gods, the patroness of the new church. That night, in the serenity of the occasion, she felt as if her sins were being washed away; she felt no longer unclean. Holy lights, flowing white shawls, long hair framing peachy cheeks, eyes chaste and pure, eyes that glimmered with hope of salvation – all those things promised folks a new beginning; they were almost persuaded that angles had come amongst them.

But angels or not, the Kuans continued their lives in their old ways, it could hardly have been different; it was their nature, their past and their future. For Siegund it was a busy time flitting between household chores, work at the slowly growing church, moments of grieving in the graveyard and visits to the Girse. She sometimes wondered which of her obligations might be the most important to be honoured, and invariably she would dash to see Hannah, hold her in her arms, kiss the plump little face, then give the babe back into Hegan's arms and dash home again.

Hegan hardly seemed to notice her sister's flying visits; she was not well and often sank into a deep moroseness from which it was hard to rouse her. Josefa could think of no reason for her daughter's ailing. She sent Claire to take care of Hegan and her child, and Claire, happy to spend her days in her old home again, lavished her affection on the young Macalay family.

Despite folk's old misgivings of the redness Sven Klaasen took Adelika to the altar after Candlemas and for the time being lived in Katrine's household. Sven thought the whole story of the redness proper nonsense anyway, though Adelika fretted that she might not be able to produce a blond or dark-haired miracle child like Hannah or Nellie.

'If I adore my woman's hair should I not also adore it on my children's heads?' he asked her.

Adelika should have been reassured. Ethel had finally told her of her real mother's tragic end. The revelation troubled Adelika, not least because all the elders knew the story. She remained the orchid of Skerra Kua, pale and remote, though folk knew better now than to whisper. They deemed it prudent to keep their thoughts to themselves and leave well alone.

It did not stop Siegund from pondering over what might be done for Adelika to take at least one of the burdens off her shoulders. She thought herself as the guardian of peace. Perhaps it was fate; perhaps it was just her overgenerous imagination that would find a way. One late afternoon, when she stood in the Harehill yard and daylight was already beginning to fade, when her eyes caressed the brooding hills, she heard them call again. Or was it the cave? No - no, not the cave; the cave was silent. There was no urgency in the call, as if her presence were not demanded but merely invited. Leisurely she ambled along without thought of direction or destiny, just walked where ever her legs would take her. A gentle breeze plucked tiny pockets of mist apart like tufts of cotton wool so that the sky was becoming clearer and revealed a pale, almost transparent full moon. Out in the hills the air belonged to her alone; the hills were her allies. She knew them well and they knew her. She felt a beautiful peace come over her.

How long she had been walking she could not say. A hilly wilderness of boulders, bracken and heather spread out before her like a ruffled carpet. The roar of the ocean seemed no more than the sound of a gushing stream. Somewhere a sheep bleated. At the foot of a rugged slope wild ponies with stumpy legs and shaggy coats grazed peacefully, their long, coarse manes gently fluttering in the breeze. The animals lifted their heads at the intruder and assessed her with large, dark eyes, shook their manes and idled a little further afield. At midsummer night they would dance, so legend had it; only the pure and righteous would be able to see them in their frolic. She knew she would never see them, for did not regarded herself as pure and righteous despite the Candlemas cleansing.

It had grown dark already. Either by chance, by fate, or by a secretly dreamt-up plan of which her conscious mind was not aware, she had come to the Bracken Hill with its reed-framed pond. She stood on its bank and stared into the still water. The scanty moonlight had no power to take away the gloom from its dark surface no more than had the faint Northern Lights that were making a timid appearance.

So, this was where Marnie had bathed. Was she really lying at the bottom of the pond? Was it she who had called? Siegund shuddered. She crept a little closer to the water. From a rock, which was almost entirely submerged, flowed streamers of dark green blanket weed like hair blowing in the wind. Green hair! Time and water - had they turned Marnie's hair green? Siegund mused over the possibility. She stood motionless now as if captured in a time warp, her reasoning once more succumbing to fantasy. The green hair was inviting her to touch it with her hands. It was cold and slimy and she drew back. It invited her to step onto the rock, to step into the soft velvet of black water.

'Blow me, what is it you want of me, Marnie?' she whispered. 'I've loved you ever since the day Claire mentioned your name, just as I love Adelika. She is well and has wed a good man. Let her be happy.' She paused a moment, expecting some sort of answer or reaction. 'Are you angry with me for liking the fiddler? He truly loved you - he still does. Be content. I know you are lonely, but Roland and I are lonely too.'

'Come to me,' she heard the water murmur.'

Siegund tested the rock with one foot, keeping the other firmly on the ground.

'What are you saying, Marnie? I can't hear you too well. What? You want me for a companion? But what of Sonwill? She needs me too! What? Ah, indeed, she's got a new Midder, just as Adelika was given a new Midder; folks know nothing of the hurt as long as all is neat and correct. It is for Adelika's sake that I've come - for Adelika's and yours.' She tried to step onto the rock with both feet, just to hear the murmuring water a little better. She gave a little cry as two hands were grabbing her waist from behind and lifted her back onto the bank.

'No, fair Siegunda, it's not the place for you, nor is it the way to ease your pain.' Roland was holding her firmly in his arms.

'Marnie called me to be her companion,' Siegund told him, still under the spell of too vivid imagination.

'She would never ask it of you. She was not evil in life; she will not be so in death.'

'We must help her soul find rest.' Siegund's thoughts were becoming clearer now. 'Let's lay down a cross of stones and pray for her. Indeed, we owe her that.'

'Aye, aye, that we shall.' He scratched his head bemused, wondering why he had never thought of it himself. 'But how can we honour a grave without knowing its whereabouts? Rumours mean nothing.'

'It is here, right here. Indeed it is; I know it is - she spoke to me.' Siegund insisted, despite having recovered her senses now.

He did not argue, for even if Marnie's grave was not here - the memory of her was. They collected the stones, twenty-five in number, one for each of the Nordic runes. And when the Northern Lights burst into brilliant display and spread the dancing veils across the horizon they both believed that the gods approved of their mission of mercy. For once - indeed, for the first time - their hearts beat entirely in harmony as they laboured quietly side by side. Sometimes Roland chanted a rhyme. Siegund did not understand it, but she refrained from asking him to explain lest the serenity of the moment should be lost. Then they stood back to look at their work: a stone cross in a stone circle, each component bearing a sacred rune, scratched onto their surfaces by another stone; Othila, Nauthiz, Kano, Dagaz, Raido, Berkana, Souelu - separation, pain, light, breakthrough, communication, rebirth, wholeness - Roland knew their collective meaning and had carefully chosen the order in which they would be most effective.

'The runes tell of Marnie's past and, hopefully, will bring peace to her, aye. Where ever and whatever she is now - let's pray that she will be content for all eternity. Unlike you and me, she shall never grow old.' He paused for a moment and then went on: 'Dyes is what we need, for the weather will wear away the scratches on the stones; aye, tomorrow I will bring dyes, but for now it must suffice.' Then he took Siegund's hand and crooned with his soft voice: 'Marnie belongs to both of us and we belong to her, aye, and I'm asking you in her presence - will you wed me, Siegunda? And if I am second fiddle to your man's grave - so be it. I shall learn to live with it, aye, that I shall.'

Her mouth fell open, though she had always known that one day he would renew his proposal; she had not expected it at this very moment and in this very place. Roland was waiting patiently for her reply, his eyes once more speaking of all kinds of things, but now she understood what they were saying. She laughed softly.

'You have already become the second fiddler on the island, Roland; Maunsie is a far better musician than you shall ever be, but a second fiddle you shall not be. Fate has chosen a future for me; I abide by its rule. Indeed, I will wed you, and I promise you I will try to be good a wife to you,' she told him.

'Then we shall be happy together, aye, that we shall.'

Roland was happy if not entirely convinced that she may not change her mind, and thus he began with all haste to make the necessary arrangements, and even though the growing season had already begun, the wedding party rowed across the swell to the mainland. How proudly Maunsie played his tunes at the head of the procession, his head held high. Josefa followed with Bruno Bideberg who took temporarily the place of the bride's father, much to Siegund's dismay, but she let it be.

In the absence of Erik and Rory, Siegund had borrowed Duncan as the brother to walk with her to church. There had been no time for sewing a new dress, nor had she had the material or know-how, but the lack of fine clothes took nothing away from the radiance in her deep blue eyes - a rag queen with flowing white shawl that smoothed somewhat the shabbiness of the last of her hand-me-down dresses. She strode out with confidence; this was her day and she was happy.

Katrine and Hanno Klaasen were standing in for the groom's parents and Roland had generously allowed Arlene to take the place of a sister by his side while one of the young fulmars walked with Krista. Tilo Volker and old Hendricks were given the honour of being witnesses to the marriage. Roland had arranged everything with purpose, had involved as many families as he could so as not to offend any of them. There would be no time for lengthy celebrations because the fields needed tending. One day was all they were willing to spare, one day and no more.

Dressed in a his old Puritan outfit with a brand-new top hat, his beard neatly trimmed, his dark eyes alert, Roland stood out amongst his friends like a general amongst tin soldiers. He briefly took stock of his unworthy behaviour when Maunsie had asked him to teach him to play, but that seemed a long time ago now. Besides, Maunsie had needed no tuition; he was born with an enviable gift. Then he thought of his mother, then of Claire, and wished they could be here with them, but his mother never left the cottage and Claire was taking care of Hegan and the bairn.

'Will you be wed one day, Maunsie?' Emilie asked when the celebrations in the Harehill barn were well under way.

'Nay, Emilie, who'd have me?' Maunsie looked into her slate grey eyes and wondered why they could not see. Her dark blond hair fell over her shoulders in generous waves, her full rosy lips were inviting and her slim figure was beginning to grow the rounded contours of womanhood. Maunsie remembered the day in the hills when he had touched his sister's breasts; he had shrunk back then.  He knew he would not shrink back from Emilie. He sighed his triple sigh.

'I would have you if you asked me, Maunsie; yes, I would wed you,' she replied seriously.

'Nay, nay, you're far too young to know your feelings and far too pretty for the likes of me.'

'Beauty and plainness - they are the same to my eyes, but I can see into your heart. You are good and kind, Maunsie. Can there be anything more beautiful than that? And - and your music pleases my ears.' Her fingertips began to probe his square face. 'Yes, if you asked me, I would wed you.'

'Nay, nay, Emmie, it's sad. One day your sight will return - and I pray for you that it will - but then you'll regret each day you are tied to me.'

'I saw you before my blindness, I liked you then. But if you prefer someone else, if my affliction troubles you, then that's alright.'

'Nay, Emmie, I like you well, I like no one better. Perhaps... if after the next harvest you still feel the same we'll speak of it again. Till then, let's say no more of it. Either way, we shall always be friends.'

Their conversation ended when Tilo Volker, with shiny bald head, stepped onto the platform that was set up for the musician. He coughed nervously, squinted at the people who somewhat surprised and vaguely amused waited for what he might have on his mind.

'What is it that has stuck your tongue to your teeth, Tilo?' Josefa prompted him, to which Potty Pattie sniggered embarrassed. Tilo coughed again.

'Well, it's like this, folk. The Bracken Hill pond...I've asked around these past days, but no one reckons to have been near the unholy place. One day there's nothing, the next day there's a cross in a circle. And the runes...they speak of rebirth and a whole lot of other things. Not a word of a lie. Go and see for yourself. What does it mean?'

Silence came over the listeners, their faces turning gloomier by the minute. Some of the people shrugged their shoulders and would rather not speak of it, others thought it had to be discussed, but no one could come up with a reasonable explanation.

'I know mostly of medical matters and little of things as that,' Josefa told them. 'Jan would have known, mark my word. But why let this talk spoil the day?'

'Ha-yee, how blind you all are,' Claire, who had brought Hegan and the bairn to the barn, exclaimed with a mild degree of impatience. 'It means that the gods have redeemed the one whose name you will not speak, the one who merely lost her way. And if the gods can forgive her - should not we, who are nothing compared with them, also do so? The devil take it; open your eyes, search your hearts. Are there not plenty of sins within us all? It's easier to fault others than to fault oneself.'

'I, for one, want to believe that Marnie is finally at rest, for she was my Midder,' Adelika said and fell to her knees to pray. It was as much a prayer to the gods as a plea to the Kuans. 'Ethel Macalay has been a good Midder to me, the best I could have had. She was right in telling me the truth, but since the day of my knowing I have carried a heavy burden with me. Many a night have I prayed for Marnie's soul. Lift the burden from my shoulders; the gods will it so.'

The Kuans looked upon the kneeling Adelika who had never spoken of her sorrow before; in fact, she had never spoken much at all. Sven, Maunsie and Emilie kneeled beside her and in this moment of silent reverence folks were persuaded to believe in the work of the gods.

Siegund moved to the Moorholm croft where Roland had made it quite clear to Arlene that his new bride was mistress of the house. With Konrad out of the way and unable to return, Arlene's status was much like that of widowhood, reduced to no more than a dependant relative. She was not such a bad soul after all, and Siegund, not exactly the most accomplished housekeeper, was glad of the other woman's help while old Midder Mulvoen, scarcely alive, sat huddled in her chair and looked on with empty eyes.

Daily, no matter how hard she had worked or how late the hour, Siegund went to the Girse croft to see Hannah. Sometimes she would go to Garwulf's grave and speak with him and pray, though those visits became fewer as time went by. Roland knew of the visits and if at times he wondered whether or not he still came second to a grave, deep in his heart he knew it was not so, no more than Siegund came second to the memory of Marnie. Having no longer any need for medicinal brandy at weekends he kept his word and treated her well.

Rory returned in June, disillusioned with the big wide world. He instantly reaffirmed his liking for Ingeborg and she for him. Times were good again as they had been before the madness came, but even in good times bad things creep along. Hegan miscarried her second child and with it the melancholy, the strange quiet madness intensified and hung over her permanently. Her ice-blue eyes stared, but they saw no one. When all of her mother's medicines failed to heal her it occurred to Josefa that perhaps Hegan either sensed or knew the truth about Hannah, but neither of the women would speak of it. Duncan sent for a doctor from the mainland only to be told that Hegan had lost the will to live and hence, there was nothing he could do. And when the corn stood high in the fields and the larks trilled in the sky they carried Hegan's body to the marshland to lie beside her father.

Duncan blamed himself for her death, deeming, as she had done, that their marriage had been cursed because of the legacy. On the day after the funeral he came to the Moorholm cottage, carrying young Hannah in his arms. His face was ashen, his voice vibrated under enormous stress.

'Are we alone?' he asked Siegund.

'Indeed, we are, Duncan,' she replied, feeling uncomfortable by his uneasiness. 'Blow me, is it such delicate matter that you must speak to me alone? Sit down, Duncan,

I'll get you a drink. It looks like you could do with it.'

'Ne drink can ease my pain, ye ken, Siegund.' He pushed Hannah into her arms. 'I know whose child she is. I've known it some time. Maunsie thought it his duty to tell me when Hegan lay seriously ill. I should have known - yer fondness of yer sister's bairn, ye ken. But yer Midder...why did she..?' He stopped a moment to steady his voice. 'The day I learned the truth, a little of me died, ye ken. Hegan never knew, fer that I'm grateful. Take care of her, she's yers now as she should have been all along. I've spoken with yer Midder and mine; ye shall have no trouble from them.'

'I'm truly sorry, Duncan. I never wanted this to happen. Indeed, I've not always liked Hegan; Midder always preferred her to Krista and me, but blow me, I never wished her harm. I was forced to play along with Midder's cruel game and to accept my loss because it was too late for me to change what she had done. I know your pain, Duncan. I felt it too. It tore me apart, but I contented myself with seeing and holding my child once a day. My unhappiness was neither your's nor Hegan's doing. Now that it has come to this, I cannot pretend, for all its sadness, that I do not cherish this moment. Forgive me, Duncan! And indeed, I will take care of her the best way I know. She shall never be deprived of love. But what will you do now?'

'De?' He seemed lost in his thoughts.

'I would not have taken the bairn from you even now, Duncan. I know you loved her.'

'But she's not mine, and Hegan has gone. There's nothing left here for me. I shall go away fer a while and try to bring my life in some sort of order again. And when I return, if I return, I shall call on ye and the bairn.' He rose from his chair awkwardly, then quickly kissed Hannah. 'Goodbye, Siegund,' he said and could say no more.

Duncan had gone. Dazed, Siegund looked at the child in her arms, the child with large dark eyes just like Roland's. A plump little hand pulled at her hair, a tiny voice crooned into her ear. She had laughed and cried when the babe had been born, now she could only cry. Sonwill was reborn. This second birth had lasted weeks - months. At last the torture had ended for her. Was it not so with the driftwood, where one man's loss is another man's gain? For Siegund the sun had risen again, it was hers to adore.

Sven and Adelika moved into the Girse croft; they too had gained from another man's loss. As for Maunsie, he had only gained an intense feeling of guilt for telling Duncan the truth, but he consoled himself with his fiddle and with calling at the Klaasens whenever an excuse could be found - and he found them often. And always, Emilie, pleased to see him, reminded him in a subtle manner of their agreement.

If the previous year had been the year of mistrust and hatred, this one was a year of weddings, carrying unity to the other extreme, for in autumn, when the work in the fields had come to an end, Rory and Ingeborg were wed. The laughing, cheerful Ingeborg brought new life to the Harehill cottage which had been silent for far too long.

Claire stayed on at the Girse cottage where her life had begun a thousand years ago, or so it seemed. Now she kept a watchful eye over Adelika, the unholy child she had helped into the world, and would soon do the same for Adelika's child, and when in late December a golden-haired boy was born, and all was well with mother and child, folks gave sighs of relief and celebrated for days. The happy event heartened all, especially Krista, and on Yule day she stammered her request, just as Hegan had done.

'Midder...., Malcolm from the Northstane wishes to pay you a visit. Will he be welcome in your house?'

'Malcolm Macalay?' Josefa asked with deliberate slowness.

'Yes, Midder; Malcolm Macalay.'

'Is that wise after....?' Josefa stopped in mid-sentence, still a little perplexed at her daughter's choice, though she had known that this day would come. She gave her back-to-front sigh. 'Be that as it may,' she said at length. 'Malcolm is a good man; he will be welcome.'

Rosemarie Leetham was born on Christmas Eve 1936 in a small village in Germany. Education in village schools was very limited in those days. In 1960 she moved to the UK where she obtained several GCSEs at evening classes and trained as nurse. In her passion for learning she read all kinds of books, fact and fiction alike, which eventually prompted her to fulfil her childhood dream to write her own novel.

Printed in the United Kingdom
by Lightning Source UK Ltd.
134622UK00001B/34-45/A

9 781434 345837